Pretty Hustlaz

Pretty Hustlaz

Blake Karrington

www.urbanbooks.net

Urban Books, LLC
300 Farmingdale Road, N.Y.-Route 109
Farmingdale, NY 11735

ISBN 13: 978-1-64556-635-9

First Trade Paperback Printing December 2024
Printed in the United States of America

10 9 8 7 6 5 4 3 2 1

Distributed by Kensington Publishing Corp.
Submit Orders to:
Customer Service
400 Hahn Road
Westminster, MD 21157-4627
Phone: 1-800-733-3000
Fax: 1-800-659-2436

Chapter 1

As Dillon drove toward the restaurant where she was meeting her friend, she made a point to glance in the rearview mirror every three minutes or so. When she checked the mirror for the third time and saw that the same black car with tinted windows was behind her, she narrowed her eyes. "Is this car following me?" she asked out loud, as if she wasn't alone in the car and someone would answer her.

She was only two minutes away from the restaurant, and she didn't want to be late, so she resisted the urge to take a random turn to see if the car would follow her. Upon further inspection, she saw that the car behind her was a Buick. Based on what she could see of the driver, she decided it wasn't anyone that she knew. Dillon continued to watch, and sure enough, the Buick stayed behind her up until she turned into The Palm's parking lot.

"That was strange," she mumbled aloud as she parked. It might have very well been a coincidence, so she didn't want to give it too much thought. Lanika didn't know business would be discussed at this lunch, but it would be. Dillon didn't play when it came to business, and she wanted to be prompt and clear headed. She stepped inside, glanced around, and determined that she had arrived before Lanika, and so she asked the hostess to seat her at an open table.

Five minutes later, when Dillon thought Lanika actually might be late, she started to rethink the proposition that she had in mind, but at that very moment, the hostess led Lanika to Dillon's table. Lanika was right on time. Dillon smiled and hugged the woman before giving her air kisses on each cheek. The waitress came right over and took their drink orders. Dillon and Lanika spent the first ten minutes or so catching up on old times.

"Ooh, I like that bag!" Lanika yelled, pointing at an elegantly dressed middle-aged white woman who had just strolled into The Palm, a cream Chanel Caviar bag hanging from her shoulder. "Treesy got that bag," Lanika said across the table to Dillon as the waitress set their drinks on the table.

Dillon pulled her lips into her mouth and tried to stop herself from correcting Lanika's hoodrat behavior. She was being a little too loud in the classy establishment that they were in, making Dillon wonder if she knew what an inside voice was. Peeking at the lady's bag, Dillon replied dismissively, "Nah, Treesy doesn't have that bag. She got a knockoff."

"Uh-uh. Her purse is real. She paid four hundred and seventy-five dollars for that bag."

"My point exactly. That's a five-thousand-dollar handbag," Dillon responded before drawing a sip from her pomegranate martini. "Truth be told, I really don't care what Treesy, Binky, and the rest of them bum-ass, syrup-drinking bitches down at that shop have or pretend to have. I brought you here because I know how good you are with administrative work and numbers. I have a very important position on my team that I need filled immediately."

"What kind of team you got?" Lanika squawked. "I mean, I need some money bad cuz my unemployment benefits are 'bout to run out, but I don't want to get caught up in no drug cartels or anything else that could get me into trouble. My kids need me."

"Hold up. Why in the hell are you talking about drug cartels?" Dillon frowned, then cocked her upper lip to the right.

"Word around the city is you moving weight with Heavy's fine ass, and with the type of shit you be flossin' in, niggas say y'all fucking with them Colombian or Mexican cartels."

"Humph. The streets are so off. I haven't spoken to Heavy's lying, cheating ass in forever, and I'm for damn sure not fucking with any drugs." Dillon chuckled. "But that's good, because that means no one really knows my business. That's exactly how I like it. You should know that you can't believe everything you hear." Dillon wasn't too shocked by the rumors, but the way people's imagination ran wild would forever baffle her. Moving weight with Heavy? That was comical. He was her ex, and even if they were still together, he'd be the one moving weight, while she sat pretty and spent the money.

Lanika and Dillon were living in two different worlds, although they came from the same one. From the time that they were born until they finished elementary school, they both resided in Charlotte's Fairview Homes Housing Project. Dillon's parents, both blue-collar workers, then bought a house in the middle-class neighborhood of University City, in Charlotte's suburbs. Lanika's single mother purchased a home for her family in the same area with the money that she had received from her married kingpin boyfriend.

At the start of their freshman year of high school, Lanika gave birth to a baby girl, and in the middle of their junior year, she had another daughter. Following the birth of her second child, she left high school, got her GED, and went to work as an administrative assistant.

Intelligent and very well organized, Lanika was a model employee, despite her sometimes ghetto and aggressive attitude. It cost her that first job. She went on to land the best jobs, but she would always lose them after giving a supervisor or a client a crazy tongue thrashing.

When Lanika first left school, she and Dillon saw a lot of one another. As time went on, however, they saw each other less and less. Dillon busied herself with college applications and all the exciting things that came with being a high school senior. She was on the homecoming court and was the prom queen. After graduating from high school, Dillon attended Winston-Salem State University for two years before dropping out.

"What I have going on surely straddles the line between illegal and legal, but it's definitely not drugs," Dillon offered. "I will say that the last person who held this position retired a very rich woman, and it's my goal to do the very same thing." She smiled brightly. There was a twinkle in her eyes that only the thought of excessive amounts of cash brought on.

"If she was making so much money, why did she retire?"

"She'd been in the business for a long time, and she needed to move to Florida to help with her grandkids. Listen, the job pays very well. You'll be able to send your kids to private school, buy a new car, and in six months you'll be able to buy a house in Ballantyne, the Palisades, or Lake Norman and fill your closet with real fucking Chanel bags and not that knockoff shit." Her disdain for fake purses was written all over her face. Dillon was doing her best to get Lanika to see the bigger picture.

Now sitting at full attention, salivating, and hanging on to Dillon's every word with newfound interest, Lanika was all in. Cheesing, she said, "This job sounds like it's popping. I want to say yes. But I need to know what exactly it is before I give you a definite answer." Lanika was literally on the edge of her seat. "I need details of what I'll be doing." Truth be told, even if it was something illegal, she was still tempted to throw caution to the wind and engage. She needed money, and she needed it bad.

Dillon reached into her cream and beige python-skin Gucci purse, pulled out an envelope, and placed it in the center of the table. "I really like my business to stay my business. So once I disclose to you what it is, if you don't want the job, there's three stacks inside the envelope. It's compensation for your time and your silence on the subject of our meeting. Got it?" Dillon raised her brows.

"Okay. Damn. Just tell me what it is already. Ya killing me."

"I run a high-class escort service."

Lanika roared with laughter.

"What's so damn funny?" Dillon frowned, her top lip raised to the right.

"You!" Lanika exclaimed. "You went through all that, and it's just a call-girl service? Hell yeah, I'll take the fucking job. Shit, when I worked the door at the strip club, niggas was always asking me to arrange private parties, aka fuck sessions, with the dancers. I did that for free all the time. I mean, some of the cool broads would kick me some cash for hooking them up, but it's definitely not something I'm a stranger to. I thought you were about to say some off-the-wall, crazy shit."

"This service is far more elite and lucrative than sex in the back room of strip clubs. I can't begin to stress to you the kind of money that is made in high-class escort services. It's enough to make a person filthy fucking rich."

And to be filthy rich was Dillon's goal indeed. She was far from broke, but she wanted more. A lot more. Working for someone was cool, and it had put her in the position that she was in now, but Dillon wanted to level up. She wanted to start her own business and earn more of the profits. Retiring in the next two years with a few million dollars in her bank account made Dillon's coochie wet. She just wanted to be rich, without a care in the world.

With the way she liked to travel and shop, not even a few million would be enough for her to live comfortably for the rest of her days, so the wheels in Dillon's head were turning. She needed passive income, a legal way to make money in her sleep. That way, each day all she had to do was wake up and worry about being fabulous and living life her way, on her own terms. Or maybe she'd get married to a wealthy man, become a housewife, and sit on her paper while she spent his.

"I'm down with that!" Lanika stated in a high-pitched voice.

"So you're on board. Great! Shit, let's get out of here, then. We have to start your makeover pronto." Dillon tossed some money on the table to cover the bill and the tip.

"What kind of makeover? Ain't shit wrong with me!"

"Your whole getup is perfect for the world that you run in, but not for mine. That quick weave, those caked-on cluster lashes, that cheap-ass Shein dress, and those Bakers shoes are a no go. Even your name doesn't work in my world. From now on, I will call you and introduce you as London."

"Damn! You changing a bitch's name too?"

"I'm not changing anything. I'm paying you to do a job, and part of your job description is to assimilate into my environment and be exceptionally gorgeous at all times. You're about to get glammed the fuck out from head to toe by some of the best in the city. The escorts aren't the only ones that have to be on top of their game. This is a business, and if you're affiliated with the brand, you have to be a bad bitch and not a regular one. An exceptional one." Dillon winked.

Dillon's unapologetic assessment stung, and Lanika smirked to keep from snarling. Sarcastically, she stated, "Oh, so it's *that* serious."

"Yes. It's very serious. Our clients are multimillionaires and billionaires. Not only do the escorts have to be on point, but all the females moving around the property have to be presented as flawless and fuckable at all times. There is no such thing as a bad day or an off day. We are a wealthy man's dream home. If they wanted to see frumpy, dumpy women, they could go home and look at their wives. Now let's go. You can follow behind me in your car."

"My friend guy dropped me off."

"That's even better. Then you can ride with me. So how serious are you and this friend guy?"

"Not too serious. We smash from time to time, and we might grab a bite to eat or catch a movie here and there. Why?"

"You may wanna lose him now. Or you can learn your cover story for your new job and feed it to him. When I say you have to be discreet, I mean it. This shit isn't legal, and none of us are trying to go to jail." Dillon shot Lanika a warning glare.

"What *is* my cover story?"

"You are the operations manager at P H I Modeling and Talent Agency. By no means do you ever tell him—or any man that you date, bed, or wed—what you truly do. Understand?"

"Understood."

London, formally known as Lanika, rode quietly in the passenger seat of the thunder-gray Continental coupe as Dillon whipped the luxury vehicle toward the outskirts of Charlotte. Being silent was the only surefire way for London to hide how geeked she was to be riding in a Bentley. "Oh my gawd," London exclaimed as Dillon turned into a neighborhood of sprawling mansions. "What neighborhood is this?"

"Trail View Country Club."

"Wow! I didn't even know that houses like this existed in Charlotte."

"See, that's why you have to leave your Westside and University area comfort zones. This city has all kinds of treasures that I bet you don't know about."

"I guess I'll get to discover them now that I'll be working for you."

"You damn right," Dillon answered while turning into the entrance of a long driveway. She stopped at a seventeen-foot iron gate, punched a combination of numbers on the keypad, and slowly moved forward as the gate opened.

"Holy shit." London's eyes bulged wide. "This is where I'm going to be working?" She gazed at the stucco mansion in awe. It had to have more than nine thousand square feet of living space.

"No, but it's not far from here."

"Oh, so this is where you live?"

"Negative. This is where you will be getting your makeover, among other things."

With her brow furrowed, London asked, "What other things?"

"Just come on. You'll see."

Nervous and excited at the same time, London got out of the car and followed Dillon up the long circular driveway. Staring at the fleet of expensive luxury cars parked in the driveway of the mansion, she stumbled and nearly fell against Dillon's back. When they reached the front door, Dillon slid a key in the lock, turned it, and opened the door as if she lived there.

"Damn! This look like one those rich ballplayers' or rappers on MTV cribs," London exclaimed as she stood between the foyer and the living room, admiring the mosaic-tiled floor, the hand-carved crown molding, and the twenty-five-foot ceiling.

"This way." Dillon led London to the lower level of the mansion, a forty-two-hundred-square-foot basement that had been transformed into a luxurious salon and spa. "The staff, the models, and I get everything from head to toe taken care of here."

A slim, five-nine, mocha-skinned female sporting a razor-sharp pixie cut approached with a warm, glistening white smile. "Hey, Dillon," she greeted.

"Hey, Toni."

"What you getting done today?"

"I'll be back later for an updo and makeup for that thing I have tonight. For now, I simply need you to take care of Pretty Hustlaz new manager, London. And, London, this is Toni. She is the owner and lead hairstylist of this very private salon and spa."

Both London and Toni shook hands. "Nice to meet you," they greeted one another simultaneously.

"Now, Toni," Dillon said with an exaggerated Southern drawl, "I need y'all to work y'all's magic and make her drop-dead gorgeous."

"You know we will," Toni responded, examining London. "She has a pretty face, good skin, and a nice shape." Toni lifted London's weave with the tips of her fingers, as if it were infected. "What kind of install is this?"

"Huh?"

"How were these extensions put in your head?"

"This is a quick weave."

"Oh Lord," Toni sighed, rubbing London's head and feeling the thick layers of glue affixed to London's gel-hardened black hair. "I'm going to have to send my assistant out for some Morning Glory to get this shit out. They can do your facial, mani, and pedi until then—"

"Before you do any of that," Dillon interrupted, "take her to the dress suite so Antice can get her measurements and pull her some stuff while you all are working on her. I'll be back in a few hours. Toni, can I borrow your truck for a li'l bit?"

"I don't even know why you asked when you know that I don't care. The keys are in the usual place. Just make sure you leave the keys to that beautiful Bentley," Toni responded.

Chapter 2

A black town car entered through the gates of one of the most lavish estates in Charlotte, the P H I estate. Only a few chosen ones had ever made it past those tall iron gates. Those who did make it in were either extraordinarily gorgeous women or extremely wealthy men. The vehicle slowly crept down the half-mile-long driveway, then stopped at a beautiful Art Deco–style courtyard in front of a massive, luxurious mansion. The chauffeur got out and opened the rear passenger door. Out stepped Dave Prescott, one of the current senators of North Carolina. He walked over to a waiting golf cart. An exotically pretty Japanese woman in a formfitting black pantsuit was behind the wheel.

"Good afternoon, sir," she greeted him with a warm and welcoming smile.

"Good afternoon to you." He peered at her lustfully. "I haven't seen you before. What's your name?"

"Amanda."

"Are you on the menu?"

"No, I'm a hostess," she replied, steering the golf cart onto the lawn and toward the back of the mansion.

"I may need some private hosting while I'm here. I pay well."

"My boss would have to okay any private work," she responded before stopping in front of the estate's guest-house.

"Check with your boss. It's been a while since I had a nice ménage. It would do me a lot of good to get one in today," he uttered while getting out of the cart. "I'll be here for the next three hours," he added, his excitement already growing. He paid like he weighed, so anyone who was about their money would be a fool to decline his offer.

"If I get the okay, I'll be back." She winked at the handsome older gentleman.

Dave was a former NBA megastar, and before that, he was the starting point guard on a championship UNC–Chapel Hill team. Born and raised in Boiling Springs, a small North Carolina town, he was considered a state treasure and was loved and adored by many. Currently serving his second term as senator, he had never held any political seats prior to being elected to the position. Before he ran for the office, he'd never even thought about becoming a politician.

His entrance onto the political stage was a calculated choice that was strongly encouraged by his wife, Mallorie. Hailing from a wealthy family with major political ties, she understood the power of putting people into elected offices. Politicians were the country's decision makers. Mallorie had learned from her father that having politicians in her pocket was a major asset: politicians could make crucial decisions that benefited her and could do her unheard-of favors. In the end, money, fame, an overfunded campaign, and starstruck North Carolinian voters had put Dave Prescott in office.

As a senator, Dave did work hard, but he played harder. His playtime was well funded too. During his years as an NBA player, he'd earned more than three hundred seventy million dollars, which he'd invested well. Add to that his wife's huge inheritance and the money that special interest groups and lobbyists slid him beneath the table, and he had already hit billionaire status. This type of wealth afforded him the opportunity to pursue some really expensive habits. His newest and favorite pastime of the past few months was hanging out at the estate, which happened to be home to twenty drop-dead gorgeous high-end escorts from around the globe.

Dave had fucked a couple of them, but lately he had had eyes only for one, Alleyne. He considered the young beauty his; therefore, Dave had spent a lot of money to block off her time daily so that she would have little contact with other male clients. Instead of a whore-john relationship, they had a married man and his mistress situation going on. The escorts had their own private rooms in the mansion, but Dave often preferred the estate's guesthouse over the mansion for his visits with Alleyne. He used the guesthouse so much that he was getting a discount on the five-thousand-dollars-an-hour rate.

After entering the guesthouse, Dave found Alleyne sitting on the couch, dressed in his favorite outfit, a La Perla ivory lace thong and strappy six-inch Zanotti heels. Alleyne's legs were crossed, her arms were folded across her bare chest, and her beautiful face was covered in annoyance.

"Why the long face?" Dave asked as he shrugged out of his custom-fitted Armani suit.

Alleyne rolled her eyes and poked her lips out like a spoiled little girl. Dave flashed that sexy white-toothed smile that had landed Alleyne in her current predicament in the first place. He put his pointer finger under her chin and gently raised her head. Alleyne looked into his beautiful slanted eyes and felt her pussy pulse right away.

Fuck! I can't stand this fine-ass, rich nigga! she scolded herself silently. She was supposed to be here on business, not getting weak in the knees after two seconds of being alone with Dave.

"You going to tell me what's wrong?" he asked again, although he knew already.

"It's broad daylight . . . You're cutting my time short . . . um . . . you want me to contin—" Alleyne began, but her words went tumbling back down her throat when Dave crushed his mouth onto hers forcefully. She let out a throaty breath, and her body folded against his. He already had her folding like a lawn chair. Alleyne parted her lips slightly and allowed Dave's long, lizard-like tongue into her mouth.

"Slsss," she hissed, her words garbled, as his hands danced all over her body. Dave pinched her erect nipples, which sent her juices gushing from her dripping wet center.

He grabbed a handful of Alleyne's hair and yanked her head back so that he could look into her eyes. "I don't want to hear you complaining again . . . you hear me?" Dave growled, then stuck his tongue out and licked Alleyne's lips.

"Mmm," she whimpered, keeping her eyes closed tightly and melting under his tight grasp. This was the shit she loved about fucking Dave; the sex was different every time. Sometimes they made love, and other times, like now, they fucked like animals.

Dave forcefully pressed his mouth against hers. His hot, minty breath sent heated sparks down her back and made her left leg quiver. Alleyne just knew her pussy was going to explode. This was one more thing Dave loved about her—the fact that she could squirt. Most women didn't have that kind of pussy control. Their tongues met once more and performed a wicked dance. Alleyne became so excited that she bit Dave's bottom lip and drew blood.

"Yeah . . . that's what I'm fucking talking about!" he growled, and he followed this with a seductive smile. "I love when you act like a nasty little bitch!" he grunted. Sucking the blood off his lip, Dave shoved Alleyne forcefully. "Get on the fucking floor," he demanded as he loosened his belt and unzipped his pants.

Alleyne was excited just thinking about Dave's nearly twelve inches of thick meat. She had tried to tell herself that she wasn't addicted to him, but the way she was salivating now was surely like a fiend waiting for a hit. Alleyne complied with his demand, stretching her body out on the fluffy throw rug in front of the fireplace. Her beautiful caramel skin against the white rug gave her a glow that Dave couldn't resist.

"On your stomach," he said, stepping out of his pants.

Before she turned over, Alleyne examined his strong, muscular frame and the long tool that was hanging in between his thighs. She licked her lips lasciviously, eased her hand under her body, and fingered her soaking wet clitoris. Dave resembled a man much younger than his age. He had a thin, muscular frame and six-pack abs and was six feet, four inches tall. His hair was still full, and his tight, soft curls hugged his scalp. For a man in his late forties, Dave resembled Rick Fox in his early Laker days.

"I like when you play with it and get that shit ready for me," Dave whispered, dropping to his knees behind her. He started at her neck, licking her nape, and then moved slowly across her shoulders and down the center of her back with his tongue.

"Agggh! Yes! Fuck!" Alleyne cooed. When Dave reached her ass, she couldn't take it anymore. she let out a stray kitten–sounding yelp. Dave chuckled and then placed his strong hands on her ass cheeks and gently spread them apart. She responded by gently pushing her ass upward toward his face, yearning for his long, wet tongue to enter her.

"You waiting for this shit, ain't you? All that fucking pouting for nothing," Dave chided, laughing wickedly. "You like when I eat that ass from the back?" he asked and then pressed his face between her ass cheeks while he held them apart.

"Yes!" she belted out, clutching fistfuls of the throw rug. Dave licked Alleyne's ass from top to bottom, then stopped at the hole for a minute and gently blew.

"Ewww, Daddy!" she cried out in ecstasy, all parts of her hourglass-shaped body trembling. In all her twenty-five years on the earth and with the plethora of men she'd serviced as an escort, Alleyne had never really experienced the mind-rocking sex she shared with Dave.

"You ready for me?" he asked, gently pushing Alleyne's perfectly round ass, urging her onto her knees. Once she was in position, Dave resumed his tongue massage. He bent his head and delved tongue first into her dripping hot box, and lapped up her juices like he needed them to live.

"Fuck me . . . Fuck me now!" she growled. All his tongue play had her overheated and feeling insatiable amounts of pleasure, but what she was really looking forward to was Dave's porno-type dick.

Dave was more than glad to oblige. He liked spending time with Alleyne, but he knew he had to get this over with. Dave was an important man, with places to be and people to see.

After lifting Alleyne off the floor, he carried her to the bedroom and placed her in the center of the California king–sized bed. He stepped back and took in her beauty. Alleyne was one of those exotic beauties that Dave loved. Born in Belize, Alleyne had a slight accent, and it and her curvy body and her beautiful eyes drove him wild every time. Dave climbed onto the bed, then moved toward her, hungry for her loving. He kissed her neck, moved slowly down to her erect nipples, and then headed slowly back up to her mouth. After wedging his hips between her knees, he entered her. They had stopped using condoms after the second encounter, and he was glad, since he felt fully the wetness mixed with heat now surrounding his dick.

"Yes! Dave, fuck me! Right there . . . harder, harder . . . Don't fucking stop. Don't ever fucking stop," Alleyne pleaded as she raked her long nails across the skin on his toned back.

"Whose pussy is this?" he grunted, pumping his ass in and out with a rhythm that had Alleyne's clitoris buzzing.

"Nobody's! Nobody's! Only yours!" Alleyne screamed as she experienced an earth-shattering, mind-blowing orgasm while tightly wrapping her legs around his slender waist.

Dave flipped her over without taking his dick out of her. "Ride this shit now," he said huskily. With her legs quaking and her body feeling exhausted from the crazy climax, Alleyne moved up and down slowly.

"Nah, you know what I like," he huffed, using his hands to move her faster up and down on his rod.

"Ahhh!" Alleyne yelped when it felt like Dave's long pole was busting into her guts.

"Don't fuck around!" he growled, using his muscular arms to push her up and pull her back down on his dick. Alleyne finally got her second wind and began swirling her hips as she moved up and down.

"I'm about to . . . ," Dave growled, but it was too late. "Argh!" he groaned, pulling her down on top of him as he shot his load while thrusting deeper into her warm, hot center.

Alleyne collapsed on top of him and listened to his pounding heart. She closed her eyes, wondering if this would ever be permanent. "I wish that I could go to sleep like this and wake up like this every morning."

"You will"—he ran his fingers through her hair—"one day, I promise."

"Dave, I'm not stupid. You're never going to leave your wife for me."

"I might. It just won't be anytime soon. It would be too difficult. She could take everything from me. Then I wouldn't have anything to spoil you with, would I?"

"I can spoil myself. I just need you to love me in the same way that I love you."

"I do love you. If I didn't, I'd get with the other girls, instead of spending all the thousands that I do every week to cover your weekly minimums so I can be your only client."

Satisfied by his answer, she moved on to another subject. "I've been thinking about leaving this place and opening my own brothel."

"Hell no."

"Why not? I have enough money saved, and three of the girls here said that they would go with me."

"If I leave my wife for you, you are going to have to leave this world behind you. Besides, it takes connections, which you don't have, to open and run a brothel under the radar—"

"Excuse me," Amanda interrupted as she stood in the middle of the room in only a thong and a pair of pumps. She had quietly entered the guesthouse and then had tiptoed into the bedroom. "My boss said that it's okay and that you'll be invoiced at the regular rate for me."

"Bitch," Alleyne squawked. She slid off Dave's softened dick, hopped up off the bed, and turned to Amanda. "What the fuck is your hostess ass doing in here with nothing on?"

"I asked her to join us." Dave stood up.

Frowning, Alleyne turned back to Dave. "For what?"

"For starters, I want to watch her eat your pussy while you suck my dick. If you don't like it, get out and I'll have one of the other girls sent in here."

Pissed, Alleyne forced a smile. "Oh no, baby, I'm not tripping. I just thought she was trying to be slick, like some of them staff bitches be doing, and trying to press up." She swallowed hard. "You know I'll do whatever you like, Daddy."

He sat back down. "Get on your knees and put this dick in your mouth."

Afraid of displeasing him, she dropped down to her knees immediately and began to pleasure him.

Dave pointed at Amanda. "You get down behind her. Let me see you work that tongue in her ass and pussy."

Dave left the mansion feeling like a new man. Whenever he could have his way with women, it made him feel like a king. Dave's wife was long past stroking his ego and making him feel special, unless she wanted something out of him. Alleyne looked at him with stars in her eyes. She wanted nothing more than to be with him, and since she was so young and beautiful, Dave felt like that nigga when he had Alleyne on her knees, crawling to him. Sure, he was wealthy and plenty of young women wanted an older man to take care of them, but given the way Alleyne came all over his dick every time they had sex, he knew she enjoyed her time with him, and he refused to believe she wanted him only for his money.

In his opinion, no woman in her right mind, his wife included, would want a broke man, so that didn't bother him. Since his balls were drained, Dave was going to stop by the country club and grab some afternoon drinks with his buddies, who were judges, doctors, and lawyers. Dave rubbed elbows with the best. He loved having people in his pocket who could pull strings and look out for him no matter what the situation or the circumstances were. He was part of an elite group.

He loved the power that his name and his wife's held. Mallorie Prescott didn't hesitate to remind people who she was anywhere she went. If she had it her way, women carrying buckets filled with roses would walk in front of her and toss rose petals on the ground for her to walk on. That was just how special she thought she was. Dave and Mallorie had become so ego driven and bigheaded that they thought they were untouchable.

Dillon's grandmother's neighborhood on the northwest side of Charlotte had a mix of poverty-stricken, poor, and lower-middle-class families. It wasn't fear that had motivated Dillon to drive Toni's Range instead of her Bentley to her grandmother's house. She just didn't want to ride through the neighborhood in a $180,000 car when some of the people didn't even know where their next meal was coming from. Although Dillon had many good childhood memories of the neighborhood, she longed to move her maternal grandmother, Lilly-Ann, out of the area. In the early nineties, when crime had begun to spiral out of control, many of the middle- to upper-middle-class homeowners had fled to the suburbs, often selling homes that had been in their family for generations.

Now, more than 75 percent of the homes in the neighborhood were leased to renters, who moved in and out so fast that no one bothered establishing a relationship or even exchanging names. The teens who lacked proper supervision, for numerous reasons, formed little violent cliques and became a menace in the community. They burglarized houses, robbed people at the bus stops, and extorted money from the mom-and-pop stores. Dillon had been so worried about the escalating crime and violence that a year ago she'd purchased a brand-new home in an upscale area for her grandmother. The gracious gift had not been accepted. Lilly-Ann didn't believe for one minute that Dillon's money came from a real modeling agency, and so she had rejected the gift. And she was well within her rights to feel that way.

For twenty years Lilly-Ann had worked as a housekeeper for the Gallaghers, one of the wealthiest families in North Carolina. They were often referred to as the Kennedys of the South. Much like Massachusetts's most famous family, it had long been rumored that the Gallaghers' great wealth was built from the illegal proceeds on the sale of moonshine and from the money raked in by the after-hours gambling houses that Fran Gallagher ran during the Prohibition era of the 1920s.

Fran, the daughter of Irish immigrants, was an outcast in her devout Catholic family because she'd given birth out of wedlock three times before the age of twenty-five. Borderline illiterate, she was pretty and had a magnetic personality and a loud, contagious laugh. Fran was also an excellent bootlegger; Irish whiskey was her specialty. The party crowd clung to her and wanted to be wherever she was. Even if Fran couldn't read, she wasn't dumb. Partying was great, but capitalizing off partying was better.

Fran made a lot of money selling her Irish whiskey at the parties and card games that she hosted weekly. With the proceeds from her illegal drinks, Fran provided a wonderful lifestyle for her sons and spared no expense when it came to their education. All three boys attended the most prestigious boarding schools and colleges on the East Coast. Fran's special blend of whiskey was in high demand not only in North Carolina but in other states as well. Juke joints, speakeasies, and crime families ordered cases of the whiskey by the dozen. By the end of Prohibition, Fran was filthy rich, and the investment that she'd made into her sons' education was paying off tremendously. Fran's sons legitimized her money through their businesses, Gallagher Properties and Gallagher's Supply Store. Not only did they clean the family fortune, but they also multiplied it.

In the mid-1960s Lilly-Ann began working for the oldest Gallagher son, Carney. At that point, Gallagher Properties was number one in Charlotte's commercial real estate market. Gallagher's Supply Store had become Gallagher's Department Store, and it was a premier chain in mid-Atlantic and southeastern states. Even with the Gallaghers' corporate and financial success, allegations of criminal activity followed the family for generations. The rumors were not unfounded, due in part to the family's ties to the Irish Mafia and its relationships with members of other criminal organizations.

The rumors did not affect the way that Lilly-Ann or the other house staff felt about the Gallaghers, especially since they were treated so well and paid more than other housekeepers. Lilly-Ann's children were always invited to playtime, parties, and sleepovers at the Gallaghers' home. Mary, Carney's wife, was so smitten with baby Dillon that she asked that she and Carney be named Dillon's godparents. Mary and Carney's granddaughter Meredith moved into their home at the age of four. Being that they were the same age, Meredith and Dillon took to each other as soon as they met.

As a young girl, Dillon would spend practically entire summers and school breaks with Meredith and the Gallaghers, even after her grandmother retired. Once Meredith left for boarding school out of state, the close-knit friendship slowly dwindled away. The girls were united once again at Lilly-Ann's seventy-fifth birthday party, which Meredith attended with her grandparents. Meredith invited Dillon out for drinks so that they could catch up on one another's lives.

From that night on, Dillon and Meredith were inseparable. Many people said that Meredith was the reincarnation of her great-grandmother, Fran Gallagher. They were eerily identical in appearance, and though Fran had been dead for decades before Meredith was born, she possessed Fran's personality and mannerisms. Meredith, who never attended college, had several profitable self-started businesses, all of which she opened before the age of twenty-three. Her most profitable businesses were a construction firm, a modeling agency, and a millionaire dating service.

When the construction firm began getting sizable contracts, Meredith had to spend the bulk of her time and focus there. As a result, she needed someone whom she could trust to help with the dating service and the modeling agency, so she brought Dillon on board. It was then that Dillon learned both companies were fronts for an escort service. A year or so after bringing Dillon on, Meredith became the target in a major securities, mortgage, and wire fraud case. At first, it seemed like the case was going nowhere; then suddenly it began to pick up steam.

Realizing that neither money nor the power of the Gallagher name could help her to escape the charges, Meredith decided to flee the country until her attorneys could work things out. Meredith's bank accounts were frozen in an attempt to flush her out of hiding. Fortunately, Meredith was a silent partner in Pretty Hustlaz Inc. an ethnically diverse escort service that Dillon started. Pretty Hustlaz was under a shell corporation that wasn't directly linked to Meredith, and therefore, its assets weren't frozen. Every month Dillon put Meredith's cut of the profits in various safe-deposit boxes at different banks across the city. Whenever Meredith sent word that she needed money, Dillon made sure that she got it.

Lilly-Ann didn't know the intricate details of Dillon's business, but she knew that the amount of money her granddaughter was spending plus her relationship with Meredith equaled trouble. The money being dirty wasn't Lilly-Ann's biggest concern. She truly worried about her Dillon getting in any kind of trouble. Lilly-Ann felt that if she accepted the house or large sums of money from her granddaughter, it would mean she was condoning whatever illegal activities Dillon was involved in.

Dillon was hurt that her grandmother had rejected the house, but she had got a sliver of relief when her aunts, Pat and Gloria, moved back to Charlotte from Detroit some months earlier and arranged to stay with Lilly-Ann. Right before the economic downturn of 2008, both sisters had retired from auto factory jobs after thirty years of service.

There was no place that Pat and Gloria loved more than Detroit, but the entire city went to hell after the recession, and it didn't look like it was going to reemerge. Instead of moving to a safe suburb or a small town in Michigan, they decided to return to Charlotte. Lilly-Ann convinced them to move in with her and save their money, since she was alone in a sizable two- story, five-bedroom prewar home. Pat and Gloria were happy to oblige their mother. They didn't like Lilly-Ann living alone, which she had done since their father's death fifteen years ago.

Pat's adult daughter wanted desperately to get out of Detroit, too, for the sake of her twelve- and fourteen-year-old sons, but it would be eight months before she could transfer within the same company to Charlotte. In its current state Detroit wasn't the place for any teenage black boys, particularly ones with a mother who worked long hours and a military father stationed in another country. Without thinking twice, Pat brought the boys with her.

Lilly-Ann loved having her daughters and great-grand-sons there. Gloria and Pat had given the interior of the house a complete makeover, installing new appliances, bringing in new furniture, and applying a fresh coat of paint. Meticulous cleaners, both women kept their mother's house spotless, and the boys kept the yard in order. Lilly-Ann's house was lively once again, like it had been when her children were young. Each morning Lilly-Ann joyfully rose at 6:00 a.m. to cook breakfast for her family. She prepared lunch at noon daily, and dinner was ready by five thirty every evening.

It was winter when the sisters moved to Charlotte, and the neighborhood was relatively quiet. But as the weather began to heat up, so did the action. The sisters were not naïve. They knew that the neighborhood had changed drastically from the days of their youth, but they had no idea it had become so violent. In the first three weeks of spring, there was violence almost daily: junkies were stabbing junkies, gangs were brawling with cliques, and innocent children were getting jumped or hit with stray bullets.

A rolling shoot-out the previous night was the reason for Dillon's impromptu visit. Pulling up to her grand-mother's brick home, Dillon spotted her aunt Gloria sitting on the porch. "Hey, Aunt Glo," she called and waved as she was getting out of the truck.

"Hey there, Dee Dee," Gloria replied before taking a long drag off her Virginia Slims cigarette, which was perched between the knuckles of her right middle finger and forefinger. Blowing a long stream of smoke out her nostrils, she smashed the butt against a clear blown-glass ashtray. "How you feeling today?" She flung her arms around Dillon and hugged her tightly.

"I'm fine, Aunt Glo," Dillon answered, squeezing her back. "What you doing smoking? I thought you quit those nasty-ass things."

"Them nasty-ass things is the only thing keeping my nerves intact after that bullshit last night."

"So, what exactly happened?"

"These silly-ass young niggas had a shoot-out in broad daylight in the middle of the street like in a fucking old Western movie. Some of 'em was walking, and some were in cars. A boy in one of the cars got shot, and the dummies in the car opened the door and pushed him out right there." She pointed to the sidewalk that bordered the yard.

Dillon glanced at the burgundy-stained beige concrete. Shaking her head, she muttered, "This is crazy."

"Hell yeah, it is, and Mama in there talking about it's going to get better."

"What makes her think that?"

"Some ole foolish shit that so-called neighborhood board and the police be kicking to them at those community meetings. They have them damn meetings every week and ain't accomplishing shit. Mama and a few other elderly people that still own their homes run to every meeting, paying dues and supporting fundraisers for a neighborhood watch that don't exist."

"Grandma tripping. She has to move now." Dillon opened the screen door. "Aunt Pat in the house?"

"No," Gloria stated firmly. "She took them boys to a hotel, since the police were over here messing with the kids that didn't have nothing to do with it. Plus, the boy that got killed, his friends are on Facebook, saying that they coming back for revenge."

"Yeah, I would've got them out of here too." Dillon stepped inside the house. "Grandma?" she called out.

"I'm in the kitchen," Lilly-Ann answered as she sat in a high-back wooden chair, peeling sweet potatoes. With smooth cider-colored skin and golden-brown dyed hair, eighty-one-year-old Lilly-Ann Rutledge could pass for early to midsixties. Old school to her heart, she was a no-nonsense type of woman. Set in her ways and stubborn, Lilly-Ann could be hard to persuade when she had her mind made up about anything. With just a stern, icy stare, Lilly Ann could make her grown children back up off her.

Dillon and Gloria knew that they were about to face firm resistance, but they were prepared for it. Along with Pat, they had agreed that they would stick together and not retreat from the goal of convincing Lilly-Ann that it was time for her to move.

"Hey, Grandma." Dillon bent down and kissed Lilly-Ann's cheek.

"Hey, gal. I ain't seen you in a month of Sundays."

"I've been working like crazy, Grandma. I've been doing two different jobs."

"Humph. Work . . . Is that what they calling hustling and peddling now?"

"Peddling?" Dillon drew back, offended. "Not today, Grandma. I don't have time for it. Why didn't you tell Pat and Gloria that I bought you a brand-new home, a home that you refuse to live in, and that you're living in the middle of a war zone by choice?"

"Why would I tell anybody about something that I don't want?" Lilly-Ann replied as Gloria walked in the kitchen.

"Mama," she interjected, "there is no way you should be living here when Dillon has bought a home in a safer area."

"I do not want a house that dirty money has built."

Sighing deeply, Dillon rolled her eyes upward. "Grandma, you keep talking about my money being dirty with absolutely no proof whatsoever."

"I worked for them white folks for twenty years, and everybody know that they wealth was built on dirty money for generations." Lilly-Ann dropped a skinless sweet potato and pointed the knife toward Dillon. "I curse the day that you met Meredith Gallagher. She's just like the rest of her family. Got all that money and still like to chase that dirty money. Just plain ole greedy. That's why she over in Europe, on the run now."

"First of all, she is not on the run, Grandma. Second, you worked for the Gallaghers for twenty years, and you didn't have a problem taking the dirty money then."

"I didn't start hearing things about their money until I started working for them. In those days I couldn't just up and quit a job. We had five children. Your grandfather, God rest his soul, didn't move into management until our children were in high school."

"That sounds good, Grandma. Now explain why you still accept the money that they send you every Christmas, birthday, and Mother's Day?"

"It would be rude to turn down their gifts."

"But it's okay to reject mine," Dillon retorted.

"Mama," Gloria said, stepping in again, "I don't care where the money came from to buy that house. It's time to get from over here right now. Pat and I were going to buy our own separate houses. You talked us into living with you instead, and we love being here with you, but we did not leave Detroit to come here and feel like we're living on the West Side of Chicago. It's becoming just as bad here as it is there."

A concerned expression washed over Lilly-Ann's face. "What are you saying, Gloria?"

"We can't keep living here, Mama. Now, if we had gotten our own houses and came here and saw how it was over here, we would've moved you in with one of us immediately. Since that is not an option, we're moving in that house that Dillon bought for you."

"I'm not! I meant what I said. I don't want that house."

"That is absolutely fine, Mama. You don't have to want it, but we are getting away from here."

"We?" Lilly-Ann's face became fraught with horror. "Who is *we?*"

"Pat, the boys, and me," Gloria answered, playing on her mother's emotions. Lilly-Ann had confided in a family member that before Pat and Gloria moved in, she was living in fear and loneliness. That confession had gotten back to the sisters, and Pat had decided to use that knowledge as ammunition.

Lilly-Ann's face twitched and sadness filled her eyes as she said, "Y'all just going to leave . . . ? That's fine. I was by myself all those years before y'all moved in." She inhaled deeply, and her chest heaved up and down, and then she swallowed hard as she exhaled to ward off the tears.

Feeling her mother's anguish, Gloria drew close to Lilly-Ann. Bending down, she looked directly in her mother's eyes. "Mama, I know you do not want to be here by yourself. We've already agreed to pay rent to Dillon and eventually buy the house," Gloria lied, saying whatever she needed to say to get her mother out of the danger zone.

"Well, if y'all do it that way, I'll move," Lilly-Ann said somberly while beaming inside. She was so happy that she'd been given a way out without compromising how she felt about the situation. She did not want to be alone again, whether it was at her current residence or one in a safer location.

Dillon stood there, shocked, thinking, *Wow. That was much easier than I expected.* "Since that's settled, I'm—"

"You just got here," Lilly-Ann interrupted. "You just cannot sit your hips still for more than ten minutes. By the way, this is *not* settled."

"Grandma, I have a really important event this evening. And what's not settled? You said that you would move to the house."

"But what about *this* house?"

"Sell it," Dillon said matter-of-factly.

"Girl, I'm not selling this house! Your granddaddy worked hard to pay for this house. We raised our children here, and you and all your cousins practically lived here too."

"Well, rent it out, then."

"I don't want no dirty-ass people tramping through here, tearing my house up."

"Grandma, I can't do this with you today. Pat and Gloria will help you figure it out." Dillon leaned down, hugged Lilly-Ann, and kissed her cheek. "I love you."

"Uh-huh. Well, stay longer, then."

"I really can't today, but I promise I'll be back." Dillon hugged Gloria and slipped five hundred dollars in her back pocket, then whispered, "That's all the cash I have on me right now. Get the estimate from the movers, and I'll get it over here."

Watching Dillon walk away, Lilly-Ann called, "You need to come back for dinner. You getting too skinny. Must not be eating."

"I do eat, Grandma," Dillon shouted, making a bee-line to the front door. "I eat clean and work out hard." Stepping out the door, she saw a black Range Rover exactly like the one that she was driving pull into the driveway.

The driver's door opened, and Dillon's ex-boyfriend, Heavy, stepped out, a sly smile on his face.

To the world, he was Andre Cuthbertson, a business-man and a music mogul on the rise. To Dillon, he was Heavy, a street dude who knew how to play the game and women as well as Kenny G played the flute. Heavy had earned that nickname on account of his size and demeanor, something Dillon had once loved.

"What up, D?" he greeted.

"Hey, Heavy," Dillon responded, her tone a bit dry, as she opened the driver's door and tossed her purse over to the passenger seat. "What are you doing here?"

"Checking on my mom's old house. The last tenants moved out a couple of months ago. I come through here once in a while to make sure ain't no junkies or trap boys posted up in there. You know shit stupid around here now."

"Yes, I do . . . Well, it was nice seeing you. Tell your mother that I said hello."

"Damn. Why you trying to blow a nigga off so fast?"

"It's not like that. I'm just really beat for time."

"I understand that, but, damn, can a nigga at least get a hug?" Heavy took Dillon by the arm and pulled her slim frame into a tight embrace. "Damn, I miss you."

"Okay." Dillon begrudgingly hugged him quickly and pulled away.

"Damn, you really be treating a nigga fucked up."

"How?"

"I tell you I miss you, and all you say is okay."

Shaking her head, Dillon let out a wry giggle. "What did you expect me to say, Heavy? You know what . . . ? Let's not do this today, and let's not go through this every time we bump into each other. It's getting quite old."

It had been more than four years since Dillon had ended their two-and-a-half-year relationship. They'd been very much in love once upon a time. Heavy grew up a few doors down from Lilly-Ann's house. Nearly all the homes in the neighborhood were owned by blacks who worked for the rich whites who lived in a nearby community. It was said that the white families created the neighborhood so that their servants wouldn't have far to travel for work. Heavy's mother worked for one of the wealthiest families, and it was rumored that he was a secret love child. As a young boy, he had the biggest crush on Dillon for years. He didn't act on it until she returned home after dropping out of college. After dating for close to three months, they got serious, and for the first year and a half, it was great, but the last nine to ten months were extremely toxic.

In the latter part of their relationship, Heavy's small-time cocaine and weed operation began to expand rapidly. Money was coming in by the thousands, faster than he could count it. Knowing that he was in the midst of a hustler's dream run, he gave all his time and attention to the hustle. At that time, it was money over everything, including Dillon, and when she complained, he wasn't trying to hear it.

There were times when Dillon would not see Heavy for two or three days, and the days that he was present in their home, it was only to sleep, shower, and dress. Loneliness and depression filled Dillon's days, along with anger from rumors of his cheating with different chicks. Heavy tried to appease Dillon with cash and pricey gifts. It didn't work; her feelings couldn't be bought. During one of his prolonged absences, Dillon decided that she had had enough. She was done talking, and she was flat-out tired of the below-the-belt, heated arguments that they were having every other day. She packed every item that she owned, moved out, and left him.

Heavy was shocked when he returned home. As soon as he stepped in the door, he knew that Dillon was gone. Her beloved art that gave the living room character wasn't on the walls; the rustic ivory-suede wingback accent chairs that she cherished were gone. There was not a single trace that she'd ever lived there. He didn't even put up a fight for Dillon. He missed her like crazy, but he didn't miss the distraction from his main goal. With Dillon gone, he could put 100 percent of his focus on getting money.

Heavy purposely remained single for the eighteen-month period following the breakup. In that time, he built a solid team, which allowed him to distance himself from the time-consuming trench work. Everything was going well until he found himself locked up after an investigation exposed his entire operation. He spent two years in prison on a five-year bid and was happy for the early release due to good behavior and his lawyers' persistence . You would think prison would have made him reform himself, but it merely made Heavy smarter with his movements. He was more cautious and kept his head on a swivel. With his free time increasing after his release, he began craving the company of a woman whom he could deal with on a serious level. There were a number of chicks that he could smash whenever he wanted. Beyond their ass and throat, he had zero interest in them.

In his pursuit of a serious female companion, Heavy dated a handful of impressive women who measured up to his incredibly picky beauty and personality standards. None of the women held his interest long, however, because once he began silently comparing them to Dillon, not one of them could stand next to her. He began to think of his ex-love quite often. The more that Dillon danced across his mind, the more he realized that he should've never let her go. She was the one person who knew the real Andre, not just Heavy. Dillon knew how hard it had been for Heavy to grow up without proper means. The poverty had been the driving force behind his grind. One thing she always loved was the way he cared for his mother.

After rebuilding everything he had lost while incarcerated, Heavy reached out to her to try to rekindle their relationship. This second time around, Dillon just happened to be on a paper chase. Pretty Hustlaz was running smoothly and was making a good profit. Dillon did everything in her power to keep her business humming. She really wanted to give Heavy another chance at first, but then she decided that any kind of close relationship with him could be problematic for the business that she was in.

It wasn't a secret that the streets had crowned Heavy as the man. He ran the cocaine game, and he was the only one bringing large quantities of high-grade cocaine into the city. Dillon knew that at any time state or federal law enforcement could be watching Heavy. She didn't want to come under any kind of investigation due to her association with him or any street dude. So at that moment she made up her mind to date only corporate guys.

Dillon did not even like standing around and chatting whenever they randomly bumped into each other. Heavy couldn't understand why she acted so funny toward him. With his ego slightly bruised and his feelings a little hurt, he told her now, "I never thought that you'd be so cold toward me. I'm not the same young jackass. Like I said before, I regret putting the money before you, and I never meant to hurt you. If you're still hurting—"

"Hold up." Dillon raised her palms toward him. "I'm so over our relationship, and much like you, I'm a different person. If I had stayed with you, I wouldn't have accomplished the things that I have. I'm very content in my belief that everything happens for a reason."

"What if it was meant for us to break up, then get back together on some power couple–type shit? You're still the baddest bitch in the city, and you already know who I am."

"Yeah, the cockiest dude in Charlotte."

"And you match my gangsta. Ya Range looks like mine, right down to the black shoes. We damn near already got his and hers whips."

"No, we do not," Dillon remarked, ready for the awkward encounter to end. "It's time for me to get it back to the owner now." She turned to leave.

"I should've known," Heavy scoffed.

Dillon turned around, her mouth twisted in a frown, ready to read him. "Should've known what?"

"That you was just stuntin' in some nigga's shit."

"Let me be extra clear with you. I don't have to explain myself to you. But since I see that you're continuing your long record of being an ass by assuming shit you don't know anything about, I'm going to straighten you out." She pointed to the truck. "That is my homegirl's Range. I drove it because I didn't want to flaunt my two-hundred-thousand-dollar Bentley in the face of people who are struggling day-to-day."

Turned on by her attitude, Heavy grabbed her hand. "You're the only person that I let speak to me like that."

Dillon snatched her hand away. "Boy, bye! Can you please move your truck so that I can get out? Now. Thanks." She hopped into the truck.

Moving backward toward his truck, Heavy shouted, "Hope to see you soon."

"And I'm desperately hoping not to see you." Dillon yanked the door closed.

Dillon had barely gotten out of the neighborhood when her phone started going off. She looked down at the screen, and her head began pounding when she saw the name Jada. Jada was a girl who had started out with Dillon when Pretty Hustlaz was just a dream. Dillon no longer allowed Jada to work for her because of her constant drama-filled life. In the beginning, Jada would work on and off, whenever she needed the extra ends, but she was never dependable. Dillon would always tell her, "Girl, you have to invest to make money. You can't ask for eight hundred to a thousand dollars and not invest in your business. Your nails should be done, your hair should be done, and you should not be in a cheap-ass motel."

Jada would always respond the same way. "I understand, D. I will get it together."

"I don't think you get it, Jada. One fuckup and this could all be over. I don't plan on going to jail for trying to help you," Dillon would warn her.

Dillon had known Jada since high school, and in the beginning she let her work—even though Jada was hooked on pills—because she had children and because Dillon did have half a heart. But more so, it was because Jada was a beautiful girl and had a lot of potential. Dillon knew that Jada could be one of her top girls even now. She also knew that was probably what she was calling her for. Jada had been begging Dillon to put her back on. But there was no way in hell that Dillon could ever forgive her after their last encounter and her *final* breaking point of the relationship.

Dillon thought back to that day. It was two days before Christmas, and Dillon and her then assistant, Nilda, couldn't reach Jada. After leaving voicemail after voicemail with no response, they both decided that Dillon should go to Jada's house and check on her. When Dillon arrived, she found Jada's two daughters, ages eight and twelve, home alone. The puzzling thing to her was that there was no Christmas tree and not a single gift in sight. Dillon knew there should have been both, considering she had purchased the tree and tons of gifts for the girls herself.

"Where is your mother?" Dillon asked, holding back tears of pity and anger but trying to maintain her composure.

"I don't know. She left last night," answered the youngest child, a bright-eyed little girl, who was obviously afraid and uncomfortable.

"Do you know who your mommy left with?" Dillon asked.

"Mommy left with the man in the red car," the child responded.

Dillon called the emergency number she had for Jada.

"Hello," said a soft, sleepy-sounding woman's voice.

"Hi. This is Dillon, and I was hoping you could help me find Jada or, better yet, a safe place for her girls to stay."

"Is there something wrong?" asked the woman on the other end, becoming a little frantic.

"I am sure everything will be fine. Jada is not home currently, and I just found the girls alone and don't want to leave them without some type of adult supervision," Dillon explained.

"I am their grandmother. I will be right there," the lady said before hanging up.

Dillon called Nilda and told her to come over to Jada's place. She had no idea how to deal with kids and hoped Nilda could help out until the grandmother arrived.

Nilda arrived pissed off. "I can't believe that stupid bitch left those kids all alone," she said aloud, slamming her car door shut. She hurried into the house.

Nilda immediately went over to the girls and knelt down. "Hey, sweetie pies. What are your names?" she said, changing her tone so that she sounded friendlier and more relaxed.

"I am Dasia, and her name is Olivia," said the youngest girl, who was small and beautiful, with soft skin and long curls. She came right over to Nilda, her curls bouncing around the dimples on her cheeks.

"It's okay. Don't be afraid," Nilda said softly, noticing the older girl was extremely quiet.

"I don't like being home alone, and we don't have lights," the eldest girl whispered. "I am not scared of the dark," she added.

"I am not scared of the dark, either, but I am scared of the man in the red car," Dasia said in a very meek voice.

"What? Why? What is wrong, sweetheart? Who is the man in the red car?" Nilda asked, pulling the young girl close to her.

Olivia glared at her younger sister, and she immediately became quiet again.

"No! Tell me what you are afraid of, baby. You can tell me anything," Nilda said, standing up. She looked Olivia in the eyes, trying to hold back the tears that were now forming. "Olivia, baby, please tell me why you are afraid," Nilda said, watching tears fill Olivia's slanted brown eyes too.

"Sometimes when Mommy is bad, he touches me and Dasia," Olivia said, covering her face.

Nilda knelt down again and had to remind herself to keep her composure. She hugged the girls and told them they were going to be safe and asked them to wait inside for their grandmother to come pick them up.

Nilda walked outside, where Dillon had been waiting and talking on the phone. "They can't stay here," Nilda said, tears running down her face, after Dillon left another voicemail for Jada and hung up.

"What?" Dillon replied.

"That nigga that Jada is with has been fucking with them little girls. They can't fucking stay here!" Nilda screamed, now overwhelmed by thoughts of her own abuse as a child. She knew far too well what the little girls were going through. She thought about being touched by different men and the pain stemming from that abuse, which she still dealt with, even as an adult.

"Dillon, we can't just let them go with the grandmother and be back here tomorrow. We have to help—" Nilda was interrupted by bright car lights approaching the house.

The red Dodge Neon was halfway in the yard when Dillon saw Nilda take off running toward the car. The car came to a halt, and as Jada stumbled out of the driver's seat, Nilda grabbed her.

"What kind of mother are you?" she shouted at Jada.

The passenger, a slim man with tight jeans and a baseball cap, started toward Nilda as he yelled, "What the fuck are you doing?" When he came within close range, he met the barrel of Dillon's .380.

"Motherfucka, nothing in this world would make me happier than to blow your fucking head off. You are a nasty bastard. You like touching little girls? You get off on fucking with innocent children who can't defend themselves?" Dillon growled through clenched teeth as the chrome of her gun smashed against the man's forehead, knocking him to the ground.

"Empty your pockets and get in the car, mothafucka, and you, too, bitch," Dillon said in a low but serious tone, with Nilda standing beside her.

"You are a worthless bitch, Jada," Dillon spat.

"How could you do this to your own kids after all you went through?" Nilda asked as she looked at Jada. It was pointless. Both she and Dillon could tell from Jada's blank stare and glazed eyes that she was high as a kite.

"Your mother is coming to get the girls," Dillon said.

"My babies ain't going nowhere," Jada uttered.

Dillon placed the gun right between Jada's eyes. "Yes they are, and you won't do one fucking thing to stop them."

A second set of headlights flashed around the corner.

"Now, get your sorry ass in there and tell those kids they will be staying with Grandma until you make a safe home for them to come to," Dillon instructed.

Jada's mother parked her car and started to get out, but Nilda stopped her. "The girls are inside. Let me get them for you," she said.

"What's going on?" Mrs. Jones asked, her face full of concern and angst.

"Everything is going to be okay, Mrs. Jones," Dillon answered, seeing the full head of gray hair on old but pretty woman. "Your daughter is just going through some things, and the girls probably should stay with you for a while. Can you take care of them?"

"Yes, of course they can stay with me," Mrs. Jones said in a sweet yet sad voice.

Nilda smiled and headed back to the house to get the girls. Evening had set in, and Nilda couldn't see well enough to pack the girls anything in the messy, dark house, but she did manage to find their shoes and a stuffed animal for each of them.

Dillon reached down and hugged the girls tightly. Then she gave them a card with her number and Nilda's on it as she and Nilda walked them to their grand-mother's car.

"You call me if you ever need anything. If you ever feel scared," Nilda assured them, with tears in her eyes.

Before they reached Mrs. Jones's car, Olivia saw Jada's face out the corner of her eye. Before Dillon could respond, the girl took off toward her mother, and then Little Dasia dashed after her sister. Dillon turned and watched the scene unfold. Dasia squealed when she ran into Jada's arms, and Olivia's tough exterior cracked as she fell into her mother's embrace. The three of them held on to each other.

Dillon felt a lump form in her throat as she watched them. Her heart ached for the girls because she knew that having a mother like Jada couldn't be easy for them, but despite all her flaws, they loved her. Dillon remembered something one of her ex-employees told her the day she left. "These chicks out here looking for a nigga to put them on a pedestal, all they got to do is just look at their kids. You might not be shit to people out in the world, but in your damn house, your kids see you as a damn queen, and they give you they love for free." Missy wasn't the most polished one of her workers, but she was one of the smartest.

Dillon looked at the girls and shook her head. She didn't want to break up their family, but she knew Jada was in no position mentally or physically to do what she needed to for her children. Just then Mrs. Jones exited the car and walked up. Dillon could see where the girls got their eyes from. Mrs. Jones's sad, soft eyes drew a person in just like the girls' did Mrs. Jones nodded and called the girls to her, and they kissed their mother and ran to their grandmother. Jada sat on the ground, smiling weakly and waving to them, as the girls climbed into their grandmother's car. Mrs. Jones's eyes began to water. She turned and took a step toward Jada, then stopped and faced Dillon.

"Dillon, get her some help. I have tried with her. I love her with everything I got inside me. I always have, but she is so much like her father, and I don't think I could bear her ending up like he did. Do the best you can with her." Mrs. Jones turned, walked back to her car, and climbed behind the wheel.

Dillon followed her, and when she reached the driver's door, Mrs. Jones rolled down her window. "Mrs. Jones, you take care of them, and if you have any problems or need anything, you let me know. The girls have my number." Dillon reached in the car and handed Mrs. Jones several one-hundred-dollar bills.

That was the last time she had spoken with Jada, although she still kept in touch with Mrs. Jones and still sent her money for the girls.

Chapter 3

"It's nice to meet you, Mrs. P—"

"Mallorie. Call me Mallorie." The woman smiled and shook the hand that Mr. Jacobs, the private detective with whom she was meeting, extended toward her.

"Mallorie." He nodded his head at her, and they both took their seats. "Tell me why you'd like to use my services." He sat back in his seat and studied the polished, elegant, and well-put-together woman.

Everything about Mallorie screamed wealth. From her manicured hands and expensive yet simple pieces of jewelry, to the mint-green pants set that she rocked with Gucci sandals that showed off her pedicured feet. Mallorie swiped a piece of hair from her feathered bangs out of her face.

"I have reason to believe that my husband is up to no good, and I want to get ahead of anything that might be going on. I am a very important figure in the community, and so is he. We have a lot at stake, and there's no time for scandals or surprises." Mallorie flashed a smile at the detective.

She was an expert at keeping her game face on. Mr. Jacobs had no clue that just the thought of her husband doing something to embarrass her had her ready to set some shit off. Mallorie was very poised and elegant, but behind the scenes, she was a force to be reckoned with. She had goals, and a philandering husband wasn't going to ruin them for her.

Mallorie thrived on attention, validation, and power. Being well respected and almost like black royalty in Charlotte fed her ego and kept Mallorie high. Wealth and popularity were her aphrodisiacs. She was somebody without her husband, but being on his arm gave her extra perks. Perks that she wasn't willing to lose under any circumstances. Her name would be attached only to greatness. There was no room in her life for anything that would knock her off track. She wasn't trying to ride the wave of scandal and humiliation to the top.

"Tell me a little about your husband."

"Well, Dave is a senator. He's a very busy man. I don't doubt that, but I just want to make sure that his time away from home is being spent on work and not on extracurricular activities. There are also some questionable sums of money being spent on I'm not exactly sure what."

Mallorie would never admit that the possibility of her husband spending ample amounts of money on a woman pissed her off more than the thought of him sticking his dick inside her. She hoped the detective would be able to give her peace of mind, and if he couldn't provide that for her, at the very least, he should be able to provide some answers. Once she knew exactly what was going on, she'd be able to put a plan in motion. It would make her day for the detective to tell her that everything checked out and Dave was indeed being a good boy.

Dan Jacobs was no stranger to doing surveillance and snooping around on spouses or significant others who might be cheating. Spouses and significant others made up a huge percentage of his clients. There were very few times that he could recall a husband or wife being suspicious, and it turned out that their spouse was completely innocent. Dan had never looked into anyone as high profile and important as the senator, and his interest was beyond piqued.

As Mallorie looked through the photos in her hand, she thought back to that first meeting she had had with Dan. The photos in her hands made her stomach churn. The money she had paid him was well spent, because it had gotten her the answers that she wanted, even if she didn't like the answers that she got. As she cleared her throat, Mallorie attempted to process everything that she was seeing. With a stoic expression on her face, she studied photo after photo, all while resisting the urge to throw up. Dave had really outdone himself.

After she had studied the last photo, Mallorie composed herself and looked up at the detective with a tense, tight-lipped smile on her face. "Well, you did your job very well. I can honestly say that I wanted to know what Dave was up to, and you delivered. I will send your final payment as soon as I get in the car. Thank you so much for your time and dedication. I've hired private investigators before, and they didn't find anything. I honestly don't think they tried too hard. Not many people want to risk getting on the mayor's bad side."

"Giving news like this is never easy, but you paid me good money, and I refused to let you down. I'm sorry you had to find out this way."

"It's fine. I knew that my husband was no angel. Even women my age can still have hope, but it was very slim. Again, thank you for your service."

"You know," Dan began as he did one final assessment to try to gauge where Mallorie's head was, "there are other things that I can do besides investigating."

Mallorie's brows lifted. "What exactly are you saying?"

"I could maybe give some of the ladies a little motivation to stay away from your husband. He may be a high-paying client, but he's not the *only* client. The wrong customer could bring a lot of undesired attention to the house, and I'm sure the ladies don't want that."

Mallorie sat up straighter. She was almost amused. "And why would you do that for me? What's in it for you?"

"Of course, there will be a small fee attached, but it's mostly because I hate to see beautiful women like you not being appreciated at home."

Mallorie thrived on attention, but even she was smart enough to know when bullshit was falling off a person's lips. She smelled like money. Mallorie looked like money, and Dan wanted in. She wouldn't mind having him on her side, but she didn't want to seem desperate. Dave's infidelity was like a knife in her heart, but she'd never let anyone see her sweat.

"That's good to know," she replied with a smile. "I'll be in touch."

With the manila envelope clutched tightly in her hand, Mallorie stood up and gave Dave a head nod. As she walked out of the coffee shop with her head held high, Mallorie was boiling on the inside and mad enough to spit nails. She wasn't sure how just yet, but Dave was going to regret the day he ever made the dumbass decision to play in her face.

"You are one gorgeous woman," said a male voice as Dillon strolled into a shoe store.

When she looked up to make sure the man was talking to her, she locked eyes with a handsome black man who was dressed casually but nice enough to let her know that he had some business about himself. He didn't have a street edge, and she could tell just from that glance that he was a square. Dillon didn't mind. As she did a quick inspection of him, she decided that as long as he wasn't unbearably corny, he might be someone who was worth her time.

Dillon's profession wasn't legal, and while she had nothing against men that chose to get their money in unconventional ways, she wasn't opposed to a man getting it the right way either. Dillon wasn't looking for love. She was looking for fun. As long as she kept her business to herself, it didn't matter what profession her playthings were in.

She blushed from the stranger's compliment. "Thank you."

"Are you single?" He gave her an inquisitive look.

"I am. And what about you? Because oddly enough, I've had men ask me that question in the past when they weren't single themselves."

The man in front of her laughed, and Dillon observed his stark white teeth. "I am very single. I'm not too sure about other men and what they do, but I'm not even that kind of person. My name is Corey." He extended his hand for her to shake.

"Hi, Corey. It's nice to meet you. My name is Dillon."

"Dillon, is there any way that I can get your number? I'd love to take you out sometime."

"I think that can be arranged." She gave him a broad smile.

When Dillon first met Corey, she knew he wasn't a slouch, but she didn't know he was a lawyer with a little status and pull in Charlotte. He was a nice enough guy, but Dillon didn't trust anyone enough to tell them that she was a madam. She felt as though she did a lot of lying and dodging questions, but that was necessary in her line of work.

After sitting in traffic for close to two hours, an aggravated Dillon arrived back at the salon to get her hair done for the night's big event. She'd been invited to the annual Citizens of Piedmont Black-Tie Gala. Each year the gala was the biggest affair on the calendar for Charlotte's elite society. A who's who of rich socialites, politicians, and local celebrities always attended, and they were always dressed to the nines. It would be Dillon's first time attending, and for her debut, she'd purchased a beautiful Charbel Zoé couture gown, along with a killer pair of Sergio Rossi stilettos. A week earlier Dillon and Toni had picked the perfect hairstyle to compliment her dress. The style wasn't difficult, but adding extensions to accomplish it would take a lot more time than she had. If Dillon couldn't get her hair the way that she wanted it, she would not be going to the gala.

Truth be told, Dillon really didn't want to go to the gala anymore. The traffic jam had deflated her mood, and she hated rushing to get ready. She was still making an attempt to go only because of her new very close friend, Corey Hutch. Dillon did not want to disappoint him, and all that she could think of was how happy he'd been when she agreed to go with him.

"Toni, is there enough time for you to do the style or something close to it?" Dillon asked as she entered Toni's styling suite.

"Yeah. I have some real nice clip-on extensions that I can put in for tonight. It won't take long at all."

"Yeah, but my face and nails need to be done." Dillon sighed. "I already know I'm not going to make it."

"You'll have time for all that. Vontray can do your face, and Mai can do your mani-pedi while I'm doing your hair."

"I don't even have my dress and shoes with me, though." Reasons not to go to the event kept entering Dillon's brain.

"Where is your stuff?"

"All the way downtown, at my condo. Before I got stuck on the fucking highway, I was going to pick it up and get dressed here."

Toni smiled at Dillon. "You kill me," she said and shook her head. "I know what you're doing. I see right through you."

"What?"

"Trying to find a reason not to go with Corey tonight. And I want you to stop it right now. Antice is still here. Send her to get your things. Then go upstairs and take a shower, so when we're done getting you right, you can slip your dress on and be on the way."

"You get on my nerves." Dillon laughed. "I really wasn't trying to back out. You know how I am. If my shit ain't together, I'm not going anywhere."

"I do know you well. Before you go upstairs, you need to see this." She turned her head. "Antice," Toni called out, "bring baby girl out here for Dillon."

Antice, a petite bombshell dressed in a quirky punk-rock getup, bopped into the room. She was the personal shopper and stylist for Dillon as well as P H I. Her own eccentric style of dress didn't exactly scream *fashion stylist*, but she was indeed a fashion genius, with a strong résumé to back it up. Unbeknownst to the masses, Antice was the person whom the celeb stylists called on to get hard-to-find pieces, because she had strong ties to many designers.

Cheesing from ear to ear, Antice struck a model-presentation pose, her arms open to the side, and said, "Presenting Lady London."

Dillon's jaw dropped. With her mouth wide open, she silently stared at London in awe for a few seconds, then stuttered, "Oh my God, oh my God. You look *so* good." She slowly walked around London, examining her from top to bottom.

Dressed in a sexy orange Gucci silk blouse, matching hip-fitting slacks, and nude Jimmy Choo Anouk stiletto pumps, London looked like she'd just stepped off the

New York or Paris Fashion Week runway. Toni had installed twenty-six inches of the best hair extensions on the market in London's shoulder-length mane strand by strand, and with a razor, she had carved out long, flowing layers. London's gluey, clumped cluster lashes had been replaced with single-strand mink lash extensions, which instantly softened her face and complimented the stunning makeup job she'd received.

"There was no doubt in my mind that you were going to be popping, but you look even better than I expected," Dillon remarked.

"Thanks. I guess." London shrugged, smiling nervously. "It was your people that did all this."

"*Yasss*, they did that," said a woman with a husky voice and a Cuban accent as she entered the room. Nilda, the former P H Inc. manager, greeted Dillon with a kiss on the cheek. "Hello, baby doll."

"Hey, Nilda."

"Hello, my loves." Nilda blew kisses at Toni and Antice.

"Hi, Nilda," they sang out simultaneously, both truly happy to see the vivacious, timeless beauty with a to-die-for curvy shape.

Charismatic and brutally honest, Nilda had no qualms about speaking her mind. "She is very pretty, and the body is grade A," Nilda offered after thoroughly observing London. "Fitting in visually won't be a problem."

Giddy, London blushed from the flurry of compliments.

"Let's see if she has enough brains to do the job," Nilda spat unapologetically. "Beauty can get you only so far."

London's smile faded, and her neck started to roll. "Hold the fucking phone. What you mean by that?"

"London!" Dillon exclaimed. "Cut it out."

"But she trying me like I'm dumb. She don't know me." London was in defense mode.

Dillon shook her head. "Ain't nobody trying you. This is Nilda, my last manager. She has been gracious enough to fly in and train you. Nilda knows more than I do about the day-to-day operations of P H I. Leave your attitude at the door, respect her, and soak up everything that she has to offer you. Okay?"

After a slight eye roll and a deep sigh, London begrudgingly replied, "Okay."

"Nilda is going to take you over to P H I now, and I'll see you tomorrow," Dillon said.

London followed Nilda from the suite, and then they made their way outside and climbed into a chauffeured black Rolls-Royce. They rode for a grand total of three minutes before arriving at a two-and-a-half-acre estate, secluded behind seventeen-foot-tall iron gates and twenty-foot privacy bushes. In the center of the estate stood an enormous ivory- and gray-limestone mansion. It had three floors, which together had to amount to about thirty thousand square feet of pure luxury. London stepped out of the car and paused, in awe, to gaze up at the magnificent structure. Toni's mansion salon paled in comparison to the P H I estate.

"Chop-chop, baby doll," Nilda said, walking past London. "Now is not the time for admiring. We have much to do."

If this old bitch keep trying me. . . , London thought, falling in behind Nilda as she strutted across the elegant travertine courtyard.

As they walked up the five steps leading to the front entrance, Nilda stopped on the fourth step and turned to London. "When you get inside, don't become a deer caught in the headlights. Act unimpressed, like you're used to seeing everything that's on the other side of this door." She frowned. "If you don't," she warned, "these bitches will eat you alive. They can sense when a fish is out of water."

When they stepped through the front doors, London held her composure, even though she was wowed by the three-story entrance hall. It had exquisite Italian marble floors, massive crystal chandeliers, and elegant double grand staircases.

"This is one of the formal living rooms." Nilda pointed to a large, open 1920s Hollywood glam–inspired room. "That's the formal dining room over there." She nodded to the left, then proceeded to show London the cigar room, the billiards room, and the gourmet chef's kitchen.

Off the back side of the kitchen was the relaxed living area. It's mauve-colored walls were adorned with abstract oil paintings. An edgy rectangular purple leather couch sat in the middle of the room, surrounded by oversize, plush, butter-soft sky-blue leather chairs and ottomans. A ten-foot-long oak and granite wet bar, fully stocked, lined the right wall.

The room's ultra-clear wall-to-wall and floor-to-ceiling windows afforded a spectacular view of the opulent back-yard oasis. The patio, paved with glistening brown and beige slate, had an outdoor kitchen with stainless-steel appliances, brick-encased gas grills, and a circular dining island, and a retractable pergola stood on one side of the space. At the opposite end of the patio were three glass-topped cabanas, in-ground firepits, a stone-wrapped Jacuzzi, and an edgeless swimming pool. Directly behind the swimming pool was a courtyard that led to a twenty-two-hundred-square-foot ranch-style guesthouse.

Nilda guided London out to the patio, where a crowd of close to thirty women and two men were gathered, sampling chef-prepared hors d'oeuvres and sipping cocktails. All the women were exceptional. Most of them were American, while the rest hailed from different places around the globe, including Russia, Nigeria, Sweden, Belize, Panama, Greece, and Brazil. A majority of the women were dressed in sexy designer outfits, while a handful of them were in sexy tailored uniforms.

"Hello, everyone," Nilda greeted. "Thank you all for getting out here so quickly. I'll be fast. I know that your time is money," she said and winked. "I'd like to introduce you to London. She has been hired by Dillon to be P H I Agency's new executive manager."

Playing it cool, London greeted the gathering with a head nod.

"London will be handling all the things that I did when I was here. That is all. Please stop and introduce yourself on the way out."

One by one, the escorts introduced themselves. Some were ice cold and barely stopped long enough to say their names. Others were kind of welcoming, shaking London's hand and chatting her up a little. Only two embraced her and gave her an authentic smile. A pair of ditzy American black chicks, Kelly and Monica, from Iowa. They had been on their way to Los Angeles to work in the porn industry when Dillon recruited them.

"You're going to have so much fun working here," announced Kelly, a thin, café au lait vixen with a heavy top.

"This place is so cool! Will you be living here too?" said Monica, a perfect dark chocolate, real-life life Barbie doll.

"I think I'll be here a lot, but I don't know about staying here."

"Watch out." Alleyne pushed past Monica and Kelly. "I have somewhere to be." She extended her hand to London. "I'm Alleyne."

Alleyne's body and face were superior to those of all the other women, and there was no mistaking the fact that she was clearly the top escort. Her beauty was so entrancing that London saw her mouth moving but didn't hear the words that were coming out of it.

"My bad," London remarked, squeezing her eyes tightly and snapping out of her trance. "What did you say?"

"I said my name is Alleyne. It's nice to meet you."

London clutched her hand and shook it. "Thank you. Nice to meet you too." She tried to pull her hand back, but Alleyne wouldn't release it.

Alleyne raised London's hand in the air and spun her around, giving her a good once-over. "You are a mean little thing. Dillon is doing you a total disservice."

"In what way?"

"She should've recruited you for one of these bedrooms instead of the office."

"Come again?"

"The bedroom is where the real paper is, and a sexy, gorge bitch like you would make a killing."

"She sure would," Kelly and Monica agreed in unison. They worshiped Alleyne. They'd agree with anything she said, even if they totally disagreed. The women followed her around like helpless puppies.

London came very close to blurting out her first thought. *Unlike you bitches, I ain't no mahfuckin' prostitute.* Instead, she snatched her hand back. "I'm good where Dillon put me. I like managerial work. I'm heavy into running shit," she smirked, with a raised brow.

"Oh, okay." Alleyne laughed and rolled her eyes. "I hear that, boss bitch. I wish you all the luck on running shit, boss." She raised her martini glass to London, then walked away, strutting better than a supermodel, her two minions on her heels.

Nilda waved her hand dismissively at Alleyne. "She is drop-dead gorgeous, but she's also the biggest piece of work here."

"It ain't hard to tell," London responded.

"And those two dumb broads think she's the best thing since Jesus walked on water. Forget about them, though."

Nilda motioned toward the uniformed staff. "These lovely ladies and gentlemen will be your backbone." She took London around and introduced her to each of them. The men and two of the women made up the security team. Four of the ladies were housekeepers, and two were culinary chefs.

On their way back into the house, London asked Nilda, "Do those women really clean this house?"

"Yes. Why do you ask?"

"I've never seen any women as pretty as those on a cleaning staff."

"Baby doll, you are going to see a lot of things here that you've never seen before. We'll finish the tour later. Right now I'm going to take you to the most important room in here."

"What room is that?"

"The money room . . . your office."

They went up to the second floor, and Nilda stopped at a heavy wooden door. She placed her right hand on the biometric scanner next to the doorframe. After leaning forward, she placed her left eye against the retina scanner. Seconds later a green light flashed, and the audible click of the locks alerted her that the door was unlocked. She opened the door and flipped the light switch, revealing a modern study loaded with tall bookshelves that were stocked with thousands of books. Two contemporary hexagonal-shaped desks faced the door. In the rear of the room four gray-upholstered wingback chairs with black piping were posted at opposite ends of a contemporary round coal-black coffee table. A tall, slim vase holding a fresh arrangement of long-stemmed pink and black roses sat atop the table.

"That's your desk." Nilda pointed to the desk on the right. "And that's Dillon's." She nodded toward the other desk.

"Oh, I can get with this." London went over to her new desk and pulled out the smoke-gray leather swivel chair and plopped down. "Ooh. The new Mac Pro desktop," she said and ran her hands over the computer screen.

Nilda picked up a small remote, pressed a button, and three ultra-thin forty-two-inch flat-screen smart TVs descended from the ceiling. By pressing another button, she powered on all three screens. "On the first screen you can watch whatever you like, but the other two are strictly for surveillance." The second and third televisions were split screens displaying each of the escort's bedrooms. Some of the screens were blacked out, but the ones that were not showed live jaw-dropping sex acts. They were slightly blurred to hide the participants' identities.

"I have to sit here and watch them have sex?" London frowned.

"No. Just glance up at the screen every once in a while to make sure the girls aren't in trouble. They have panic buttons in their rooms, but just in case they can't get to them, you have to be on the lookout."

"What do I do if I see something going down?"

"Radio security. Then press RECORD to save the video."

"Isn't it recording already?"

"Yes, but it loops and records over every twelve hours."

"Okay, but how will I know which girl is being attacked, since I can't see their faces?"

"The room numbers are in the bottom corner of each screen."

"Why are some of the screens blacked out?"

"Because they don't have a client at the moment. The cams in the room are on only when they have one, and it's your job to activate them when the client goes in. I'm going to show you how to operate all the technical stuff after I show you how to work the books."

Nilda opened a computer file containing a list of hundreds of different companies. "Every company here is a front for an individual client. When clients book a girl, they will give you only the name of the company. You'll invoice the company for various model services. The rates are twenty-five hundred dollars an hour, with a two-hour minimum. If they want to use the guesthouse, it's five thousand dollars an hour, with a three-hour minimum. Each girl must make a minimum of twelve thousand a week or pay rent to the house, but it's very rare for any of them not to make the minimum. This group regularly makes triple the weekly minimum."

"Sheesh, that's a lot of dough for some ass."

"The money isn't just for any old ass. It's for premium pussy and premium privacy. And while we're on the subject, the men and the women that come here are wealthy and powerful. A few belong to criminal organizations. The majority of them have people on standby to handle their problems." Nilda looked London square in the eye. "My point is these clients don't like their secrets getting out, and they will go to deadly lengths to make sure they don't."

"I understand."

"And another thing that you need to understand is these girls are not your friends. I don't care how many expensive gifts they give you for your birthday and holidays. They're your work associates, nothing more."

"Got it." London nodded.

Alleyne lay across her bed, flipping through a magazine. She stared at one of the models carrying a Chanel purse, and she decided that she wanted one. Not only did Dave have phenomenal dick, but his pockets were long and deep, and she got whatever she wanted. Alleyne had

Chanel bag money, but she didn't want to buy her own bag. What was the point of being with a rich man if she had to spoil herself?

"Knock, knock."

Alleyne rolled her eyes upward at the sound of Monica's voice. "Come in," she stated in a flat tone.

Monica opened the door and took one step over the threshold. "Hey, girl. Sorry to bother you, but I'm all out of Bitter Peach. Can I have just two squirts of yours?" Monica begged as Alleyne frowned. She'd never ask to borrow perfume from someone, but they weren't her.

The women lived in the same house, and they had the same profession, but no one could tell Alleyne that she wasn't better than the other women. She walked around with her nose so far up in the air, she should have been able to smell rain coming.

"Sure." She didn't even bother telling Monica that begging for another woman's perfume was borderline bum-bitch behavior. She had got tired of trying to teach some of the women in the house how to act. Attention from Dave had created a hell of a monster within Alleyne. Before she fell in love with him, she'd been a decent person with a decent attitude. Now she was giving diva, and most of the girls in the house disliked her.

"Thank you so much," Monica gushed. "One of my favorite clients is about to come through. I'm low-key hoping his ass will get to the point where he just pays to block off my time, like Dave does with you. Getting the same amount of money to do less work sounds like a win to me."

Monica snickered. "Every man isn't going to do what Dave does. They can probably afford to, sure, but that doesn't mean they will. Dave loves me, and he can't stand the thought of me with another man. It makes him insanely jealous."

"Damn, that must be nice. So, I bet your next stop is out of the brothel, huh?" Monica replied, with stars in her eyes.

It was a shame how dumb she was. Those were Alleyne's thoughts as she watched the woman spray more than two squirts of her perfume.

"Okay, Miss Mama, that's enough. You said two squirts, not that you wanted to bathe in my shit."

"Sorry." Monica smiled sheepishly, putting the perfume back on the dresser. "Well, I'm about to go pull out all my best moves for mister, and hopefully, he'll fall in love with my ass too. I don't think he's leaving his wife, though." Monica really thought that Dave was going to leave Mallorie for Alleyne. Foolishly, Alleyne thought it too. The delusion was real.

"If you ask me, any man that stays married to a woman that can't satisfy him sexually is stupid," Alleyne declared. "All of them need to let these old hags go and get with someone that can keep them satisfied."

"I second that! Well, let me get going." Monica sashayed out of the room while Alleyne daydreamed about not having to work in the mansion anymore.

Dave would move her into a gorgeous high-rise condo, and he would spoil her relentlessly. Mallorie's time in Dave's life was coming to an end. Alleyne was going to see to it that Dave chose her.

Chapter 4

"You are so beautiful." Corey Hutchison ogled Dillon as she approached him outside the Ritz-Carlton. "Hmm, and your body in that dress . . . Girl, you are making me want to do some things to you." He grabbed her by the waist, embraced her tightly. With lust in his eyes, Corey smoothly slid his hand down her back and squeezed her ass.

Wearing a sheer, sequined champagne Charbel Zoe gown, Dillon looked smashing. "Thank you, Corey. You're looking extra handsome in that tux, my dude."

"I swear, if I didn't have some big announcements to make, I'd snatch you up and take you home and do that thing you like."

Giggling like a schoolgirl, Dillon blushed. "And normally I'd let you, but after all that I went through to make it here tonight, some people other than you are going to see me."

"The way that dress is fitting you, I'm not letting you leave my side."

"Is that right?" She smiled sexily.

They didn't call one another boyfriend and girlfriend, but they were the closest thing that each of them had to a boyfriend or girlfriend. Not to mention they did all the things that people labeled couples did. Corey would've loved to give Dillon the label of his girlfriend. She, on the other hand, was very hesitant to fully commit to him or any man, mostly due to all the committed men who patronized her business. Dillon wasn't sure if she loved Corey, but she did have a lot of love for him.

In a lot of ways he was her ideal man. Corey was fine, to say the least, and although he wasn't hood, he had a li'l hood swag, kinda like Drake. Corey was a stellar student in college and law school. He graduated from both with top honors. Corey passed the state law bar exam on his first attempt, and now, at the age of thirty-five, he was the youngest junior partner in his law firm's long history. Not only had he been born into money, but he had made a good living as a corporate attorney. So, he wasn't the kind of man to just sit back and do nothing because financially he didn't have to. He had a grind and hustle to him, and Dillon like that.

"So, what kind of big announcements do you have to make?" she asked as they intertwined arms, entered the building, and were met with the flashing lights of cameras.

Stopping on the red carpet for pictures, Corey told her, "I'll share one of my announcements as soon as he gets here."

"Who is he?" Dillon asked through clenched teeth while smiling for the picture.

"I'm going to introduce you to my father."

"Oh, shit. We finally get to meet your mysterious-ass father."

"You got jokes, huh?"

Corey had learned the identity of his father only two years earlier, when his mother had called them together and made a deathbed confession to them both. She didn't want Corey to grow up the spoiled child of privilege because of his father's celebrity status, and she didn't want the father thinking that she was trying to trap him with a child to get his money. Upon meeting Corey, his father was excited, because he had always wanted a son but had produced only daughters from two different marriages. Corey was hurt that his mother had kept his father a secret from him, but it didn't change how he felt about her one bit. He excitedly pursued a relationship with his father, but he wanted to do it privately before letting the world know. After two years of bonding and cultivating a wonderful relationship with his father, he was ready to let the world know the identity of the man he now proudly called Dad.

Extravagant decorations, rare flowers, and expensive ice sculptures were spread around the ballroom. Old money pretended to embrace new money while secretly admonishing it. Most of that foolishness was carried on by the women who came from long centuries of wealth. The majority of them had done nothing to earn the wealth that they arrogantly threw in the faces of those who hadn't been rich as long. The men did not worry themselves with such trivial things; they were too busy networking, politicking, and checking out the younger women.

All eyes shifted to Dillon and Corey when they entered the ballroom. Official couple or not, they looked magnificent together. People were constantly stopping Corey as they moved about the room. Many shook his hand and told him how they appreciated his work in the community. Corey was very active in helping the city's poor, disadvantaged, and disenfranchised youth, especially the young minority males. Corey had spearheaded several programs geared toward helping minority males achieve success, including a program that provided aid and mentoring to boys from the day they entered elementary school until they graduated from college. Another program that he was heavily involved in helped troubled young adult males get back on track by providing job training and by partnering with companies that were willing to hire young men with criminal records.

A commotion drew everyone's attention toward the entrance, where Charlotte's distinguished mayor, Richard Tynes, and his entourage were walking in. Dillon did a double take when she saw Heavy looking dapper in a tuxedo and holding hands with the mayor's daughter.

"Son of a bitch," Dillon muttered.

"Did you say something?" Corey asked.

"Oh, I was saying the mayor's daughter, Mariah, has a nice dress on."

"Isn't that your ex, Andre Cuthbertson, with Mariah?"

"Yes, and I didn't realize you knew his last name."

"Of course I know his name. I've done business with him before."

"I didn't know that."

"Dillon turned her head and saw the mayor and all his people coming straight at her and Corey.

"Corey! My boy." The mayor, who had light skin and salt-and-pepper hair, gripped Corey's hand tightly, shook it firmly, pulled him into an embrace, and patted him on the back. "You ready for that big announcement?"

"Yes, I am, Mr. Mayor."

"I'm not going to be here long tonight. I have another engagement, so we're going to make it in about thirty minutes."

"Grab me when you're ready. I'm on your time."

With a charming grin, the mayor gave Corey a thumbs-up, then led his large crew of followers in the other direction. Heavy went out of his way to speak to Corey and Dillon as he passed by.

"How are you, Dillon?" He threw his head back.

"I'm great."

Reaching all the way around Mariah, he gave Corey a pound. "What's up, bruh?"

"Nothing much. Just coolin'. It's nice to see you looking good."

"You too, my brother." Heavy winked at Dillon and kept moving.

"He irks my soul," Dillon muttered.

"I need to watch my back for Andre."

"Why?"

"The way he was scoping you out, I think he wants you back," Corey joked.

"He already knows that it ain't happening."

The room began to rumble again as someone else with star power entered. Dillon couldn't see who all the fuss was about, since a dozen paparazzi had circled the medium-sized group, trying to get the best shot.

Recognizing a few faces in the group, Corey said, "Perfect timing." Then he pulled Dillon in the direction of the chaos. As they approached, the gala organizers and security began ushering the paparazzi out. Feeling her cell phone vibrating in her clutch, Dillon let Corey's hand go and stopped short a few feet from the group. Dillon was looking down, struggling a bit to remove the phone from the tiny clutch, when she heard Corey say, "Hey, Pops."

Dillon looked up and saw the man whom Corey was hugging. *Holy shit*, she thought. It was Dave Prescott. She immediately became lightheaded.

Luckily, before her knees buckled, Corey swooped over and slipped his arm around her waist and began proudly introducing her. "Pops, this is Dillon, my friend that I've been telling you about. Dillon, this is my pops, Dave Prescott."

Dave Prescott's eyes widened a little; naturally, he was shocked to see the madam of the lavish brothel that he frequented standing before him. Being his smooth, charming self, he played it cool. "Nice to meet you, Dillon. I've heard nothing but great things about you."

"I wish I could say the same. I don't know how Corey could keep it a secret that our state senator and the best-shooting point guard ever is his father."

The two shook hands like they'd never met.

"Corey, aren't you going to introduce me to your lovely friend?" asked a refined older lady in a lilac Elie Saab gown.

"Yes, ma'am," Corey replied. "Dillon, this is my step-mom, Mallorie Prescott."

Dillon extended her hand. "Nice to meet you."

With a tight-lipped smile, Mallorie shook Dillon's hand, saying, "Nice to meet you too. You look so familiar. I feel like we've met before."

"I just have one of those faces. I get that a lot."

"No, darling, a face as pretty as yours is rare," Mallorie uttered with a sly look. Truth was, she knew exactly who Dillon was and what she owned. Having her husband investigated had paid off greatly for Mallorie. It had taken four weeks and nearly two hundred fifty thousand dollars. But it had paid off, and she knew at some point she would make her knowledge known. However, now wasn't the time. This was something that Mallorie had to do in a very calculated manner. There was a lot at stake.

One of the mayor's aides dashed over to Corey. "The mayor is going to have to leave earlier than we originally planned. He wants to go ahead and make the announcement now."

"We'll be right over. Let's go everybody." He caught Dillon's eye. "You too." He snatched Dillon by the hand. With his father and stepmother leading the way and the Prescott camp behind him, Corey confidently marched toward the stage.

Dillon grabbed a champagne flute from a passing waiter's tray, tossed her head back, and drained the liquid from the flute. She sat the flute on a white linen–covered table next to the stage.

As Corey and company lined up across the back of the stage, the mayor stepped up to the podium with a smile. "Good evening, ladies and gentlemen. I promise to be brief. Looking out into the crowd, I know that I am among some of my biggest supporters. Many of you helped me to get into office ten years ago with your huge campaign contributions and your tireless volunteer work." His eyes began to get misty, so he paused for a few seconds to collect himself. "It is with great sadness that I inform you I will not be seeking another term as mayor of this great city."

Moans of "Aw!" and "No!" rippled through the crowd of truly disappointed people. Mayor Tynes had done great things for the city.

"With much greater joy, I have the pleasure of telling you first that I'm formally tossing my hat in the race to seek my first term as governor of this great state."

The crowd erupted in cheers and applause. The mayor's wife and daughter kissed and hugged him. Others onstage patted his back and congratulated him.

Once the room calmed down, the mayor turned back to the crowd. "At this time, I would like to introduce you to the next Democratic candidate for mayor that I'm fully endorsing. He is a hardworking young man. He used academics to carry him from Charlotte to the halls of Harvard Law School. Once this young fellow made it in the world of corporate law, he didn't forget where he came from. He returned to Charlotte and helped dozens of youth turn dim futures into bright tomorrows. It is with great honor that I present to you the future mayor of Charlotte, North Carolina. Corey Hutch."

Again, the crowd, especially the liberal young socialites, went into a frenzy. Like the mayor, Corey was swarmed by well-wishers and family. During the chaos he became separated from Dillon, allowing her to quietly slip offstage. *Ain't this 'bout some bullshit*, she thought as she walked as briskly as she could in her skintight gown to the ladies' room. Inside the bathroom she finally removed the phone from her clutch, but she didn't bother checking the missed call. Dillon sat the phone, along with her license, two credit cards, and ten folded one-hundred-dollar bills, on the bathroom counter, then retrieved one of the Xanax bars that she'd stashed at the bottom of the clutch. Dillon put the pill under her tongue, then placed all the contents, with the exception of the phone, back into the clutch.

Returning to the ballroom wasn't an option. Dillon went to the hotel's bar, which happened to be one of the city's hot spots. Of course, the heads of those dressed business casual turned when she glamorously sauntered in such a formal gown. Unfazed by the attention, Dillon went straight to the bar.

The white male bartender, who looked to be in his midtwenties, rushed over to take her order. "What can I get for you?"

"I need a glass of water right now."

"Bottle or tap?"

"Bottle. But can you pour it in a glass?"

"Sure." He pulled a bottle of Acqua Panna from the cooler, poured it in a water glass, and served it.

"Can I get a vodka tonic with Grey Goose Le Citron?"

"Be right back."

With the tip of her tongue, Dillon flicked the pill from the floor of her mouth onto the middle of her tongue and drank the water.

The bartender sat the vodka tonic in front of Dillon. "Anything else?"

"Another one please." She passed him her Discover Platinum. "And open a tab." Dillon tossed the entire drink back and checked her phone. There were two missed calls from Nilda. Dillon got her second drink, took a seat in a secluded corner, and dialed Nilda.

"Hello," Nilda answered.

"Hey, Nilda. I'm sorry I missed your call. This gala has truly been insane."

"That's okay. I found what I was looking for. Is the gala a good insane or bad insane?"

"I'll let you be the judge. I just found out that Dave Prescott is Corey's father and Corey is running for mayor. Oh, and did I mention my ex is here?"

"Ay, Dios mío, Mami!"

"Oh my God is right," Dillon laughed. "How are things going there with London?"

"Pretty good. She is actually a sweetheart once you get to know her. A little rough around the edges, but a sweetheart nonetheless."

"Do you think she'll be able to handle the girls?"

"Oh yes. Alleyne came at her during the introduction meeting, and she handled herself quite well."

"Good for London. Alleyne has been crossing the line a lot lately. Call me again if anything else comes up. If not, I'll see you tomorrow."

"Hasta luego."

Dillon polished off her second drink and headed back to the bar for another one. While waiting on the bartender to fill her order, Dillon felt a tap on her shoulder. She turned to the side and came face-to-face with Heavy. Damn. This nigga had a nerve to really be looking and smelling so fucking good. Dillon had seen him dressed up in a suit only when was going to court or to one of his homies' funerals. However, this was different. He was really wearing this new mature boss look very well. But Dillon knew that under this well-dressed man was a person whom she knew all too well. A lying, cheating, self-centered narcissist.

"Now a nigga see why you don't want to come home to Daddy," Heavy said. "You got a thing for the golden boy."

"I don't have a thing for anybody. Corey is my good friend."

"Yeah right."

"Again, something that is none of your business. Did I come ask you if our mayor knows that Charlotte's kingpin of coke walked in holding his daughter's hand?" Dillon said as the bartender placed her drink in front of her.

"Ha ha. You're such a funny lady."

"So I've heard."

"Does future Mayor Golden Boy know that you own the most . . . ? Let me get it right. How did old dude say it? Oh yeah, the best damn whorehouse this side of the Mississippi?"

"What the fuck are you talking about?"

"I know all about the Queen City's best-kept secret. I mean, what kind of kingpin would I be if I didn't know what went on in my city?"

Playing it cool, she raised her glass. "Cheers to false secrets, unfounded rumors, and innuendos." Dillon downed her drink and summoned the bartender over with her hand. "Can you close my tab please?" Giving Heavy a mean side-eye, she said, "I'm done here."

"My man, can you bring me a double shot of Patrón?" Heavy asked the bartender. Once the bartender agreed, he turned his attention back to Dillon. "If you don't mind me saying, you looking damn nice. I mean more beautiful than I've seen you."

"No, I don't mind a compliment from you," she answered, a little mellowed out from the Xanax and the drinks. "It makes up for all the days that I never got any when we were together. And it was kind of hard to see me dressed up when you were in prison."

At that moment the bartender came back with Dillon's credit card and receipt. She picked up the credit card from the receipt tray, signed the receipt, and handed the bartender a one-hundred-dollar bill. "That's for his drink too." She nodded at Heavy. "The rest is for you."

"Thanks. I really appreciate it," the bartender told her.

"Not a problem. Have a good night."

"I appreciate you paying for my drink." Heavy smiled as he leered at her. "You gon' make me drink alone?"

"Aw, no, I don't want that."

"Well, sit back down for a while."

"Oh nah, but I will make sure to let your date know that you don't want to be alone right now." Dillon patted him on the back and walked off, laughing hard. As she walked away, she remembered a gut-wrenching conversation they had once had.

Heavy walked into the apartment that he shared with Dillon and saw her sitting on the couch, with a menacing look on her face. Her arms were folded underneath her breasts, and she was looking at him like she wanted to kill him. Heavy was tired and not in the mood for a lot of back-and-forth. His pockets were just as heavy as his name due to almost nonstop hustling. The only sleep that he'd gotten in the past two days was when he dosed off few a few hours after he slid up in some pussy.

"It's nice to see that you remember where home is," Dillon spat before hopping up off the couch. "Two days, Heavy. Since when is it okay for a man in a relationship to stay away from home and not communicate with his girlfriend for two days?" Dillon was furious. If she had any solid proof that Heavy was cheating, she was going to cut his dick off.

Heavy groaned. "Please not now, Dillon. A nigga is tired as hell."

"And how is that my problem? There's a bed upstairs, but you choose not to come home every night and sleep in it."

"What is sleeping going to get me?" he barked. "Don't shit come to a sleeper but dreams. I'm trying to get this money up. I can sleep later."

"Heavy, I can't keep putting up with this. I don't see you for days at a time. Most times, you don't even bother to call me and let me know if you're safe. I also know firsthand how some of these hoes in Charlotte like to gossip and get information wrong, but if any of the rumors I've heard about you are true, you have to know that I'm leaving you." Just the thought of him cheating made Dillon sick to her stomach.

Heavy was tired and irritated. Maybe being single was best. Yeah, he dabbled in new pussy every now and again, but for the most part, when he said he was out getting money, that's what he was doing. The way Dillon was acting, she liked it when he was broke. She couldn't have been okay with a broke man sitting up in her face all day every day. Dillon had no desire to look like a fool in her relationship, and Heavy had no desire to compromise on where he was going in life.

"You're going to do what you're going to do, and you're going to believe what you want to believe," Heavy replied wearily. "At this point, it really doesn't matter."

Dillon's mouth almost hit the floor. Any other time that she had threatened to leave Heavy, he had begged her not to go. He had made false promises about staying home more and spending time with her. Dillon was almost too stunned to speak. But she had to say something. "Oh, I get it. You start making a little bit of money, and now you're feeling yourself. You're ready to shit on the ones that had your back when you didn't have shit."

Heavy laughed sarcastically. "And that's why I'm not going to stop getting this money, because people don't hesitate to throw your broke days or what they did for you back in your face. You're bitching about the fact that I don't want to be that lame-ass nigga anymore. I'm not going to apologize for putting myself in a position to have more and to do better. If you want to find a man that works a regular nine-to-five or one that doesn't work at all, be my guest, Dillon. But the threats are getting a little old."

Heavy walked past Dillon, heading toward the bathroom so he could shower, and once again, she was speechless. He had never talked to her like that before. He had really looked her in the eyes and admitted that if he had to choose between her and the money, he damn sure wouldn't choose her.

Dillon came back to the present with a chuckle. She couldn't believe that she had once given Heavy such a hard time about leveling up. Money was always going to be the motive, and if she had to choose between money and that fairy-tale bullshit, life could keep the fairy tales. A lot of people claimed that money couldn't buy happiness, but she wasn't so sure about that. Since she started getting to a real bag, it had taken her a lot to act out of character or feel sad and depressed.

Back then, she'd been in love. She would have lived in Heavy's skin if he had let her, and the blow to her ego had crushed her. The fact that he had chosen the streets over their relationship had ended up turning Dillon into a savage. Ironically, it was her changed ways that would make all the difference if they decided to give one another one more chance. She was certain it would work this time because now Dillon simply couldn't bring herself to care about what a man was doing. There was a time when she and Heavy had been super happy, and oddly enough, it had been when they were both broke. Wasn't that some shit?

Oh, well, it was water under the bridge. Dillon could admit that just maybe she'd done too much in her relationship with Heavy. Maybe she should have been more understanding and patient. Back then, it hadn't been about the money, but now, shit . . . he had better be glad that she wasn't the clingy, fall-in-love type. Now she just stood back and let him watch from a distance.

While exiting the bar, she ran right into Corey. "What are you doing out here?" Dillon slurred. The thoughts that she was having about Heavy disappeared just that fast.

Corey could tell by her speech and her glazed eyes that she was lit. "I was looking for you. Why did you run off like that?"

"There was a lot going on. With all those people huddling around you, I was too overwhelmed. I should have told you that I was stepping out for some air."

"Sorry about that. I should've warned you that it might get crazy in here."

"Congratulations, future mayor. You totally blindsided me with that one. I've never heard you talking about running for city council let alone mayor. Talk about things that I didn't see coming. Whoever would have thought?"

"I knew that one day I would get into politics. I never thought that I would do it at this young age. The circumstances are just right, what with the mayor running for governor and my father standing behind me. Enough about all that, though. You ready to go?"

"I sure am, but can you leave? Shouldn't you stay around and mingle and start the process of networking?"

"Yeah, I came here only to make that announcement. You know this isn't my type of scene at all. As soon as I said what I had to say, I was ready to leave."

"That's what I love about you." Dillon had to concentrate not to stumble when she walked. The combination of Xanax and alcohol had her higher than a light bill.

Palming her ass, Corey pulled Dillon close as they strolled to the hotel exit. "So you do love me?"

"You're twisting my words. I said I love an attribute that you possess. That was a very nice try, however."

"You sure know how to stick a knife in a man's heart and twist it around."

"You know you my people."

"I wanna be more than just your people, though."

"Yeah, right, Corey."

Flashing camera lights blinded them as they stepped out into the hotel's courtyard, and reporters bombarded Corey with questions.

"How does it feel to get the mayor's support?"

"Are you ready to lead a city at such a young age?"

"Who is your girlfriend?"

"Are you engaged?"

Corey whisked Dillon back into the hotel. "Give me your valet ticket."

Dillon placed the ticket in his palm, and he rushed over to the nearest bellhop. The bellhop took the ticket out to the valet stand, and when Dillon's car was brought around, they made a mad dash through the reporters and cameramen. Dillon rushed into the passenger seat as fast as her dress would allow, and Corey ran around to the driver's side. Once they were both inside the vehicle, the valet attendants closed both doors forcefully, and Corey whipped the car away from the hotel entrance, cameras snapping in the rearview.

Dillon gave a sigh of relief. "And you think that I'm actually going to sign up for this insanity with you?"

"It's not always going to be like this."

Dillon wanted to scream, *I run a brothel, and your freaky fuckin' father is one of our best clients*! Instead, she calmly stated, "Corey, you're about to make a run for mayor. You're not going to have time to be with me or anyone on a serious level. Honestly, I don't want or need the scrutiny that is going to come. I don't want to stop seeing you, but I'd just like to keep it on the low, like we've been doing."

"To be honest with you, I'm tired of sneaking around like some kids. I'm not going to keep doing it either."

"That's the beauty of life, especially here in America. You are free to do whatever you want."

Not wanting to ruin the night by pressing the issue, Corey decided to let it go. He placed his hand over hers. "I'ma fall back on that." He kissed the back of her hand, then said, "This is a special time for me, and I want to celebrate it with you."

They drove to Corey's place, a spacious twentieth-floor bachelor condo in the heart of Center City. As soon as they entered the condo, Dillon slipped out of her gown and into a white tank and a floor-sweeping silky coral skirt. Corey traded his tux for a much more comfortable white V-necked tee and baggy khaki cargo shorts. He went out onto his humungous concrete balcony overlooking the city and beckoned Dillon to follow him. An assortment of chef-prepared meats, salads, and sides sat atop a sizable table covered with black linen. The orange-red flames of the four sixty-inch-tall dark purple candles that had planted in each corner of the balcony danced against the darkness. Bottles of Clicquot rosé chilled in a sterling ice bucket.

Dillon stepped out onto the balcony barefoot, with a fresh vodka tonic in her hand. "Wow. Corey, what is all this?"

"My homeboy Chef Vegas and his people put this together. I was going to invite some friends and family over for a little party to celebrate, but when I saw you in that dress, I was like, 'Nah, I don't want nobody else here but us.'"

"Yeah right."

"Yeah right what?"

"You changed your mind just to be alone with me."

"You see all that food on the table, and there's a lot more in the kitchen."

"That was sweet of you to think of me on your night."

"Lately you're all I think about." He kissed her neck.

Dillon shivered. The Xanax and vodka tonics coursing through her bloodstream intensified his every touch. Holding on to her glass and her breath, she stood still as Corey stroked her face and hair as he continued to kiss her lips, ears, and neck.

Cradling her head in his hands, he looked into her eyes. "I wish you could feel what I'm feeling for you."

"I do feel it. I feel you."

"If you feel the way I do, why are you playing?"

"I'm not. The time is just not right."

"When will it ever be right?"

For a moment Dillon contemplated giving in. It felt so right. But it was far too complicated now, what with him stepping into politics . . . not to mention his father. Her mind was made up. She was not going to commit on this night or anytime in the near future. Dillon didn't want to shut him down and kill the wonderful vibe. Not to mention they hadn't had sex in weeks, and she was extra-horny. His kisses alone were causing small eruptions of hot cream to dampen her thong.

"Corey, I thought you wanted to leave that alone for tonight and just enjoy the moment?"

"I do. But."

She placed a finger on his lips. "No buts. You haven't even had one drink tonight. Pop open a bottle of champagne and get like me."

"I'm with that." He kissed her lips. "This is probably the last time I'll be able to get fucked up for a long time. I need to put something in my stomach first. I haven't had anything since breakfast." Corey stepped over to the table and pulled a chair out for Dillon. "You need to eat something too. I don't know how many you had at the Ritz, but you've smashed three vodka tonics since we got here."

"Damn, nigga. What are you? The alcohol-intake monitor?"

"Don't do that, Dilly. You know I'm not on it like that."

Dillon sat down, polished off the drink in her hand, and raised the glass to Corey. "I needed every drink that I've knocked down and some more. I just want to get shit faced and duck reality for the rest of tonight."

"I want you to get shit faced too," Corey laughed. "You real nasty when you get fucked up."

"And you love it." Dillon winked as she placed crab cakes and steamed asparagus on her plate.

Corey pulled out a bottle of aged scotch that had been gifted to him when he made junior partner at his firm. After cracking it open for the first time, he drank shots while eating and talking to Dillon. As she peered at him while he spoke, it began to dawn on Dillon how much Corey and Dave Prescott favored each other. Before the gala she would've never thought to make the comparison. Corey was actually a young dark chocolate version of his father. He'd inherited Dave's sharp cheekbones, piercing dark eyes, and long, thick lashes.

Dave being Corey's father was a big part of the reality that Dillon was trying to escape for the night. She didn't have a clue how she was going to handle that situation, and the mere thought of trying to figure it out was stressful. Dillon couldn't help but think that Dave's political camp was somehow involved in Corey's sudden foray into politics.

"I'm still confused about something." Dillon stood up, grabbed a bottle of champagne from the ice bucket, and popped the cork.

Corey leaned over, slapped her ass, then squeezed it. "What's confusing you, baby?"

"You." She filled a long-stemmed flute with the bubbling pink liquid and offered it to Corey.

"Nah." He waved the flute away. "Let me get that." He grabbed the bottle from her. After turning it up, he took a big swig. Then he asked, "How am I confusing?"

Resting one hand on the table to maintain her balance, she tossed half the flute of champagne back with one swallow. "We have talked about everything, and I mean everything," she said in a drunken slur, waving the flute around. "And not one good goddamned time have you ever talked about running for shit."

"Sometimes, when chance and opportunity fall into your lap, you have to see where they lead."

"Richard Tynes endorsing a rookie for his beloved seat doesn't happen by chance. Bet that." Dillon drained the remaining liquid from the flute.

Corey refilled her flute. "So you feel like there's more to it."

"I sure do."

"Speak on it, then."

"It's not hard to peep game, knowing your father happens to be everybody's favorite basketball star turned senator."

"The mayor isn't endorsing me just because Dave Prescott is my father. They cool, but they ain't that cool."

"He'd do it for Mallorie Prescott."

"Come on, Dillon. You reaching. What sense would that make?"

"Perfect sense."

"Who the fuck is she that makes you think that she would have the mayor's ear over my dad?" Corey took a big swig from the bottle. Laughing, he joked, "Unless something is going on between Mallorie and the mayor. I know the mayor ain't got the balls to try my pops like that." He doubled over in a fit of laughter.

Dillon was not amused. "So, you serious or nah?"

"About which part?"

"Mallorie's ability to influence the mayor."

"What makes her so influential in your mind? I need to know. Let me hear this."

"Her money."

"You mean my dad's money."

"Oh no, no." Dillon waved her finger at him. She pushed some plates to the side and hopped up on the table and sat there. "Mallorie is worth a whole lot more paper than all Dave Prescott's NBA contracts and endorsement deals combined."

"Fuck outta here," he blurted. "She don't do shit but shop, look pretty, and use my dad's last name to raise money for all them charity boards she on."

"She does not need your dad's money." Dillon threw up two air quotes. "Mallorie is one of the Bowies from Northern Virginia."

"What does that mean?"

"She's the heir to billions, and her name holds enormous weight in political circles. When the Bowie family finances a campaign, it damn near guarantees a win, and you already know that type of support isn't free."

Corey's smile faded. His demeanor quickly shifted from jovial to serious. If Dillon's words were true, the mayor's endorsement wasn't based on Corey's intelligence, résumé, or the hours-long conversations he and the mayor had had about the future of Charlotte and Corey being the right person to guide the city to prominence. "It's crazy that I've never heard about a black family with that much money and power."

"They're not considered a black family by some. Her great-great-grandfather got rich in the forties by passing for white. Some of the family is still passing, even though it's so fucking unnecessary in twenty twenty-four."

"Yo, how do you know all this?"

Smiling coyly, she sipped from her flute. "I know a lot of things about a lot of people."

"So I've noticed, but you never say how or where you get your information from."

"And I never will."

"Just something else to add to all the other shit you're so secretive about," he hissed.

"You know what . . . ?" Dillon hopped off the table. "My bad for running my mouth. I wasn't throwing shade. It's just . . . it's just . . . Never mind."

"It's just what?"

Dillon didn't want to say any more, the liquor had already made her say much more than she would have said sober. "Nah, I've said enough. Congratulations and good luck." Leaning over, she softly pressed her lips against his. "That's all I've should've said. I don't want to bring you down on your night, so I'm going to go on home." Dillon opened the sliding-glass door.

Corey jumped up, and in a few quick steps, he caught up to Dillon. After grabbing her by the elbow as she crossed the threshold of the door, he spun her around. "Ay, stop tripping. You too drunk to go anywhere." Holding her by the waist, he commanded firmly yet so sensuously, "Now, tell me what were you about to say."

"It was nothing." Dillon attempted to keep going.

"Stop that." Corey tightened his grip on her midsection. "Don't pull away from me. Talk to me. What were you going to say?"

"I just want the best for you."

"*You* are the best for me." He kissed her before she could speak. Corey pushed at the waistband of her skirt until it slid down over her hips and collapsed at her feet. Then he grabbed the bottom of her tank, yanked it up over her head, and tossed it across the room, leaving Dillon in nothing but a peach lace thong. He nudged her on into the house, then slid the door closed behind him. Corey kissed, sucked, and groped Dillon's body while guiding her across the room to an oversize armchair. Caught in the throes of ecstasy, Dillon followed with zero hesitation.

"Sit down," he whispered so sexily in her ear that she damn near melted onto that chair. Standing back, Corey looked at her lustfully while he removed his clothes, then dropped to his knees. Grabbing her by the top of each calf, he pulled her forward until her ass was hanging over the edge of the armchair, and pushed her legs open. Corey slid his tongue beneath the G-string and tickled the slit of Dillon's pussy lips, causing her to pant heavily.

Pushing the G-string aside, he licked her from anus to clit, sending shock waves through her body with each stroke. "Oh, Corey," Dillon moaned loudly as Corey teased her wet opening with his index, then slid it in. He massaged her G-spot while nibbling and sucking her clit. Gently he worked his finger into her anus, and once all the way in, he moved both fingers back and forth in both her holes simultaneously, driving Dillon mad.

She loved and hated what Corey was doing to her. She loved the shear unadulterated pleasure that made her shiver uncontrollably. Dillon hated the loss of control, though. When he worked her like this, there wasn't much Corey couldn't get her to agree to.

Corey pulled his index finger from her pussy and slipped it into her ass. He moved his two fingers back and forth in her ass rapidly as he dipped his tongue in and out of piping hot hole.

"Oh shit. Oh shit!" Dillon screamed. Warm liquid trickled down her hard, thumping pussy walls. Dillon inhaled, water filled her eyes, and every muscle in her body locked up. "Ahhh," Dillon yelled as she exhaled. Tears leaked from the corners of hers eyes, and cum splashed from her pulsating pussy walls.

Assured that he'd put it on her, Corey grinned sexily as he stood up and looked down at Dillon as she trembled from the aftershocks of such an explosive orgasm. Like his father, Corey was well endowed. His thick, erect dick stretched halfway down his thigh. After allowing her a few moments to recoup, he took Dillon by the hand and said, "Stand up for a sec, baby."

Dillon slowly stood, her legs wobbling slightly beneath her. Corey took a seat on the chair and pulled her down on top of him. Planting her knees on the chair, she straddled his lap, then slid down onto his rock-hard pole, taking as much of him as she could inside her. Starting out slow, she went up and down his shaft, and then she steadily picked up speed. Bouncing at a fast pace, she squeezed and twerked on his wood as her ass cheeks jumped. Corey looked at her like she was unbelievable. Her tight, moist box had him ready to blast off, but he couldn't. Not yet. Taking control, he grasped her by the waist, stopping her movement.

"What's wrong, baby?" Dillon panted.

"I just want to slow down for a second. You keep riding me like that, I'm going to nut."

"Isn't that the point?" She licked his neck and flexed her inner muscles.

"Yeah." Corey slapped her ass. "But not yet. You feel too good. I want it to last longer. I want to really feel it. Like this." Holding her by the waist, he slid her up and down his shaft in a nice slow motion. "Don't do anything. Let me drive for a little while."

Nodding her head, Dillon bit down on her bottom lip. "Mm-hmm."

"You like the way this dick feels?"

"I love it."

"Oh, you love?"

"Yes," she whimpered.

"You love my dick, but you don't love me?" he said, thrusting upwardly.

"I love you too."

"Why won't you be mine?"

"It's too complicated."

"I can't accept that." Pumping harder, he moved her up and down faster. "You saying you love me. You know that I love you. Shit, I adore you." He slipped two fingers into her wet ass and continued thrusting everything that he had into her physically and emotionally. "Be mine. You know I'll take good care of you."

"I know you will."

"Say you'll be mine."

"I can't."

"Yes you can. Say you will. I'll never hurt you."

"You won't?" she questioned.

"No."

"Okay."

"Nah, I need to hear you say it. Tell me you're mine."

"I'm yours," she squealed as she exploded again, coating his dick in thick white cream.

Rapidly pumping, Corey tensed up tightly as euphoria raced over his body and he released a mind-numbing nut deep inside Dillon.

Chapter 5

"What do you have planned for the day?" Mallorie sat at her vanity, with a tube of mascara in her hand, while she watched her husband with narrowed eyes.

Dave's shoulders lifted into a shrug. "Same things I do every day. Business meetings mostly. Why?"

"No reason." Mallorie didn't have much to say. She had had her eye on her husband more than usual.

Mallorie came from money, and because of that, she would have never been able to peacefully marry a man that her family didn't deem worthy of her hand in marriage. It had always been Mallorie's dream to marry a powerful man and to be that bitch. Her name belonged in the headlines. Being the wife of the mayor fit her dreams indeed. She was living the life that she had always wanted to live, and she wasn't going to let anything ruin that.

Sure, Dave had cheated on her. Most men cheated. Her father had more than one baby with more than one woman. It was just something women in her family had learned to deal with. Mallorie would have loved to be the one to break that generational curse, but why should she let a man who couldn't keep his dick in his pants mess up her dreams? On the other hand, they were married and were supposed to be a united front. Instead, Dave stuck his dick in any young woman with a slit, and it was beginning to repulse Mallorie.

She needed solid proof of his philandering before she gave him an ultimatum, however, and she had finally found it. All she had to do was wait for the perfect time to burst her husband's bubble. And he wasn't the only one who was going to feel her wrath. Mallorie had a few tricks up her sleeve, and she wasn't going to let up until she came through like a tornado and caused a whirlwind of damage. God help anyone that was stupid enough to get in her way.

"Don't forget we have dinner with the Hugheses tomorrow night," she reminded him as she zipped her makeup bag shut.

"I haven't forgotten. I saw James yesterday at the country club."

Mallorie chose not to respond. She wanted to keep the peace until she decided that she wanted to make Dave aware that she wasn't as dumb as he thought she was, but looking at his smug face lately was making her stomach turn.

He was really under the impression that he was getting away with his bullshit. Just picturing him getting what was coming to him was enough to make a smile ease across Mallorie's face, which confused Dave when he glanced over at her.

"What's funny?" He truly looked confused.

"Nothing. Have a wonderful day at work."

Dave stared at Mallorie as she stood up and sauntered toward her walk-in closet. These days, smiling was something that she rarely did. But it wasn't the smile that had him eyeing her with skepticism. It was the fact that she looked like the cat that had swallowed the canary. Mallorie was smiling as if she had a secret. Like she knew something that no one else knew. Dave decided that he had bigger things to worry about besides Mallorie's strange behavior. Just then his phone rang, and when he saw who was calling, he looked over his shoulder and stepped out of the bedroom.

Mallorie didn't miss the fact that Dave left the room when his phone rang. Men were so stupid. They were so obvious about the bullshit that they did. There had never been a time when Dave didn't take a call in front of her unless he was hiding something. Mallorie had been to the rodeo before when it came to Dave's infidelity. Even though status and image were so important to her, she was starting to wonder if she should take a different approach. The approach of outing her cheating husband and taking him for every penny that she could get. If he wanted to play in her face by screwing young cum buckets, she could play in his pockets and make him regret the day he ever crossed her. The wheels in Mallorie's head were turning.

When Dave was out of earshot, he spoke. "Hello?" he said in a hushed tone as he walked down the hallway.

"Hi, Daddy," Alleyne purred. "I miss you."

Dave sucked his teeth. "What have I told you about calling me before you know I'm at the office? I do have a wife, you know," he whispered. "Do you think I can take your calls when I'm in the same room with her? I shouldn't even be taking them while I'm in the same house with her."

"You won't have one for long." Alleyne's syrupy sweet tone had disappeared, and her voice had some bite to it. "I love you, and I know you love me. I'm being patient, but I need more, Dave. I deserve more. She can't even make you happy. Her feelings shouldn't matter. She can't even do her wifely duties correctly."

There had been several times when Mallorie was home and Alleyne and Dave talked on the phone. There had even been times when he went into the bathroom and masturbated while she talked dirty to him. That had told Alleyne all that she needed to know. When a man was in the house with pussy, but he chose to get a nut from phone sex with his mistress, his wife was doing it for him. Alleyne knew that Mallorie didn't do it for him. Mallorie didn't deserve Dave. Alleyne did. She wasn't sure why Dave was acting so brand new all of a sudden.

"I'm not about to stand here and explain to you why I have to move a certain way with my *wife*. Someone that you knew about from day one. Unless there's an important reason as to why you're calling me, I'll see you later."

Dave ended the call and shoved the phone into a pocket of his slacks. Sometimes women were more damn trouble than they were worth.

A distinctive, familiar dinging sound roused Dillon from a deep slumber. Peeking through one eye, she looked around and realized that she was in Corey's bed. She could not recall how she got there. Corey was knocked out cold, his mouth wide open, completely unbothered by the loud humming of his phone, which was vibrating across the nightstand, just inches away from his head. The dinging sound that had awakened Dillon sounded again, and she realized that her cell phone was going off as well. Recognizing that it was the text message alert on her phone, Dillon jumped out of the bed and felt like someone had struck her in the head with a cast-iron frying pan. *What the fuck?* She grabbed the side of her head, then followed the sound of her phone into the living room as it went off again.

Seeing their clothes strewn about, empty champagne bottles scattered on the floor, and a huge stain on the chair that they'd had passionate sex on hours earlier only brought back a slight recollection of the previous night. Her promising to be with Corey and dropping the *I love you* bomb flashed through her throbbing head.

"No the fuck I didn't," she muttered and angrily snatched her phone from the coffee table. Dillon pressed the text message icon on the phone screen and saw there were several new messages.

The first message was from Gloria. Dillon, the packers, and movers will be here at ten thirty. The remaining balance is seven hundred dollars.

She opened the next message. It was from Toni. Hey, girlie, Antice and I are going to breakfast at our spot, followed by some shoe shopping. You must come with and tell us all about last night. Saw some pictures and it looked like it was totally epic! XOXO

Dillon glanced at the top of the phone screen to find out the time. It was eight fifteen. She needed to leave ASAP, and as more memories of the drunken sweet nothings she'd told Corey flooded her mind, she decided that it would be best if she got out of there without waking him. Looking around, she saw that everything that she needed to make a quick exit was within arm's reach. Quietly she threw her clothes on, grabbed her keys, her clutch, and her gown, and rushed out.

A pounding headache nearly blinded Dillon on the short drive to her nearby penthouse. When she got inside, she went straight to the medicine cabinet and retrieved a bottle of Excedrin. Dillon swallowed four of the pills at once, then took a quick steaming-hot shower. After drying off, she entered her clothes' room, a bedroom that had been converted into a mega walk-in closet. Dillon was not in the mood to get dolled up. In need of maximum comfort, she slipped on a white fitted Gucci tee, a pair of sexy fitted white Gucci sweatpants, and a pair of beige Gucci flip-flops with pink-leather trim.

Dillon snatched the first sizable handbag that caught her eye. She didn't care what it was as long as it could hold three smartphones, an iPad mini, a billfold, and a makeup pouch, the usual items Dillon carried with her on a daily basis. On her way out she pulled seven stacks from the hallway safe, which was discreetly hidden behind a faux wall vent.

In the building's garage a refreshed Dillon hopped into her white Mercedes ML350 and headed to her grand-mother's home. When Dillon arrived there, both of her aunts, the boys, and her grandmother were in the kitchen having breakfast.

"Good morning," Dillon greeted as she entered the kitchen.

"Hey," everyone sang out, cheesing from ear to ear.

"Aren't you a glowing beauty," Pat remarked.

"She sure is," Gloria added.

"Thanks," Dillon replied. The super upbeat energy in the kitchen was a little weird, but Dillon just figured they were happy about the move.

"How are you feeling this morning, baby?" Lilly-Ann asked Dillon.

"I'm fine, Gramma." Something was *definitely* up. Lilly-Ann didn't call her sweet names unless she was trying to butter her up.

"Sit down and have some breakfast."

"Thank you, Gramma, but I'm meeting my friends for breakfast in a few."

"Well, sit a minute and have a cup of coffee," Lilly-Ann pleaded with a smile.

"Okay. What is up with y'all?" Dillon sat in the empty chair next to her grandmother.

Smiling extra hard, Lilly-Ann said, "Why have you been hiding that good-looking lawyer boyfriend of yours?"

"Huh? What are you talking about?" Dillon was genu-inely confused.

"Don't go acting all shy. My friends have been calling me all morning," Lilly-Ann boasted.

"Calling you for what?" Dillon was totally perplexed.

"They saw you on the front page."

"The front page of what?"

"The *Charlotte Observer*. You and the youngest mayoral candidate in the history of the city."

"Where is the paper?"

"I got it right here." Lilly-Ann picked up the folded newspaper from the table and handed it to Dillon.

With all eyes on her, Dillon opened the paper. "Holy effin' shit!" she gasped as she gazed at the picture of her and Corey holding hands on the red carpet and read the headline below it: IS THIS CHARLOTTE'S FUTURE MAYOR AND FIRST LADY?

"You better watch your mouth!" Lilly-Ann popped Dillon on the hand. "I don't care if you are dating the next mayor."

"I'm sorry, Gramma, but this is crazy." Dillon's heart began pounding, and her airways started to tighten. She knew an anxiety attack was imminent. "I gotta go." Dillon pulled a stack of money from her purse, and without counting it, she handed it to Gloria. "Love y'all."

Dillon raced out of the house, climbed into her truck, and immediately popped a Xanax. After taking a few moments to compose herself, she sped across town to Peterson's Diner. Antice and Toni were already seated in a booth and eating when she walked in. When they saw Dillon approaching, they both smiled widely.

"Hey, Michelle Obama," Toni joked.

Antice burst into a loud laugh.

"Ha ha. Real fucking funny," Dillon muttered as she slid into the booth next to Antice. "I guess y'all have seen today's paper."

"Yes, and the blogs," Toni replied.

"The blogs?" Dillon frowned.

"Honey, *yasss*," Antice said. "They all want to know about the pretty black girl that killed in that Charbel Zoé gown."

"I just cannot believe this, on top of all the other bull-shit last night." Dillon was trying her best to take it all in, but she just kept hoping that she'd wake up from this nightmare. Everybody and their mama was going to be digging through her life now.

"So what else happened last night?" Toni asked.

"What didn't happen?" Dillon sighed, rolling her eyes. "I should've stayed my ass far away from that damn gala and Corey."

Antice furrowed her brows. "Damn. Was it that bad?"

"Here's the condensed version . . . You already know this nigga is running for **mayor**. Dave Prescott is Corey's father, and my ex-fiancé, Heavy, was Mariah Tynes's date. Corey pressed me all night to be his woman, and during a good pissy-drunk fucking, I think I agreed to be his."

Antice dropped her fork. "Wait a minute, bitch. You just said a whole fucking lot. We need the longer version, with details."

"Yes, we do," Toni agreed.

Over breakfast Dillon detailed the entire night out for her closest girlfriends. She gave them every detail, from walking the red carpet to waking up and sneaking out of Corey's condo that morning.

When she finished, Toni asked, "So what are you going to do about Corey?"

"Leave him the hell alone. What else is there to do?"

Toni raised a quizzical eyebrow. "Why?"

"Come on, Toni. You already know I didn't want to commit before he went off the deep end and decided to run for fucking mayor of Charlotte. I damn sure ain't going to commit now. I'll end up catching a fucking case.

I don't need that many eyes on me. People are nosey as hell and will stop at nothing to find out every detail about me, including how I take my coffee. No thank you." Dillon frowned. Corey's announcement was still putting a damper on her mood many hours later.

"Well, you did tell him that you would be with him." Antice smiled, batting her long lashes at Dillon.

"I was drunk, and he was blowing my back out. As a lawyer, he should agree that I made that promise under duress."

"Speaking of backs getting blown out, what's up with you and Heavy?" Antice asked. "I saw a few pictures of him and the mayor's daughter, and he's still looking fine as ever, and he was blowing that back out for years."

"Girl, that was my second time running into him this week, and he keeps saying how much he's changed and that we need to talk." Dillon frowned again. "I just can't deal with all this right now. All I want is to fade into my normal obscure life and forget about all this bullshit. As a matter of fact, I'm done talking about it for the rest of the day. I feel another headache coming on." Dillon rubbed her temples.

"Sounds like you need to just relax with us today," Toni said, "and enjoy some retail therapy."

An hour later Dillon sat in the premier designers' shoe salon at Neiman Marcus, surrounded by shoes, shoeboxes, and handbags. On her left foot was a strappy fire-red suede Aquazzura pump, and on her right foot was a red and beige Valentino Rockstud pump.

"Which one, Antice?" Dillon asked as she stood up so Antice and Toni could examine the shoes.

"Hmm," Antice hummed, squinting and twisting her lips like she usually did when she was concentrating. "Bitch, they both look so fuckin' good, I can't even choose. What say you, Toni?" She looked over her shoulder at Toni.

Toni circled Dillon, her attitude on ten. "Honestly, I don't like either one," Toni announced sassily.

Forever the devil's advocate. Dillon rolled her eyes. "That shit doesn't surprise me. If it ain't about you twisting this wig of mine, you don't give one fuck," Dillon snapped, flopping back down in the chair.

"Mm-hmm," Antice agreed, handing Dillon a pair of Gianvito Rossi pumps this time.

"Your ass just can't be like the rest of us rich hood bitches and buy some simple red bottoms or some Giuseppes? You fucking with Italian m'fuckas nobody ain't never heard of," Toni sassed, sucking her teeth for emphasis.

"Shut up, Toni. I do have to be different. Yes, that's right. I ain't that run-of-the-mill chick, and besides, I have about every style of Louboutins that has come out. I'm sick of them shits, and plus, they fucking hurt like shit," Dillon retorted. She followed up her words with a chuckle to let her friend know it wasn't that serious.

"Lucky bitches have all the nicest shit and all the fun too," Antice shot back, laughing too.

"C'mon. I gotta get checked out. It's been fun relieving some of my issues by shopping, but I need to go check in on Nilda and London," Dillon said, winking at her friends.

Antice began gathering up all the boxes, stacking up the ones that Dillon wanted to purchase and setting aside the ones Dillon had rejected, but then a small commotion behind her made her stop. All three ladies turned toward the sounds.

"Wait, is that a celebrity rolling up in here?" Toni asked, immediately and instinctively sweeping her hands through her hair.

"Sure seems like it, the way all the commission whores are racing over there," Antice said, squinting for a better look.

Dillon stepped around Antice so she could see as well. She wasn't the type to be starstruck by any celebrity, because she was used to hobnobbing with the best of them, but her curiosity had been piqued.

"It looks like some older bitch," Toni said once she got a clear view of who all the commotion was for. "It's Mallorie Prescott, and she's walking this way."

Antice stood up straight, and her eyes went wide. Everybody in the city knew who this lady was and what she represented. "Um . . . Dilly . . . um . . ." Antice was trying to give Dillon a warning, but she couldn't even find the words.

Dillon spun around, and before she could react, she came face-to-face with Mallorie Prescott and her throng of bodyguards.

It was an intense few seconds of hot, evil glares exchanged between Mallorie and Dillon. It seemed as if time had been suspended and everyone in the store had had a pause button pushed, halting their movements.

With Mallorie and Dillon now toe to toe, the differences between them were stark, but what they had in common was now apparent.

Mallorie was clearly from old money, or what they called generational wealth. Her wealthy air was as effortless as the low-key Chanel blazer she sported and her St. John slacks. The sixteen-carat canary diamond ring that gleamed on her wedding ring finger told the story as well. Not to mention the neatly coiffed chignon that sat at the nape of her neck.

At this particular moment Dillon felt like a hoodrat compared to Mallorie, although Dillon was no slouch herself. It was just that the Gucci sweats she wore now seemed a little too tight and a little too hoodratty for her to be standing toe to toe with such a classy lady. Even Dillon's three-thousand-dollar Michael Kors Casey

Python bag paled in comparison to the vintage Chanel Caviar bag Mallorie had slung over her shoulder.

At the black-tie gala, all had been well, but Dillon could practically feel the heat radiating off Mallorie now. She was willing to bet that this encounter would be anything but friendly, and she was confused. This was only her second encounter with Mallorie, and Dillon had never done or said anything out of the way to her.

"I made a special trip here just to see you," Mallorie said, with a small grin creasing her lips.

"Why? You just saw me last night," Dillon stated in a polite tone while cocking her head to the side.

"Oh, sweetie, you know, it seems like I met you long before last night. I know more about you than you'd like to think," Mallorie shot back, her voice even but flat.

"Look, lady, whatever your hang-up is, take that shit up with Corey or someone else," Dillon said, getting ready to push past Mallorie.

Mallorie reached out calmly and, with one swift motion, caught Dillon by the arm.

"Uh-uh! Get the fuck off her!" Toni yelled, rushing over. The three bodyguards who accompanied Mallorie stepped closer. "You see this shit?" Toni said, turning to Antice with a helpless look on her face.

"I didn't come here to fight with you like some street trash. I came here to give you fair warning," Mallorie said, fire blazing in her eyes.

Dillon shrugged her arm away from Mallorie. Dillon's jaw rocked feverishly, but she listened as Mallorie moved her mouth close to Dillon's ear.

"Stay away from my husband. As a matter of fact, you should just go ahead and ban him from your little establishment, because, see, I have people in high places who will have you locked up for the rest of your little wretched whore life," Mallorie snarled, all the while with a small smile on her face.

Dillon's heart pounded in her chest, and blood rushed to her face. She felt so small now. Standing there with a bag filled with cash meant nothing when a real rich woman, one who had real wealth, which she probably had never worked for, confronted you and made you feel like you were back struggling in the hood.

Dillon's guard was up, and she was on high alert. The only people who should know about the brothel were the ones that utilized the services and the ones that worked there. Having someone like Mallorie know way too much about her business wasn't a good thing at all, but Dillon was as stubborn as Mallorie. She'd never let the nervousness that she felt shine through.

"How about you stop by my little establishment and take some classes on how to please your husband? Then maybe . . . just maybe . . . he will stop coming on his own and will fuck you again once you learn what it is that he likes and needs. Now, get the fuck away from me," Dillon retorted, also smiling, as if she and Mallorie were exchanging pleasantries.

Mallorie laughed. "Oh, you are a funny one. But that's okay. I'll see how funny you are when my brother, Chief Abrams, the chief of police, stops by. He might be interested in learning about your business," Mallorie shot back.

"Chief Abrams is your brother? Isn't his skin a little dark for him to be your brother?" Dillon looked Mallorie up and down.

"He's my half brother. One of my daddy's many dirty little secrets, if you will. However, I've always treated him good, and he cherishes me for it. Therefore, if I say, 'Sic 'em,' he'll hunt you down like the dog you are." The sinister grin on her face made Dillon aware that the woman meant business.

"Do whatever the fuck you want," Dillon growled in Mallorie's ear. "If your sweet Dave doesn't go there, he'll find another place and another woman who will do all the freaky shit he likes. At least my girls are clean and constantly tested. So, you'll have nothing to worry about during your once-a-year anniversary fuck."

Although she was smiling outwardly, Malorie was thirty-eight hot on the inside. Nobody had ever dared talk to her in such a manner. Not even her husband's past mistresses. Quite a few of them she had paid to disappear. The two or three that couldn't be paid off, because they were so in love with the great Dave Prescott, seemed to have vanished into thin air.

"Now, you have a good day, Mrs. Prescott! It was so nice seeing you again!" Dillon said loudly. "C'mon, ladies. I changed my mind. Let's get my shoes and then do a little more shopping," Dillon called to Antice and Toni, all the while keeping a grin on her face.

Like Mallorie, she was hiding her true feelings. The moment Mallorie mentioned Dave visiting her establishment, Dillon knew that it meant big trouble. And that meant Dave had to go. She wasn't going to let Mallorie know that, though. She had to stick it to Mallorie for coming at her the way she did. Having her face plastered on the pages of the newspaper of one of the fastest-growing cities in America as the potential future first lady was more than enough drama for Dillon. She didn't need a wealthy scorned wife whose brother was the city's highest-ranking officer on her back. She wasn't even done running her errands for the day, but this couldn't wait, and she didn't want to give orders over the phone. Dillon wanted to look Alleyne in her eyes when she told her what she needed to tell her. The other things that she had to do could wait. Her livelihood was at stake.

Dillon paid for her shoes at Neiman Marcus, left Antice and Toni, and drove to her palatial brothel. She stopped in the office first. Nilda was guiding London through the books.

"Hello, love," Nilda greeted Dillon.

"Hey, Dillon," London said cheerfully.

"Afternoon." Dillon placed her purse on her desk. "Nilda, cancel Dave Prescott's company file right now. Do not book any more appointments for him."

"But he's on the way right now."

"When he gets here, have him brought in this office. He is not to make it to Alleyne."

Dillon blew out of the office, raced up to Alleyne's room, and knocked on the door.

"She's not in there," said Dria, an eye-pleasing Albanian woman with endless legs, as she walked past.

"Do you know where she is, Dria?"

"In the lounge room. Cute pants, Dillon."

"Thanks," Dillon replied before speed walking to the steps.

Perched in the center of the purple couch like the queen bee she imagined herself to be, Alleyne dangled her wrist in front of Monica and Kelly. She proudly showed off a wide-strap, braided platinum bangle set with flawless full-cut diamonds. The extravagantly beautiful piece of jewelry had been delivered that morning. It was a gift from Dave.

"This is so nice," Kelly cooed as she admired the bangle. "How much do you think it cost?"

"Probably, like, thirty-five hundred dollars," Monica blurted out.

"Bitch, you sound stupid," Alleyne scolded. "This is a forty-thousand-dollar work of art. I understand that you low-budget hoes ain't used to this level."

"Forty thousand," Kelly gasped. "Yeah, girl, that's definitely your man. Johns don't buy gifts like that."

"Johns are not serviced here," Dillon said from the doorway, startling the three women. "P H I provides only models for clients' companies. Need I remind you to stop using that pimp-whore language?"

"Yes, ma'am. I'm working on it," Kelly replied, staring at Dillon's attire in disbelief.

"Stop with that 'ma'am' shit. I've told you about that."

"My bad, Dillon. You looking real cute in your Gucci sweats, though."

"You sure do," Monica added. "I've never seen you this dressed down."

"Me neither," said Kelly.

"I didn't plan on anyone here seeing me, but something urgent came up. And speaking of that, Alleyne, I need to talk to you alone."

"About what?" Alleyne questioned with a royal attitude.

"Not to-fucking-day, Alleyne," Dillon barked, fed up with Alleyne's obnoxiousness, which had grown to new heights since Dave had begun paying her weekly minimums and then some. "You two beat it now," Dillon roared at Monica and Kelly. The pair jumped up and rushed out of the lounge room. "You really been smelling yourself lately. I should've checked your ass a long time ago. You giving me attitude, and you don't even know what I want to talk about."

"Excuse me if you thought I was being rude," Alleyne replied facetiously.

"I wanted you to hear this from me first, because I know that you and Dave are closer than the normal model and client."

"Oh, girl, he's my man. There is no model-client relationship."

"Whatever you wanna call it," Dillon stated dismissively.

"What do you mean, whatever I want to call it? Men don't send gifts like this"—she held up her wrist—"to jump-offs and randoms."

"I'm not here to debate what y'all are or who he is to you. I just came to tell you that Dave is not allowed here anymore."

Alleyne leapt up off the couch. "Why the fuck not?"

"His presence here threatens the business and our freedom."

"You can miss me with the shade, Dillon. I knew sooner or later you bitches were going to start hating. Y'all some old jealous-ass hoes."

Dillon prayed silently, *Lord, please keep me from wrapping my hands around this bitch's neck.* "Two things that I'm not," Dillon said through gritted teeth, "is jealous and a hater. I would love for Dave to keep coming through, dropping that cash. In case you forgot, when you eat, we eat, but Dave's wife has found out about his visits here, and she wants them to stop. Or else."

"Or else what?" Alleyne scoffed. "You're going to let a bitter wife dictate your business?"

"She isn't just some typical bitter wife. She can make shit go bad around here real fast. If it does, I'll be the one getting the time and losing the money."

"If you're going to tuck your tail and run like a weak bitch when a wife starts making threats, you might as well close up shop right now."

"Like I said, dumbass, his wife has a little power and enough weight to fuck us with no remorse."

"That's cool. I was already planning my exit from this joint. I'm about to buy a house, where my man can see me for free."

"That's absolutely fine. You can leave right now, but you better wait six months before you start seeing him again."

"Six months," Alleyne shrilled. "Once I'm gone, you can't run me."

"I don't want to run you. If his wife catches y'all together anytime soon, even outside of here, she's going to associate you with me."

London walked in. "Excuse me. Dillon, your guest is in the cigar room."

"Thank you, London." Dillon turned back to Alleyne. "We will finish this shortly."

"I'll be in the guesthouse, since my man paid for it already for the night."

Shaking her head in disgust, Dillon left the room. London spun around to exit the room next. Before she could, Alleyne called out to her. "Ayo, pretty girl London."

London paused and turned around. "Yes?"

"They don't play fair here. I'm about to open my own brothel service. I'm going to need a bookkeeper. You might want to strongly consider jumping over to the better ship. Before this ship starts to sink."

London looked at Alleyne and shook her head before responding, "Nah. I'm good right here."

Chapter 6

Dillon frowned at the car that drove beside her. Its driver was honking the horn clearly trying to get her attention. She was less than a mile away from the mansion, in a residential neighborhood, and she had no clue why someone would be trying to get her to stop her car. She looked over at the brown-skinned man who was driving the black Tahoe. He pointed to the shoulder of the road, urging her to pull over.

Maybe he was trying to tell her that something was wrong with her car. Dillon reached inside her purse and grabbed her .22 and placed it in her lap as she eased her car onto the side of the road. She had no clue who this guy was, but if he tried any funny business, she was going to shoot his ass without thinking twice about it. Dillon gripped her gun as the man pulled up behind her and got out of his car. She stared at him, trying to see if she could place his face, but she drew a blank.

"Dillon?" he asked as he crouched down and looked into her window. His eyes landed on the gun in her hand.

"Do I know you?" Her tone was less than friendly.

"You don't know me, but you might want to. Does your boyfriend know you own a brothel?"

Dillon's top lip curled. "You're real bold, and you must have a death wish! I know that isn't what you pulled me over for. Who the fuck are you?" she growled.

"I work for Mrs. Prescott."

Scoffing, Dillon placed the gun in her lap. "I've never seen a woman so pressed because the man she married would rather screw everybody but her. I don't know what kind of pussy she thinks I am, but she will not bully or harass me. If she's your client, she must be paying you well to do her grunt work. It better be worth it, because if I catch you following me again, I will handle it how I see fit."

Dan smiled at Dillon's warning. "This is a gorgeous car. You seem to live a very luxurious life. All of this will come to an end if you end up in the slammer."

Dillon picked up the gun in her lap and cocked it back, sending a bullet into the chamber. Dan backed away from the car with his hands up. With a frown on her face, Dillon watched him get into his car. Mallorie had a lot of fucking balls, and it was beginning to piss her off. Dave had better get a handle on his wife before Dillon did so herself. She wasn't about to allow people to keep threatening her with jail, but the possibility of serving time was very real.

If word about the brothel got to the wrong people, Dillon's ass was grass. Meredith was tucked away somewhere safe, and she was on the front lines. If shit hit the fan, Dillon would be the one carted away in handcuffs. And she was as solid as they came, so in the event that she did get in trouble with the police, she would never rat on Meredith. That wouldn't happen, so Dillon would have to take the fall for being a madam. She was beyond stressed. *First things first*, she thought. First, she needed to handle Dave ASAP.

"Good afternoon, Dave," Dillon said as she walked into the meeting room.

Dave stood up and removed the stogie he was smoking from his mouth. "Afternoon, Dillon."

"Sit, sit." She took a seat in the leather wingback chair opposite Dave. Dillon opened the gold-trimmed wooden case that sat atop the table next to her chair. It had been an hour since Mallorie's minion had pulled her over and tossed a few threats her way, and Dillon was a tad bit calmer. She picked up a cigar, dipped it in cognac, and lit it. Dillon took a small pull off the cigar, then spoke. "Dave, I hate to be the bearer of bad news, but you can't come around here anymore. I have to cut all ties between you and this brothel."

"Why? Because Corey is my son? I can assure you that I'm not going to tell him about this place or that I knew you prior to last night."

"No, it has nothing to do with him. As much as I care about Corey, you know better than me that I can't continue in that relationship without exposing this place or myself."

"Well, what's the problem?"

"Your wife. She tracked me down at Neiman Marcus today to inform me that she knows all about this place and me. She knew exactly who I was before the gala. And to add insult to injury, some guy was following me earlier, and he asked me to pull over. He proceeded to get out of the car and threaten me with jail time. He said Mallorie was his client."

Dave was deep in thought. "My wife must've hired some new investigators," he said finally. That was why she'd been walking around looking all smug and acting strange lately.

"What about her brother, the chief?"

"How do you know about that?"

"Your wife threatened to tell him about my operation if I continue to let you patronize my fine establishment here, and we both know I can't have that. I'm not sure if she thinks she's really that tough or if I look soft as hell, but the balls that she's coming at me with is insane."

"Damn. Mal must really be pissed off. She doesn't tell anyone about her dark-skinned brother. Don't worry. I'll get her off your back. What are you going to tell Alleyne, since I can't come around anymore?" Dave was disappointed, but he was sure he could work around coming to the house. And even if he had to take a break from Alleyne, getting pussy had never been an issue for him. Alleyne could be replaced by morning.

"I told her the truth. She's not taking it well. She says she's moving out. I just ask that you two cool your heels for the next six months, so your wife won't associate anything that you may be doing with this house or my girls. Alleyne doesn't get it. She thinks I'm hating. I just don't want to jeopardize everything I've worked for over a disgruntled wife. She's making it her business to track me down, as if I'm making you fuck Alleyne. I'm trying to be patient, but it's wearing very thin, I can assure you." She didn't even care to mention that if she had to get other people involved, Mallorie would be sorry. Other people meaning Meredith.

"Alleyne has a lot of growing up to do, but don't worry about her. I'll smooth her over with some gifts and money for a new place." He stood up. "I'll get going, so I won't cause you any more trouble. I'll take care of my wife and Alleyne, so maybe one day in the future, we'll be able to do business again. You know I'm a very discreet person. I just happen to have a very nosey wife."

"Maybe." Dillon stood, shook his hand, and escorted him to the door.

Pausing in the massive doorway, Dave turned to Dillon. "Maybe you should close this place or distance yourself from it for the next year. My son does love you.

You would be a valuable asset to him during his run for mayor."

Dillon chuckled. "See you around, Dave."

He left, and she waited a minute before shutting the door and returning to her office to retrieve her things. Little did Dave know that she absolutely planned to distance herself from P H I, but it would be to do her own thing. More money in her pocket meant she wouldn't have to remain in the brothel business for years on end to maintain her lifestyle. Once her bank account reached a certain number, Dillon wouldn't mind sitting pretty and being a housewife. She'd never allow herself to depend on a man without her own money to fall back on.

But being married or seriously dating a man with a li'l bank, while her money sat in numerous accounts and drew interest, sounded like a great idea to her. Maybe if Corey was still single once she reached her financial goal, they could make something happen. It would be her pleasure to be the mayor's wife once she was no longer partaking of things that could have her thrown in prison.

London was alone when Dillon entered her office. "Where's Nilda?"

"She said she wanted to rest for a little bit while you're here. We've been going hard since yesterday evening."

"I can hang around. How are things going so far?"

"So far so good," London told her.

"How are the girls treating you?"

"Okay, I guess." London shrugged. "They're not being rude or overly polite. That Alleyne chick is a piece of work, though."

"Why do you say that?" Dillon quizzed.

"She's been saying off-the-wall shit since yesterday, and when you walked out of the lounge room half an hour ago, she told me that I should come work for her at the brothel she's opening."

Dillon's phone rang before she could say something in response. She picked it up from her desk and looked at the screen. Blocked ID. "Who in the hell is this?" Dillon muttered as she pressed ACCEPT. "Hello?"

"I see you follow directions well."

Dillon recognized the voice. "Mallorie?"

"Yes, it's me. I like how you sent my husband away quickly. Too bad you can't control your whores."

"What are you talking about?"

"That Belizean whore just called me, claiming my husband is her man and hurling the most horrible insults at me. She's ruined my day, so now I'm going to ruin your lives. I'm giving you fair warning."

"For what?"

"My brother returns from vacation in a few days. You have until then to shut that whore mansion down. If you don't, I'll tell him everything." Mallorie hung up.

Dillon slammed her phone down. "I'll be back." She bolted from the office and ran straight to the guesthouse. One of the things that pissed her off the most was that Mallorie had hung up before Dillon could go in on her. Mallorie's issue should be with Alleyne and Dave. Dillon didn't like the fact that Mallorie kept coming at her like she was some weak little mouse. She didn't have a pussy bone in her body, and Mallorie was going to make her act out of character. She was much too classy to get downright ratchet and ghetto, but she would if she had to. Especially if her freedom was at stake.

Alleyne was smoking a cigarette and pacing the living-room floor when Dillon burst into the guesthouse.

"Bitch, have you lost your fucking mind?" Dillon screamed. "Why are you calling Dave's wife? You're a silly-ass ho!" She then socked Alleyne square in the face. She was so mad that she was practically foaming at the mouth.

Alleyne wasn't no punk. She came back with a quick two piece to Dillon's right eye. The women traded wild punches and flung each other around the room, breaking tables and shattering expensive vases and glassware. At some point Dillon lost her footing and fell down. Alleyne seized the opportunity; she pounced on top of Dillon and began to pummel her with blows to the head and face. Dillon tried with everything she had to gain the upper hand, but Alleyne was too much to reckon with. They both seemed to have some pent-up anger and aggression, and in the process, they were going at it like wild animals.

Dillon attempted to block the blows Alleyne was raining down on her while frantically patting the floor with her right hand until she found a long, thick shard of glass. Before she could think about the consequences, she plunged the broken glass into the side of Alleyne's neck, right through an artery, in an effort to get Alleyne off her. Warm blood gushed out of Alleyne's neck like a geyser, covering Dillon and everything nearby in blood. Alleyne collapsed on top of her. She died instantly.

Dillon shoved Alleyne's lifeless body off her. She sat up, gasping for air. It took a few minutes, but when she got herself together, she locked the front door and ran up to one of the bedrooms and retrieved one of two satellite phones that she kept stashed there. Dillon called the only number programmed in the phone.

After five rings a female voice answered. "Hello, love."

"Hi, love. I have a problem."

"What kind?"

"Slow singing and flower bringing."

"Where are you?"

"I'm on the property, in the second house."

"Hold tight. I'll send someone. Do you need anything?"

Dillon looked down at herself; then she thought about the scene on the first floor. "Yes, I need fresh clothes, shoes, and lots of strong cleaning supplies."

Dillon went into the bathroom, stripped out of her blood-soaked clothes, and stepped in the shower. For thirty minutes under nearly scalding water, she scrubbed every drop of blood from her hair and body. When she stepped out of the shower, the doorbell was ringing. After covering herself with a plush cream terry-cloth bath sheet, she rushed downstairs. When she looked out the peephole, she saw the man that she knew to be Meredith's cousin Sean with two other men. Sean was long rumored to be an Irish mobster.

She opened the door, and the trio stepped inside. They greeted her with simple head nods. After immediately observing the scene with just a glance, Sean handed Dillon a brown paper shopping bag containing a gray tee, blue jeans, and a pair of gray New Balance.

"Get dressed fast. You have to get out of here. Before you go, tell me everything that led up to this." Dillon stood there and gave Sean the full rundown. While she was telling him about the Mallorie and Alleyne situation, an idea popped into her head, an idea that could kill two birds with one stone.

Loud knocking at the door of Mallorie's swanky Center City condo woke her from a deep slumber. She looked at the alarm clock on her nightstand. It was five in the morning. *What in the hell?* she thought, slowly rising from the bed, now regretting her decision to stay at the condo following the Hornets' playoff game and a few rounds of drinks with girlfriends. With her head pounding from all the alcohol she'd consumed hours earlier, she now wished that she had had her driver take her on to her Weddington mansion.

The loud banging continued until she yanked the front door open and came face-to-face with four uniformed officers. "Why in the hell are you pounding on my door at this hour?" she demanded. Mallorie was still groggy, and the pounding in her head had her attitude on a thousand. She didn't care if the president of the United States was at the door. She'd curse his ass out for knocking like a lunatic as well.

Shocked, the cops stared at her silently.

"Why are you looking at me like that?" Mallorie asked, then looked down and saw that her hands and ivory silk pajamas were smeared with dried blood. "Oh, dear God," she muttered as the smell of the blood hit her nose, and Mallorie resisted the urge to throw up. To her knowledge, she wasn't hurt. So why in the hell did she have blood on her? If it wasn't hers, who did it belong to?

"Do you live here?" one of the police officers asked.

"Y-yes, I do. Well, this is one of my residences. I don't come here all the time, but I got in this morning, after a night out. It wasn't too long ago, actually." While Mallorie spoke, she was trying to piece together what could have happened.

"Are you here alone?" asked the same officer.

"Yes. No one has keys except me and my husband, and he's not here. I came straight in and went to sleep. I didn't have anyone here with me." Mallorie's heart was racing. She had been drunk when she got in, and she'd gone straight to bed. She might have had too much to drink, but Mallorie was certain that she hadn't had blood on her when she got into the bed. So, how had she got blood on her while she was sleeping?

"We got a disturbance call," one of the other cops said. "We need to look around now."

The officers pushed past her and fanned out around the condo to check the rooms. It wasn't long before one of them yelled out, "In here. I got something."

The other three officers and Mallorie converged on a bloody bedroom, where Alleyne's dead body lay in the center of the floor. When Mallorie saw the body, she couldn't hold back any longer. She turned her back to the officers and the body and threw up the contents of her stomach. Mallorie had never seen a dead body before, and she had damn sure never seen one in her home. She was completely mortified, but the officers seemed unmoved. They waited patiently for Mallorie to stop vomiting.

The first officer questioned Mallorie. "Who is she to you?"

Mallorie wiped her mouth as she reluctantly turned back to look at the body once more. "Nobody I know. I've never seen her a day in my life."

"Yeah right," another officer said. "Cuff her while I call homicide."

Even though everything seemed to be moving in slow motion, the events after her arrest were all pretty much a blur to Mallorie. She felt as if she was having an out-of-body experience, and it didn't feel good. It felt like she was in a nightmare that she couldn't wake up from. Hours later Mallorie was booked into the Mecklenburg County jail on suspicion of murder. After taking a mandatory shower, she sat on a couch in the television area. Completely traumatized and unable to wrap her head around the situation, she stared off into the distance. How the hell did a dead body end up in her condo? How did she become covered with blood? There was no reasonable explanation.

A white female who had strawberry-blond hair and was dressed in jailhouse orange plopped down beside her. "Hi. I'm Lacy." She extended her hand to Mallorie.

Mallorie looked at her hand like it was diseased and didn't shake it.

"Well, alrighty, then." Lacy pulled her hand back. "What are you in for?"

"I'm not in for anything. This is a nightmare that will soon be over."

"In case you are in here longer than expected, you'll need a friend in here." Lacy leaned in closer to Mallorie, making her frown. "I'd suggest choosing the right friend. It's not easy in here. If you want someone to have your back, I'd suggest you be a little nicer. And having someone to watch your back and keep the other women off your ass doesn't come cheap."

Mallorie scoffed at the comment. She was so focused on wondering how in the hell a dead body had made its way into her home that she didn't even consider the possibility of being in jail, among hardened criminals, for more than a few hours. Mallorie could be very snide and condescending. In her world that was enough. Mallorie's words could cut like a knife, and her razor-sharp tongue was often how she got her point across. In her world, women didn't resort to physical violence. Mallorie wasn't a fighter, and these women in here could eat her alive, but she refused to let Lacy or anyone else see her sweat. If she let them know she was out of her element and gave the impression that she was weak, they really would be on her ass, and Mallorie couldn't have that.

She was banking on getting out on bond, but she couldn't be so sure. Nothing about what was going on in her life at the moment made sense to her. "Thank you so much for the offer, but I don't need any friends. As I said before, I won't be in here long. This is all a big misunderstanding."

"I'm sure you won't be, since your brother is the chief of police." Lacy was sitting so close to Mallorie that Mallorie could feel her hot breath on her neck, and it made her skin crawl. Smiling wide, Lacy winked. "Enjoy your stay here in Pod C. We love law enforcement and their family members."

"Dria!" Dan called out, as if he knew the woman who was walking out of Starbucks. He was a private investigator, and he was great at what he did, but there was no getting onto the P H I estate. Dan had to spend a lot of his time staking the mansion out in order to catch one of the girls leaving, which they rarely did. But today was his lucky day.

The Albanian beauty turned in the direction of the voice, wondering who was calling out to her. Dria rarely dealt with anyone outside the house. She had come to the States at the age of twenty in search of a better life. Her family was back in Albania. Besides the girls that worked in the brothel, Dria didn't deal with many people, and she fed a lot of them with a long-handled spoon. Being a loner was the best thing to be when one wanted to avoid drama and unnecessary bullshit.

Dria studied the man walking toward her. Maybe he was going to ask her if she was single and try to get her number, because she'd never seen him a day in her life. So, that had to be it. But how did he know her name? Dria had slept with quite a few men since her first days working at the brothel, but she generally never forgot a face.

"Hi. How are you doing?" Dan asked with a smile, like they were old friends.

"Do I know you?" Dria looked him over with a slight frown. He definitely didn't look like the type that could afford services from P H I. Dria had been an escort long enough to know that most wealthy people didn't wear their money. On any given day their attire was bland, plain, and nothing to write home about. But their aura screamed wealth. This man. No. He wasn't that.

"You don't know me, but I know a lot about you. Like how you send money home to your family in Albania every month. How they think you're over here in the States, working at some big, hotshot job and making enough money to give them a better life. When really all you do is sell ass."

Dria jerked her head back. "Who the hell are you? How dare you speak to me that way!"

Dan chortled. Dria was highly offended, and he was highly amused. "I'll keep this short and to the point. I have a client, and it would make her day if that whore-house that you work in is shut down. In fact, she has reach, and if she pulls the right strings, immigration will have your ass back in Albania before you can blink. Do the right thing. Go ahead and cut ties before you find yourself in some deep shit. Dillon is going down. Don't go with her."

Dan walked away from Dria, who stood there with her mouth hanging open. She wasn't sure who he was or how he knew what she did, but he had to be legit. Dria had never talked about her family in Albania with anyone. The money she made working in the brothel had not only changed her life, but it had changed theirs too. Dria didn't care how she made her money. She was damn proud that she had come to this country with nothing, and now she had more money than she ever would have made by being a waitress or doing some other mediocre job.

In a daze, Dria walked back to the car that was waiting for her. Out of all the things that could have happened on her impromptu coffee run, that encounter was the last thing that she had expected. The thought of losing everything was enough to make bile rise in her throat. Dria wasn't sure what Dillon had going on, but she wasn't going down for anybody.

Chapter 7

Mallorie was the type who never let anyone see her sweat, but this was a predicament that she had never experienced, and it was unsettling. She was too rich, prim, and proper for a tiny, cold, rank jail cell. She willed herself not to cry as she sat in the interrogation room, waiting for her lawyer to arrive. She had refused to answer any questions until Corey was present. Although he was now running for mayor, he was still a junior law partner and was good at what he did. Mallorie was sure that she would be vindicated of all charges against her and would be leaving the jail soon, but in the terrible event that she did have to fight a criminal case, Corey could pass the case off to one of his business associates, so there would be no conflict of interest.

She tried to appear confident, because she was pretty sure that she was being watched, but Mallorie was about to shit bricks. How in the hell did a dead body end up in her condo? That question had crossed her mind a hundred times already, and she didn't have anything close to an answer. Mallorie's head was pounding, and she was shaking so hard that her teeth were damn near chattering. This had to be a mistake. Of course it was. She hadn't killed anybody, and before last night, she hadn't been to the condo in almost three weeks. She rarely ever spent the night there. She imagined that sometimes Dave took his whores there. The ones that didn't work in brothels.

That thought made her stomach churn and her lip curl. She was much too classy and gorgeous to be married to a man who had sex with prostitutes. Cheating was one thing, but spending time in a brothel took the betrayal up a notch. It made Mallorie sick to her stomach to think about her husband penetrating women who had had sex with hundreds of men. Mallorie held her breath, and her eyes widened. Was this something that her husband had done? But why in the hell would the senator have dead bodies lying around their condo?

Mallorie made every effort to recall every detail about arriving at the condo last night, but all she had done was walk in, go to the bedroom, and fall onto the bed. Who could have called about a disturbance? Yes, she'd been drunk, but Mallorie would have surely heard if there was any kind of commotion going on. It would have woken her up out of her sleep. The condo had been quiet, and she'd slept like a baby. None of it was making a lick of sense to her. Leaning forward, she put her face in her hands. She was fucked. How in the hell did she get blood on herself? Things weren't looking good for her, and she was smart enough to know that.

Finally, the door opened, and in walked her brother, Chief Abrams. Mallorie breathed a shaky sigh of relief as he closed the door behind him.

"What in the hell is going on?" he asked in a hushed tone while his eyes roamed over his sister's face. Mallorie could be a lot of things, but a cold-blooded killer wasn't one of them. At least he didn't think so. She could be hell on two feet, but she cared way too much about her image to ever do such a thing.

"I . . . I honestly don't know. I went to the Hornets' game last night, and I had a little too much to drink, so instead of going home, I decided to stay at the condo. I got there around five in the morning, and I was so hammered that

I went to bed in my clothes. I woke up to pounding at my door, and it was the police, saying they had got a call about a disturbance." She paused to take a deep breath. "Somebody set me up," she insisted and looked at her brother with eyes full of fear. Damn. Someone had to really hate her guts to go this far, to frame her for murder.

"Why would anyone want to set you up for murder?" he asked with a frown on his face. "And you have no idea who Alleyne Cantos is?"

Mallorie's blood ran cold when she heard that name. "Alleyne?" All the color drained from her face, and her brother knew that she knew who this woman was.

"Yes. Who is she to you?"

"She isn't shit to me," Mallorie spat. "But she's having an affair with Dave. You might want to ask him about this." Mallorie was all for protecting her husband's image, but she wasn't going down for murder for a soul.

It was one thing to pretend for the world that she had the perfect marriage, but she wasn't lying to the police. Not when someone was trying to frame her. Aside from a few phone conversations, she hadn't had anything to do with this woman.

Chief Abrams narrowed his eyes. "Dave was having an affair with this woman?" He inhaled a deep breath and shook his head. "This is a fine mess that you've found yourself in the middle of."

"And you and Corey have to get me out of it," she retorted. "You know me. I couldn't kill anyone," she stated snidely, with her nose turned up in the air.

Watching her mannerisms and the anger that flashed in her eyes, even her brother had to rethink his stance. To keep her family's perfect little image intact and to keep a young, beautiful woman away from Dave, maybe she had done the unthinkable. Now he wasn't so sure he'd put it past his sister. She could be an evil bitch when she wanted to be, and there was nothing she cared more about than being praised and adored by many. Mallorie wanted the perfect life.

Just then Corey came bursting into the interrogation room, and he looked just as confused as Chief Abrams had looked minutes ago. "Mallorie, what's going on?"

Two more detectives entered the room, ready to question Mallorie. They were tired of waiting. Chief Abrams had had his time alone with her, and now they wanted to get to the bottom of the city's newest high-profile homicide.

The first detective, a dark-haired man, spoke up. "There was a call about a disturbance at Mrs. Prescott's condo. When the officers arrived, Mrs. Prescott answered the door covered in blood, and there was a deceased woman in the second bedroom."

Corey had heard a lot and seen a lot in his career, but it was hard for him to keep the shock off his face. He turned toward his stepmother, and tears filled her eyes, more out of frustration than fear. She just needed someone to listen to her and understand that this was all some crazy misunderstanding.

She repeated to Corey the same thing that she had said to her brother about going to the Hornets' game and having too much to drink. "Can't you look at the security cameras in the lobby? They will tell you what time I arrived at the condo and that it was my first time being at the condo in almost three weeks. I have no clue how that woman even got in there, but she had to already be there and dead when I got in."

"And you didn't notice a body in one of your bedrooms?" the second detective asked in a dry tone.

"No I didn't!" Mallorie snapped. "I stumbled inside the apartment and fell face-first onto the bed. Can't you determine how long she was dead and then look at the time that I entered the condo? Damn it. She had to already have been there. Do your job. Go find some evidence, instead you're sitting around and blaming me."

"So, you have no idea how this woman ended up in your condo? You have no relationship with her?" asked the second detective.

Mallorie blew out a frustrated breath. "I was just told that the woman's name was Alleyne. I've heard that name before, and we've had conversations on the phone, but I never met her in person. Alleyne is a whore. Was a whore. She is a sex worker, and she was having an affair with my husband. Her boss, Dillon, owns a brothel, and I—"

Corey's head swiveled in Mallorie's direction. "Um, excuse us," he interrupted her. "I understand that you have to ask questions, but is my client being placed under arrest?"

"I don't see how we can let her go when she was the only person found in a condo with a dead body, and she's admitted that the woman was sleeping with her husband. Mrs. Prescott is very wealthy, and so she poses a flight risk. She has the means to flee the country."

If Mallorie hadn't been sitting down, she would have fainted. She began to tremble again while Corey spoke on her behalf. There was no way she could be forced to stay in this godforsaken place.

"Can't she be placed on house arrest? I understand that it seems as if the case is cut and dry, but Mrs. Prescott is a pillar of the community. She's donated millions upon millions of dollars to various charities. Her husband is a senator of this state, and her brother is the chief of police. I am her stepson, and I'm running for mayor. Jail is not the place for her. Please release her and allow her to stay on house arrest until the trial. She will not run."

The detectives remained silent, because while it brought them a slight sense of joy to have someone like

Mrs. Prescott in jail, they knew that it could also bring a lot of headaches. And in the end, it wasn't completely up to them anyway. It was up to the judge if he wanted to grant her bail or not.

"We'll let the judge determine that," the dark-haired officer finally responded.

Chapter 8

Dillon walked into the small, intimate café that Corey had insisted on meeting her at. No matter how hard she had tried to tell him that she didn't have the time to meet with him, he had refused to take no for an answer. Knowing what had transpired with Mallorie made her intrigued about what he wanted. A sinister grin crossed her face when she thought about all the threats Mallorie had hurled at her. She had talked down to Dillon and had treated her like she was beneath her. Now, her ass would be begging a judge and a jury not to lock her ass up and throw away the key. Dillon felt she was a genius for the plan she had concocted. Alleyne had made her some very good money, but she had ended up being more trouble than she was worth, so she'd had to go. And if she could take Mallorie's ass with her, that was all the better.

Dillon ordered a frappé and a blueberry muffin, made her way to the back of the room, and sat at a small table. If Corey had begged to meet her just to try to convince her to deal with him on a serious level, and not to give her the rundown on his stepmother, she was going to be pissed. As Dillon sipped her frappé and people watched, she noticed Corey pulling up and thought back to the sex they had had the night he announced that he was running for mayor. They'd had a good time for sure, but Dillon knew she couldn't become dependent on this. It was something that she needed to prevent from happening again anytime soon.

She wanted a corporate, legit guy, which Corey was; however, the one that was for her would be quiet and under the radar. Corey was too public and in the spotlight. Truly, it was best for both parties if they didn't continue. At least that was what her mind was telling her, but her heart was beginning to betray her. There was something about Corey that she really liked, and she was starting to catch feelings for him, no matter how hard she tried to fight it.

As Corey headed to the back, where she was seated, Dillon noticed the tight expression on his face. He was definitely in a serious mood. It had to be due to Mallorie. She had known this moment would come, but she was going to play dumb. Dillon hit him with a big smile.

"Hi. Is everything okay? You look a bit tense."

Corey glared at her as he sat down. The way his eyes bored into her face, Dillon almost became uneasy. He knew something. She wanted to shift in her seat, but she didn't want her body language to convey that she was uncomfortable. Dillon knew she had to play it cool.

"You gave me a lot of little slick-ass excuses as to why we can't be together, when all you had to do was be honest and tell me that you're a madam. You're a madam that runs a fucking brothel, and my father is one of your regular customers. My stepmother has been arrested for that woman's murder, and either she's an excellent actress or she was framed."

Dillon's breathing was stifled. Damn, he knew a lot. Dillon felt like she was slipping, because she hadn't anticipated this, but she continued to appear cool, calm, and collected before responding. "Now, wait a damn minute. I get that you're upset about Mallorie, but you come in here tossing a lot of accusations at me with nothing to substantiate any of the shit you're spewing. I'm sorry your people seems to be in some serious shit, but don't lay it at my fucking doorstep. Now we can deal with the other accusations, if you want."

Dillon felt like she was buying herself a little time, but it was looking like she'd have to come clean about the brothel part. Mallorie was for sure talking, and if that was the case, her entire operation would be news in no time at all. *Fuck!* she thought to herself.

Corey frowned up his face, as if he was disgusted by her. "Do you own a brothel or not?" he asked with some bass in his voice.

He wasn't playing with her. Dillon had never seen him be so assertive and domineering, and if her entire world wasn't crashing down around her, she might have been turned on.

"First of all," she said, playing dumb, "can you tell me who was murdered?" Dillon glared at Corey while pretending that she really didn't know what was going on.

Corey was trying his best to read Dillon, but just like with Mallorie, he thought, either she didn't know what was going on or she was a damn good actress. "Alleyne Cantos, one of your *employees*, was found murdered in my father's condo. Mallorie was in the condo at the time."

Dillon gasped. She opened her mouth, but she didn't say anything. Working overtime to appear confused and shocked by the news, Dillon covered her face with her hands. "I . . . I don't know what to say." She uncovered her face. "Murdered?" She repeated the word with a frown, as if she just couldn't fathom the thought.

"Yes, *murdered*, and they are trying to pin it on my stepmother. Now, I'll admit that it doesn't look good, but she swears that she came in drunk and went straight to sleep. The only other person with access to that condo is my father. So, I will ask you again while I try to make sense of all this. Do you run a brothel?" Corey was staring at Dillon as if he no longer knew who she was, and technically, he didn't. He felt as if he didn't know anybody around him. The closest people to him were hiding a hell of a lot of secrets.

"I do," she answered with some bite in her tone. "It's not something that I can go around shouting from the mountaintops. In the line of business that I'm in, discretion is key. Why would I tell you that your father was one of my clients?"

"Because I'm your fucking friend, and that would have been the decent thing to do. You actually pimp women out? No wonder you knew you couldn't be on the arm of a mayor."

Dillon closed her eyes and rubbed her temples. "I know you're upset. Maybe you have a right to be upset that I kept my profession from you, but me telling you about your father's affair wasn't my place, and there are many reasons that I'd choose not to be on your arm. Don't get too ahead of yourself."

"And you threatened my stepmother?"

Dillon scoffed at his comment. "I threatened her? Are you fucking kidding me? She was the one tossing around threats and saying she was going to expose me and sic her brother on me."

"So, you killed Alleyne? To keep your business from getting out?" he asked knowingly, and she gasped.

"Are you out of your fucking mind?" she snapped. "You just sat your ass over there and accused me of murder? I know you've learned a lot of disturbing things, but that doesn't mean you get to sit there and talk to me crazy. I didn't have an issue with Alleyne. Your stepmother did! I don't know what happened to her, but don't bring that shit to me! Your father had way more to lose than anyone if this shit got out. I'm the last person you need to be sitting over there blaming."

Corey felt as if he was losing it. He really didn't think his stepmother was capable of murder, and his family didn't need this scandal. Corey hated to be selfish, but this couldn't have come at a worse time. Tears began to form in his eyes, and the hurt showed on his face. His father's indiscretions were sure to affect his run for mayor. This would be the biggest scandal that Charlotte had seen in a long time. Dillon wasn't who he had thought she was, and neither was his father. It had been a hell of a day for Corey.

"I just don't understand how you were running a brothel. It's like I don't even know you. I was blind-sided, and I'm sure I looked like a fool to you. You and my father were keeping secrets from me and acting as if everything was all good. It just all makes sense now. The way you disappeared after my announcement."

Dillon rolled her eyes. *No, this nigga isn't crying real tears!* He wasn't even the one in real trouble—that was her—and yet here he was being an emotional wreck in public. She stood up before speaking. "Look, I'm not about to sit here and listen to this bullshit. I'm sorry that I didn't tell you about all my illegal endeavors," she said in a hushed tone. "If that makes you feel some kind of way, then I apologize, but I'm not going to be on the receiving end of your emotional outburst. It doesn't matter if I told you the real reason or not, but I told you countless times that we could never be. You're welcome," she hissed. And then she walked off.

Dillon's heels clicked on the linoleum floor as she strutted hard toward the exit. She was furious. The blowup with Corey wasn't even at the forefront of her mind. She couldn't care less about that. But her cover had been blown. That was what mattered. Bitch-ass Mallorie had been running her mouth, and Dillon was going to have to shut down shop. Her brothel was no longer a hidden dirty little secret. It was being very much talked about, which could cause her to lose a shit ton of money, and she wasn't pleased about it.

Unless . . . Dillon reached her car, climbed behind the wheel, and drummed her fingers on the steering wheel. All she had to do was buy a little time and get the heat off her. This might just be the perfect reason to fall back from working with Meredith before starting over from scratch and doing her own thing. She just had to play it cool and not end up in jail before her plan could come to fruition.

Chapter 9

"I thought I told you to turn this off," Nilda scolded when she entered Dillon's living room and found her watching the news as she sat on the sofa.

Alleyne's murder and the scandal that surrounded it were all over the news. It was even been reported that the police had swarmed the mansion, aka the whorehouse, and run up in there, but everything had been gone. They had found nothing. The only information they had on the brothel besides the address was that it was run by Dillon. She was sure they were trying to obtain a warrant for her, but if they didn't have her home address to serve her, it was of no use. For the moment. She was lying very low and trying to figure out a way out of this mess.

Dillon chastised herself for setting Mallorie up in the first place. It should have been common sense that the bitch wouldn't be able to do any time, and she was going to tell everything she knew. Shit was all bad for Dillon. Alleyne's bullshit was now the last thing on her mind. Dillon thought she had handled her issue, but she had, in fact, made everything worse.

"What else am I supposed to do?" Dillon muttered. She drained the wine from her glass, wishing that she had something much stronger. "I need to go somewhere else and start over," Dillon added, answering her own question. "I don't know people that are connected anywhere else, though."

"Just wait for all of this to blow over," Nilda said and sat down beside Dillon on the sofa. "No one has proof of anything. There was nothing at the house, and no one caught you or your girls in the act. I know you have enough money to just sit back for a bit and wait for this whole mess to be forgotten about. Another scandal will soon take its place. Patience, my dear. Patience. Move smart and not based off greed or emotions. Trust me, these powerful men don't want to be any more exposed than you do. They will make this go away soon enough."

"And Dria? That bitch came in here and packed her things like someone was after her ass. She was spooked. It's like she knew something was going to happen, and I can't even ask the bitch what went down."

"Dillon, you have to stop stressing."

"That's way easier said than done."

Dillon did have money put aside for a rainy day, but the thought of spending without replacing didn't sit well with her. She almost wanted to arrange for some of her most loyal clientele to continue to meet with the girls, but Dillon had no way of knowing if she was being watched.

"I need food," Dillon mumbled as she stood up. She could have ordered something, but she had been hiding out inside, drinking wine and having a pity party all day. She needed some fresh air.

"Do you need me to come with you?"

"No, I'm fine. Thank you for offering."

Dillon walked out to her Bentley and got inside it. All the wine that she had consumed had her a bit tipsy, but she was so preoccupied that she barely felt it. She couldn't believe her luck, but as her grandmother used to always say, all good things must come to an end. She had had a great run as a madam, and she would have to accept that those days might be behind her.

Dillon pulled up at one of her favorite Thai restaurants, climbed out of the Bentley, and hit the LOCK button on her key fob. She barely noticed the gentleman getting out of the car beside her until he spoke.

"That's a pretty nice car you have there, beautiful."

Dillon looked over to see who the deep voice belonged to, and to her surprise, it was Heavy. She hadn't seen him since the night of the gala, and she had to admit that hearing his familiar voice gave her some calm. He had grown his beard out, and with him standing nearly six feet two and being stocky, it gave him a young Suge Knight kind of vibe.

She gave him the once-over. He was definitely looking good in his dark denim jeans, black cashmere sweater, and black Polo boots. The ice around his neck was giving the sun's rays a run for their money, and his sparkling white teeth and his clear butterscotch skin were still his best attributes. His hair was now cut low, and even though there was a short distance between them, Dillon could smell the cologne that he wore. His whole aura had her in temporary awe as she looked over at his Porsche truck.

"Thank you. It's good to see you," Dillon said after shifting her gaze to him. The effects of the wine were now a little more apparent, and Dillon felt like her head was spinning. She hadn't been enthralled with a man since her drunken fling with Corey, but seeing Heavy had her on something.

"I know our last encounter didn't go as well as I was hoping. But, D, I really have grown, and I hope that you will give me a chance and will get to know the new and improved me at some point." His eyes swept over Dillon's body, and she could tell he was still pleased with what he saw.

Her surveillance of him continued. His nails were clean, his watch was up to par, and his car and clothes were on point. With everything she now had going on, maybe it was time to give him a second chance. It wasn't like the so-called professional corporate guys had been the right decision. Hell, they did just as much dirt, and with none of the loyalty. Shit, at least you could depend on the street niggas to have your back when shit got hot, she thought.

"Yeah. It has been a while since we've really talked," she observed. "How have you been?"

"As good as a man can be without the right woman by his side," he tossed at her flirtatiously.

Dillon's smile was small. He was looking good and was a sight for sore eyes, but she was far from thirsty. He didn't need to know how much she was feeling him off two seconds of conversation.

"So I see you still eating at our spot."

"*Our* spot? I'm sure I was the one who turned your non-exploratory-eating ass onto this place."

"Yeah, I'll give you that. You definitely had a nigga eating shit he couldn't even pronounce."

They both shared a laugh at his comment.

"I'm starving. Would you like to join me for a bite to eat?" he said.

Dillon shook her head lightly. "Thank you for the invitation, Heavy, but it's not a good time right now. I'm beyond stressed, and I just want to grab some food and go back home and eat while watching my favorite TV shows." Dillon thought about how pathetic she sounded. She hated sounding vulnerable.

"Damn, Ma. It can't be that bad. You're saying you'd rather go home and eat alone than be in the presence of a real nigga with great conversation? You should never be so stressed that you cheat yourself out of a magnificent time."

Dillon's eyebrows shot up. "Magnificent?" She had forgotten how cocky he could be. "Damn, did you really just refer to your company as magnificent?" She laughed.

"Hell yeah, I did. You know I'm not like these other niggas," he replied in a serious, slightly arrogant tone. It turned her on.

"What the hell? I guess a bite to eat won't hurt."

Heavy smiled, showing those white teeth, and she smiled back. Maybe he would make her forget her problems, even if it was only temporary. They headed inside the restaurant, and the hostess seated them in a booth.

"So are you still fucking wit' ole boy?" Heavy asked.

Dillon smirked. "Now that we're seated is a fine time to ask me if I'm still dealing with someone."

"That's because you know it really doesn't matter. I'm just making conversation."

"Well, to answer your question, no, I'm not. We decided to take a break. Do I dare ask about the status of you and Ms. Thang?"

"Well, I'm no longer a disrespectful nigga. So trust that if I was in a relationship, I wouldn't be sitting here with you. That thing with the mayor's daughter was strictly a business move, and that business has concluded. I would never be lunching socially with a female if I had a woman."

That comment almost turned Dillon on again, but she wouldn't allow herself to be swayed so easily. Heavy was a sharp one, and the nigga was a smooth talker. He had the gift of gab, but he wasn't about to get Dillon caught up in the hype again.

"Cute," was all she said.

"You care to talk about what it is that has you so fucking stressed?"

"I certainly don't. Talking about it is reliving it, and I don't care to do that right now. I came out to get some fresh air and forget. Let's talk about something else."

He already claimed to know that she ran a brothel, and the story had been on the news. Most dope boys didn't sit still long enough to watch the news, but rumors ran rampant in the city of Charlotte. There was a chance that he already knew and was simply playing dumb. Heavy had never been dumb.

The conversation came to a brief halt when a waiter came over to take their orders. When the waiter walked away with their orders, their conversation resumed.

"Okay. We can talk about where you're going to let me take you on our first official real date."

"This innocent bite to eat and conversation is turning into something a tad bit more complicated. The factor that has me stressed, which I don't care to speak on, is something that will probably be stressing me out for a bit. Dating isn't on the agenda for me at the moment."

Heavy shook his head. "You are really sitting here, telling me that you plan to allow yourself to be stressed? Kind of shit is that, D? Problems come, baby. That's life. We don't sit in them, and we don't dwell on them. That's not gon' solve shit. We stick our chest out, hold our head up, and we handle that shit. We don't let it handle us." He stared into her eyes intensely, and Dillon's panties became moist from arousal. He was turning her on in the simplest of ways. It had been way too long since she'd been turned on by a man who wasn't speaking or acting in a sexual manner. She had almost begun to think it was impossible, but here he was doing it.

"Who is this *we* you speak of?" she asked coyly.

"Bosses." Heavy said the word with conviction.

His answer made Dillon smile. She was really feeling this new and improved Heavy, and she found herself captivated by him. He had big-dick energy for sure, and she knew it was warranted.

"I like that." Dillon smiled.

The waiter appeared with their order. Heavy continued to ask her questions and make clever comments as they ate. Considering all that was going on in her life, Dillon found herself smiling, and she was glad that she had come out. Had she stayed inside the house, hiding from the world, she would never have run into Heavy again, and that would have been a shame.

Dave ducked as the glass that Mallorie tossed in his direction came barreling toward his head. After a lot of persuading, begging, cashed-in favors, and the greasing of some palms, Mallorie had been released on house arrest two hours earlier. When she had got to the house, she'd taken a long, hot shower, and then she'd begun to consume one stiff drink after the other. By the time a weary-looking Dave had entered their upscale home, Mallorie was two thirds in the wind and pissed. She had had way too much time to sit and think about the shame and the scandal that was now attached to her name, and she was livid. How would she ever be able to show her face again in public? Dave and his wandering dick had ruined her life.

"This is all your fault, you cheating bastard!" she screamed. "I *hate* you. I should have let the whore have you and just divorced you while taking half of everything you own! But no, I tried to fight for my family. I tried to fight for my marriage, and this is the thanks that I get! Trying to fight for a bitch-ass nigga who never fought for me got me fucked in the end!" she roared.

Dave pinched the bridge of his nose. He was not in the mood for theatrics from Mallorie. Not when everything he had worked so hard for was about to blow up in his face. He was supposed to retire in a few years and bow out gracefully on his own terms, not be run out of his spot in office due to scandal and shame. "Mallorie—" he began, his tone full of warning, but his words were halted by a slap to the face.

As the side of his face stung from the hit, he grabbed Mallorie's wrists and held on to them tight. "Do not put your fucking hands on me again. I understand that you've been through a lot, but don't get beside yourself." He glowered at her. "Put your hands on me again, and I will put my hands on you back," he threatened before releasing her wrists.

"You are a worthless, cheating piece of shit. You are beneath me, and I hate that I married you. I hope you lose every fucking thing."

"Be careful what you wish for. If I'm not mistaken, you were caught in the same place as a dead woman."

"A dead woman that you were fucking! She was your whore. For all I know, you used to take her there and have sex with her. The police better watch the security footage, and they better do something to come to the conclusion that I didn't do this shit. And when that miracle occurs, I will take that as a sign from God, and I will get as far away from your black ass as I can."

Dave walked over to the bar, so he could indulge in a stiff drink himself. Emotions were running high. Like his wife, he was overcome with shame and embarrassment. Never did he think his cheating ways would come back to bite him like this. And what was worse was that he and his wife, even his son, were all side-eyeing one another, trying to figure out who was telling the truth. This had been one of the worst days of his life, and he knew he was in for one long-ass ride.

Mallorie wasn't done. ""I will never forgive you for this. As long as I have to go through this, your life will be hell!"

"My life was already hell," Dave grumbled.

"You think this shit is funny! I am literally being accused of murder! And who is the person that's dead? Your whore! Someone that was bold enough to call my phone about my sorry-ass husband! People will probably assume that I have all the motive in the world to kill that bitch. My life is literally over." The dam finally broke, and Mallorie began to sob. She hated Dave, and she hated Dillon in that moment. She also hated Alleyne, but that bitch was already dead.

"I'm not going to let you go to prison for this," Dave promised. "There has to be some kind of an explanation." Seeing Mallorie cry made him feel bad. He loved his wife. He was simply a man. A man who had an insatiable appetite for beautiful, freaky young women.

There was a time when Mallorie had made his toes curl in the bedroom, but he had soon begun to think that she pulled out all her best moves to get him, not realizing that those were the same moves that she needed to keep him. Truth be told, Mallorie could have sexed him like a porn star, and he probably still would have cheated, but it wouldn't have been to the extent that it was.

"Yes, like, maybe it was you who killed her?" Mallorie gave him an accusatory glare.

Dave chuckled. "Are you serious?"

"Yes, I am. Who else has access to the condo?"

Dave pinched the bridge of his nose. "I really don't feel like doing this right now. Why would I kill Alleyne?" He gave his wife a weary look.

"Why?" she screeched. "Because she was getting beside herself, and she no longer knew her place," Mallorie scoffed. "She could have become more trouble to you than she was worth."

"That's not a reason for me to kill her. She may have gotten out of line, but I could have gotten her back straight," Dave replied arrogantly, making Mallorie's upper lip curl.

"I can't stand you." She stormed out of the room, wishing that she could kill Dave with her bare fucking hands and get off by pleading insanity. Lord knows, if she felt anything, it was certainly insane.

Chapter 10

Dillon walked into her grandmother's house, prepared to hear the lecture of her life. As soon as she rounded the corner and her grandmother came into view, Dillon noticed the way her grandmother's lips were twisted to the side.

"I knew this house was bought with dirty money. I knew it, and you tried to act like I was crazy all these years," Lilly-Ann squawked. "What in the world have you gotten yourself into? This is the biggest mess that I have ever seen. What is wrong with you, girl? Weren't you raised better than this? You let greed and the love of a dollar turn you into someone that God is not pleased with."

Dillon spoke slowly, so her tone couldn't be interpreted as disrespect, as she said, "Grandma, with all due respect, I am grown. You may not agree with all the decisions that I made, but I made them. I tried to do a good thing by getting you out of a messed-up neighborhood, and you make it clear every chance you get that you don't want anything to do with my dirty money. That's noted. You don't have to worry about me offering any more of it. In fact, why don't I just stop coming around?" She meant every word of what she said.

Lilly-Ann's mouth fell open as Dillon turned around and walked back out of the house. She was in her feelings heavy, and she just wasn't in the mood for bullshit. Dillon loved her grandmother, but she was too much sometimes. Dillon groaned as her phone rang. She snatched it up, but a smile spread across her face when she saw who it was that was calling. Heavy. Or, better yet, smooth-ass new Heavy. Just like that, her mood was better, and she hadn't even answered the phone. That man had some kind of magical power. Dillon knew she needed to be running away from it, but she was running toward it. She had missed him making her feel like this.

"Hello?"

"There goes that sexy-ass voice. How are you doing today?"

Dillon bit her bottom lip as she blushed from his compliment. "I'm doing okay. What about yourself?"

"Just finishing up some work, and it hit me that you never agreed to let me take you out, and I can't have that. I have season floor seats to the Hornets' games, and I also have a boat that we can take out on the lake. We can have some drinks and conversation on the water. You can choose one, or you can choose both. I'm here for it all."

Dillon's interest was definitely piqued. Heavy wasn't just a regular street nigga; he was *the* street nigga. No one could do anything in this town without his say-so. He sat at the top of the food chain. His pockets ran deep. She knew this much for sure. It had been years since they had been together, and she wondered just who she was dealing with now. Nothing about him screamed low level, but Dillon wasn't at the bottom of the totem pole either. It would take a lot for a man to be on the same level as her, and she knew where Heavy stood. Dating down had never been her thing, and it would sadden her if she didn't deem him worthy of dealing with because of his lifestyle. For that reason, she almost didn't want to know. He wasn't broke. He couldn't be. Not with season tickets to the game. Not with the car he drove, but still . . .

"You said you were finishing up some work. What are you claiming is your business?"

"Very funny," Heavy observed. "Dillon, we both know I'm a man of many talents. I handle my business, yes, but I handle it in the right way. I own a cigar bar, a few hookah lounges, and Heavy Logistics Trucking Company. I'm retired from the streets somewhat, but I make my presence known when it needs to be. My shit is long. And you know I'm far from new money." It was as if he'd been able to read her mind.

Dillon was glad he couldn't see her face and the way her jaw had dropped. This man had really come up since the time when they were together. His pockets were even heavier than she had fathomed. The basketball game was a little too public for her, so she opted to go with the second choice. "The game is a bit short notice, but I can do the lake."

"Sounds good. I have to shoot to LA tonight, but I'll be back in two days. We can set something up for the day after the game. I'll be in touch before then."

"Goodbye, Heavy." Dillon was already smiling too hard for her liking. She didn't want to mess around and sound excited. She was glad she'd given him the time of day before finding out what he did for a living. That move, added to the fact that she had her own money, meant Dillon wouldn't have to worry about coming across as a groupie.

Nonetheless, Dillon had no clue what she was even doing with Heavy. A man was the last thing she needed, but she just couldn't tell him no. She never could. That was why she found herself caught up in him yet again. It also didn't hurt that he was rich as fuck, and she was on a short hiatus from making money. Dillon had even thought about having her girls do some legit modeling with Pretty Hustlaz Inc., but she knew men who wanted ass. And they would pay top dollar for it. She didn't know men who would want her girls for anything other than that. She had the powerful connections, but her girls possessed the pussy. They didn't even need her now. They could go out and seek men on their own, and where did that leave her?

Dillon had plenty of money stacked for a rainy day, but she was still young, and that rainy-day money would run out before she wanted it to. Heavy was a great connection to have, but her girls were out of commission for the moment. It was hard for Dillon not to worry. As she was thinking about her finances, an unknown number called her phone, and she almost didn't answer, but she decided to do so at the last second.

"We need to talk." She recognized Dave's voice right away, and a frown crossed her face.

"We don't have shit to talk about. Your snitching-ass wife has me hot as hell right now. As a nigga that couldn't even keep his affairs in order, what do you have to say? What do we have to talk about?"

"We need to talk about Alleyne and what may have happened to her. I know my wife and her had a few run-ins, but Mallorie couldn't have possibly killed her."

"And you're telling me this for what? I don't have shit to do with that. Whatever happened, it's between you and your wife."

"Do you know how this entire ordeal is ruining my family? It's not just me that's fucked up here. My wife is facing prison time, and my son's run for governor is pretty much ruined before it even gets started."

"And, again, what are you telling me this for? The last I spoke to Alleyne, I told her she needed to leave. I cut ties with her because your wife was running up on me in public, making all kinds of threats and shit. Alleyne wasn't happy about what I said, and she left. Next thing I know, I'm hearing that she's dead, and she's in *your* condo. For all I know, she left here and went there. And that has nothing to do with me. What I do know is that I'm fucked too. So I guess we're all fucked."

Dave's head was pounding. He didn't know what to think. He knew he hadn't killed Alleyne, but what if she had left Dillon's and shown up at the condo? What if Mallorie had killed her in a drunken rage without meaning to? This really was all his fault. He'd been caught cheating before. What man hadn't?

Each time in the past when Mallorie had caught him in some shit, they'd argued, she'd pouted for a few weeks, and then they had fixed it, because their name and image were the most important things to them. Mallorie wanted her husband to be faithful, but if she couldn't have that, she'd settle for appearing perfect in the eyes of outsiders. She wanted to have the perfect American dream of a life. She wanted people to covet her family. His cheating had never come back to bite him like this before. Mallorie was in hot water now because of it, and he was next in line. The press was camped out around his house, and his phone had been ringing off the hook.

If Dillon really didn't know anything about Alleyne's murder, who in the hell did?

Chapter 11

Dillon sucked her teeth as she stared at the name on her cell phone screen. Every time she saw Corey's or Dave's name on her phone these days, she got an instant headache. Dillon's first thought was always to ignore the call, but this time she ended up answering it in a dry tone. "Yes?"

She was met with a brief moment of silence. "I know you may not feel that I have the right to ask you for a favor, but I'm not asking. I'm begging. Can you help me to clear all of this up? Can you please testify at Mallorie's trial and just tell the court whatever you may know about Alleyne. I mean, she was a sex worker. Maybe she had enemies. Maybe something will come to you."

Dillon attempted to be patient and not to lose her cool. "Corey, before this, we were friends, and I don't have anything against you, but you can't be serious right now. You want me to get on the stand and admit to being a madam. You want me to try to clear Mallorie's name, and then who is going to clear mine when charges are brought up against me? You act like this incident happened in *my* home. I don't know one thing about what happened. I'm not sure how I can help clear anyone's name if I don't know anything."

Corey sighed deeply. "Did I ever mean anything to you? Or was I just a part of some game?"

"What kind of game, Corey? What could I have possibly gained from being your friend when you didn't even know the truth about what I was doing? People keep secrets all the time. Get over it. I wish your stepmother the best, but there isn't anything I can do to help her." Dillon ended the call and tossed the phone on the passenger seat of her Bentley.

She often prided herself on being smart, but maybe framing Mallorie for Alleyne's murder hadn't been the smartest thing to do. It was the reason she was out of business and losing thousands of dollars a day on discreet, wealthy men coming to her establishment to buy pussy. Dillon arrived at the lake and pushed her worries to the back of her mind. She was about to go on a date with a freakin' billionaire.

If she played her cards right, this could go very well for her. Heavy was handsome and paid, he had a way with words, and he appeared to possess the ability to handle a woman like Dillon, but she didn't believe in fairy tales. She didn't trust men enough to believe that one would come along and save the day. He hadn't galloped in on a white horse, and she wasn't a Disney princess. Men lied. They played games and opened the door wide enough to let disappointment seep in. It was life's norm.

Falling head over heels for Heavy wasn't an option, but maybe running through his pockets just a bit was. They could both have some fun, and in the end, her pockets would be laced. It was a win-win situation. Dillon parked beside a black Escalade, which she assumed belonged to Heavy. He was a billionaire, so surely, he had more than one vehicle. She had spent more than an hour on Google and Instagram learning everything that she could about the man, and when she'd seen his estimated net worth was 3.4 billion dollars, she had damn near lost it.

When she exited her vehicle, she looked around and spotted him standing on the dock. Dillon made her way toward him with a small smile on her face. The boat came into view, and she was impressed. It wasn't huge, but it was a nice boat. There was an older black gentleman already on the boat, and she assumed that he would be the one at the helm.

She greeted Heavy with a smile, and he looked at her like she was a steak and he was a starved man. He loved the class and style that Dillon exuded. She wore a purple wrap dress that clung to her in the right places and flowed loose and free in other places.

"You look delicious," he said, flirting with her and making her grin grow.

"Delicious? That's a new one. Thank you."

Heavy took her hand and led her to the boat. Once they were on the boat, Dillon took a seat and stared out at the water. She could get used to this. The life she lived off her Pretty Hustlaz Inc. money was far from a mediocre one, but she wanted to be on Heavy's level. Dillon preferred getting her own money, but being a kept woman couldn't be too bad. And she would never be like Mallorie or Alleyne and let feelings get in the way of her bag.

"You like the view?" Heavy asked as he took a seat beside her.

"I love the view. It's breathtaking."

He opened the large picnic basket that sat at his feet and pulled out a bottle of chilled champagne, along with two champagne flutes. "I say we pop this bottle and toast to new beginnings."

"And what are those new beginnings?"

"To new friends, new adventures, and new money."

"I like that."

He poured champagne into both flutes and handed her one, and then they clinked their flutes together. Dillon sipped from hers, reminding herself to be soft with Heavy. She didn't have to dim her light completely—most men found her feisty nature sexy—but she didn't want to be too overwhelming. Dillon could tell a man like Heavy was an alpha male. She'd get further with him by coming off as the type that wouldn't fight being submissive. He liked knowing she wasn't a pushover, but he also wanted her to be a woman and let him lead. For the type of money that Heavy possessed, she could stroke his ego for sure. That was never a problem. She took another sip of champagne.

"I find it hard to believe that you're single. Is it by choice?" she inquired. What she really wanted to know was what he was hiding that no woman wanted to be with him. Her cell phone vibrated inside her Birkin bag, and she peeked over and saw that London was calling. Hell, now she was back to being Lanika. Dillon ignored the call and made a mental note to call her back. She turned her attention back to Heavy.

Heavy shrugged one shoulder. "Honestly? I guess I've never been focused on settling down after we broke up. I was focused on getting the hustle and turning all my street money into legal money. Starting businesses with my background is hard work, and as soon as I got those up and running good, I dove into other things. When I do make the time to have fun, I just look at it as fun. When fun is over, it's time to get back to work. I never tried to take it to anything else. But now . . ." He stared at her, making her hold her breath. "Now I feel like maybe I was supposed to wait."

Dillon sat quietly, letting what Heavy had told her sink in, trying not to get caught up.

"That's understandable," she said about a minute later, breaking her silence. "I've actually dealt with that a lot, but people think it's weird because I'm a woman. Like, I can't put my business first and worry about a man way later, down the line."

"How'd you even get into that shit?" Heavy asked, and Dillon looked him square in the eyes as she answered.

"A lot has changed since the old days, Heavy."

"I agree." Heavy nodded. "But I mean that's not something you can just find on a résumé, so something made you decide to do it."

Dillon maintained her eye contact. "I knew that a woman would always be a man's weakness. And I decided to capitalize off it."

Heavy nodded, and this calmed her nerves. "Respect," he said.

Dillon could tell that he was intrigued, but she wasn't sure if he was disgusted. In her opinion, street niggas shouldn't do much judging, but she was also aware that there was a double standard in this world.

"So you're a pimp?" he teased.

"Pimp? I prefer 'madam.' My girls' dates don't always include sex."

Heavy gave her a smirk, knowing how this shit went. All escorts didn't have to participate in sexual acts, but most did. And even if they didn't have sex with the men, a lot of them had to take part in sick-ass fetishes and sexual fantasies that would make the average woman feel disrespected and insulted.

"Madam," he repeated slowly. "If that's what you prefer. Hell, it's all the same to me, and no shame in it, in my opinion. There are a million ways out here to get money, and that's one of them. I know I'm a street nigga, but I know niggas who have wealth on an entirely different level than the average street nigga. Every hustler doesn't become a kingpin. Most don't make too much more than a smart muthafucka with a good-ass job. They get money fast and blow it faster. So, when I began to see niggas with real money—I'm talking real wealth—and I saw the kind of money they would spend on tricking . . . Man, shit, I see why you got a Bentley."

Dillon smiled. Telling him her thought process behind it was easy, and she was thankful for that. "Exactly. And the money that my girls made was far from average. In fact, one of my best clients was the senator."

Heavy's eyes narrowed, and she could see him putting things together. "Yo," he exclaimed in an animated fashion. "Well, that explains why you were with the cornball at the gala. Does he know?"

"He does now," Dillon confirmed. "Things are a little crazy right now, so I've been laying low and not doing anything, which is why I was so stressed the day we met. I'm scared to make any moves. The senator and his wife are involved in one hell of a scandal, and I don't think they'll be letting it go. They're going to use their power and connections to make sure someone else goes down with them. By the time this blows over, I'm sure my girls will have moved on without me."

Heavy stared at her, curiosity in his eyes. "Dillon, let me ask you a serious question."

"What is it?" she asked.

"Since you started your . . . business, have you ever got down for money? I mean, if you did, again, there's no judgment."

Had Dillon slept with men in the past and been given money and gifts? Sure. A lot of women had. But she had never actually put a price on her pussy and been a working girl. That was something that she was proud of.

"Never," she stated with finality. "I didn't have to when I had a stable full of bad bitches who were making me thousands of dollars per hour on a daily basis. I just got to sit back and reap the benefits. As you stated, the wealthy will trick some very good money on something that they like. They are more than willing to pay top dollar for discretion. Clean, gorgeous women with amazing bodies that don't cause them any trouble and run their mouths when it's over? There were men that visited my brothel the way some addicts visit their dealer."

"Say less." Heavy smirked, knowing that was directed at him. He was now looking at Dillon with a hint of lust in his eyes. "I knew you were a fucking boss. That's sexy as shit. I can't promise you consistency the way you were getting it before, but I know married niggas and niggas in relationships who will, as you say, pay for discretion. They can't risk being caught, and they don't want to do the whole side-chick thing. I can definitely get some of your girls work at least a few times a month if you're interested."

Dillon's mouth almost hit the floor of the boat. "Are you serious?"

"Hell yeah. That's really the dream. Aside from the woman basically being a prostitute and all. But the main thing that gets niggas jammed up is the woman running her mouth. If a man knows he doesn't have to worry about that, he'll do what he needs to do or pay what he needs to pay to get it."

Dillon was so happy, she almost screamed. Instead, she kept it classy and raised her champagne flute in Heavy's direction. "This sounds like it could be the start of a great business relationship."

"Some people don't like mixing business with pleasure, so let's just say I'm a friend looking out for a friend. That way you won't ever try to deny me the pleasure part of it when I want my relationship with you."

Dillon smirked. "Pleasure, huh?"

"Yeah. Dillon, you know I've never been one to mince words. I want what I want. And I want you."

Dillon sat quietly, unsure what to say. She had to admit, she wanted him. But she had to focus on the task at hand.

Dillon and Heavy continued catching up on old times while getting real tipsy on the lake. She knew she didn't want to leave when she was almost disappointed when they got back to the dock. Heavy promised to hit her up, and he hugged her goodbye after walking her to her car. With a smile on her face, Dillon got behind the wheel. Before she left the parking lot, she checked all her missed calls, and it dawned on her that she had to call London back. She made the call.

London answered the phone anxiously. "Damn, bitch. I thought you were ignoring me."

Dillon rolled her eyes. "I'm sure you know better than most that I'm going through hell over here. The phone isn't always the first thing on my mind," she stated dryly.

"I get that. I really do, but I need to know if I should start looking for another job. My unemployment benefits have officially ended."

"Being that I promised you a job, I will send you three thousand dollars via Cash App. That will have to hold you over for a few weeks, while I see what else I can cook up. If I'm not able to get back to work soon, then you'll just have to find another job."

"That's understandable. Thank you for being willing to look out for me. I was desperate."

"Sure thing."

Dillon ended the call, hoping that she'd be back in business sooner rather than later, and this time, she didn't plan on sharing the proceeds with Meredith. She would be the head bitch in charge.

Chapter 12

Mallorie knew as soon as she saw Corey's face that the news wasn't good. He walked into her grand living room, where she was on her second glass of wine, and it wasn't even noon. Mallorie lived on a sprawling estate, but now that she was confined to her home and her yard, it seemed like a prison. Even in her depressed state, she knew that her prison was better than a real prison, but Mallorie felt as if she was suffocating.

Before all of this, she enjoyed bossing people around and being served, but now she couldn't even get in her car and go shopping on her own if she wanted to. The press was still camping out outside her home, and when she wanted fresh air, she had to wait until it was dark out to go into her backyard for some peace. She refused to watch the news, so Mallorie drank, ate, read books and magazines, and stared off into space all day.

She had hired a private investigator to see what Dave was up to, because she didn't want to be embarrassed. Never in a million years had she thought she'd end up more than embarrassed. Every time she thought about what people must be saying about her, Mallorie had to resist the urge to vomit. Her life had truly been turned upside down. She wasn't sure she could ever come back from this scandal.

Dave wasn't on house arrest, but he'd been hiding out, as well, after giving a statement that basically asked people to respect his family's privacy at this time. He hadn't been accused of murder, but now everyone knew that he'd been stepping out on his wife with a sex worker. It wasn't exactly a story about him that he wanted to get out.

"What do you have for me?" Mallorie asked anxiously as Corey sighed and sat down. He wanted to be angry at his father. He *was* angry at his father for potentially ruining his chance to be mayor of Charlotte.

"Not much," he reported sadly. "We can conclude from the coroner's report that when she was found, Alleyne had been dead for at least eleven hours. If she died no earlier than six p.m., that can be a good thing, because you were at the game during that time. But the security cameras in the condo lobby and elevators have no footage after five p.m. It's like someone got to the cameras and erased the footage or something."

Mallorie didn't know if she should be happy or sad. "Well, there is proof and witnesses that I got to the arena at approximately six-oh-five p.m. I couldn't have killed Alleyne, changed my clothes, and made it to the arena in five minutes. So, that has to be a good thing. So that's all we need, right? I have an alibi. The cameras don't matter."

"That is a start, but it's not enough for me to be confident. Someone let Alleyne inside that condo. Someone killed her and left her body there. If there are no signs of forced entry, and you and Dad are the only ones with keys—"

"Then they better look at him," she said snidely, cutting Corey off. "I have an alibi, and I couldn't have possibly killed that whore, because I was at the game. In front of hundreds of people. I should be in the clear," Mallorie stated with a smug smile on her face. "My alibi, my name, and my connections should be more than enough to get me off. If I can't beat this, then you just might not be fit to be a lawyer."

Corey wanted to tell his stepmother off, but he refrained from doing so. He could understand her being mad at his father, but he took no pleasure in any of this. In trying to clear his stepmother's name, he might be setting his father up to be targeted, and that was not what he wanted. Even if his father was a selfish, cheating bastard who might ruin his career.

"I will take that information to the DA and hope that all charges are dropped."

"You have to do more than hope, son. Do you know who we are? True enough, your father has shamed the family name, but we did a lot of good for this city before the bullshit. If you want a career in politics, you have to learn the gift of gab. You have to learn how to grease palms and make deals. Make this happen for me. There is no hoping. You either will or you won't."

"Yes, ma'am," Corey responded in a flat tone before standing up and leaving the house.

Once he was gone, Mallorie sipped her wine, a smile on her face. She didn't give a damn if Dave rotted in prison, as long as she didn't have to.

Dillon smiled wide as she approached Tonia, one of the women who had worked at the brothel before it was closed down. When the women had had to leave the mansion, Dillon had put them all up in hotel rooms. She could have found a house for them to live in, but she wasn't sure if she would be back in business, so Dillon hadn't made that move. She had been conversing with the girls regularly and encouraging them to chill for a moment. Dillon didn't like sitting still any more than they did, but she was trying to look out for them all.

"Hi, Tonia! I have great news," Dillon sang as she slid into the booth at one of her favorite coffee shops.

"Does it involve me working? Because while I appreci-ate the break that my vagina has gotten, I'm not ready to be unemployed just yet."

"It does. I have a date lined up for you this evening. Two hours of your time at one of Charlotte's finest hotels, and he booked the presidential suite. I showed him all you ladies' pictures, and he chose you. I have a new friend that's connected to some very rich people, namely rappers and businessmen. Maybe even a few athletes. Looks like I might be back in business."

Tonia clapped her hands together lightly. "That's what I'm talking about. It's time to get back to the money. I need all the details."

Dillon didn't want to leave paper trails, so she went over all the information with Tonia verbally. It was only one job, but Dillon was grateful for it. Heavy had come through for her sooner than expected. When the meeting was over with Tonia, she called Heavy to finalize everything and to thank him once again.

"You can thank me by giving me some of your time before I go on a business trip tomorrow. What do you say we go out to dinner tonight?"

"I'd say it's a date."

For the first time in a very long time, Dillon was excited about a man. She rushed home to get her hair done and to have a mani-pedi. She had been neglecting herself since she'd been in a slump, and she needed to step her shit all the way up for Heavy. After a few hours of being pampered, Dillon got dressed. Then she stared at her reflection in her bathroom mirror, feeling like a princess, as she waited on Heavy to come pick her up. One of the many clues that made her aware that she was falling for him was that she had let him know where she lived. She was usually very guarded and cautious, but not with Heavy. Hell, the man was a billionaire. What did she have to be skeptical about?

Her phone rang, and Dillon frowned at the blocked number. She almost didn't answer, but she decided that maybe she should. Meredith rarely ever called her personal phone, but in case it was her, Dillon didn't want to ignore the call.

"Hello?"

Silence.

Dillon's brows rose as she waited to see if anyone was going to say anything.

More silence.

"Hello?" Dillon wasn't trying to hide the fact that she was agitated. "Look, I—"

"I know you know something about Alleyne's death, bitch. You will not get away with this. If it's the last thing I do, I will bury you."

Dillon frowned at the threats coming through the phone. She was certain that the person on the other end of the phone was a man, but he was using some kind of device to distort his voice.

"Fuck you!" Dillon snapped before ending the call.

This entire situation was giving her a massive headache. She just wanted it to be over already. Dillon refused to let the caller ruin her night. No one had any proof that she had murdered Alleyne. What Dave and Mallorie were doing was just speculating. If they thought they could scare her into confessing, they were out of their minds. They could speculate until the cows came home. They didn't have shit on her.

When her doorbell rang, she knew it was Heavy, and Dillon bit the inside of her cheek as she walked to the front door in her black Yves Saint Laurent heels. The off-the-shoulder emerald-green dress she wore was absolutely stunning, and she knew she would turn heads for sure. Dillon opened the door, and Heavy's appreciation for her appearance was evident in his smile.

"Damn, you look good."

"I don't look delicious?" she joked.

"You look delicious as hell. A nigga might fuck around and say, 'Fuck dinner,' and eat you instead."

Dillon's body warmed up from the blatant flirting that Heavy was doing. He said he liked to have fun with women. So far, he'd been the perfect gentleman, and he'd scratched her back in a major way. Dillon didn't see the harm in maybe letting him sample the goods. Shit, she wanted to have a little fun too. She deserved a little fun.

Dillon stepped outside and closed the door behind her, and Heavy led her out to the Escalade. She was pleased to see that he had a driver for the evening, and the man was standing outside the car, with the rear passenger door open, waiting for Dillon.

"Thank you." She smiled as she got in the back of the SUV, feeling like a princess for real.

Dillon didn't date mediocre. Corey had a very prominent job, and he was running for mayor, so she was used to men of high caliber, but Heavy took things to another level. He always had back when they were together. She could never see herself dating anyone who wasn't on his level or above, and even with all the high-profile clients she had, Dillon didn't run across black billionaires every day. She loved money. She loved money a lot, but she had no desire to date outside her race for it. So, having found a black billionaire, Dillon felt that she'd struck gold. After Heavy, she couldn't date a man who didn't have at least a few mil.

"One of my homie's business associates is coming into town tomorrow," Heavy revealed as they drove to the restaurant he had chosen for their date. "I can give him your information. He's coming over from Italy. He plays ball over there, and he'll be in Charlotte for three weeks. While he's here, I know he's going to want some company a time or two. His girl just had a baby, and she's staying in Italy with the baby. His money stretches longer than overseas ball. He manages one of my artists, so he's gets ten percent of everything li'l homie makes."

Dillon nodded. She appreciated Heavy always letting her know that the men he referred to her could afford her girls. She wasn't lowering the price for anyone. If they couldn't afford her rates, they couldn't afford her girls. "I can't begin to tell you how I appreciate your help. I was really starting to get scared for a minute. I'm scared to use my old connections right now, so I thought it was over for me. The average Joe Blow can't afford my girls, and I'm not the type to solicit rich men off the street."

"I got you." Heavy winked at her. "I love to see a woman doing her thing. I love to see *anybody* doing their thing, really. There's enough money out here for us all to get a piece of the pie."

"I second that. I've met a lot of men, and in my profession, I often see why I feel men can't be trusted, but you are something else. I've never quite met a man like you."

"And you never will. I'm top of the line, baby."

Dillon couldn't stop herself from blushing. At her age, who in the hell still felt giddy around men? She felt like a schoolgirl with a crush.

At that very moment, Dillon's phone started lighting up nonstop with notifications, and though she really wanted to ignore it and give Heavy her undivided attention, something in her gut told her to look. Dillon unlocked her phone, and the first thing she saw was a newspaper article that Nilda had sent her.

Senator Dave Prescott has been forced to resign from his position as the murder investigation of his mistress continues. The young woman, who sources reveal may have been an escort, was found murdered in the senator's condo. After getting calls about a disturbance, police arrived at the scene to find Senator Prescott's wife alone with the body and reportedly covered in the victim's blood. However, reports say that at the time of the victim's death, Mrs. Prescott was at the Charlotte Hornets basketball game. This could very well support her claim that she had nothing to do with the murder. Stay tuned for more details as this bizarre story continues to unfold.

Dillon's heart jolted. This wasn't good. Dave and his wife were on their way to losing everything, and something was telling her that they were the type who refused to go down alone.

Chapter 13

After their dinner was over and they were once more in the car, Heavy looked over at Dillon. "I think it' s tacky as hell to bring up prices on a date, but with the bottle of champagne that I ordered, that meal was more than four hundred dollars, and you acted like you didn't enjoy it. By the time we got to the restaurant, your mood had shifted. Was it something that I said?"

Dillon's eyes grew large. "Oh, no, Heavy." She shook her head. "I'm so sorry if I'm coming off as rude. I shouldn't have checked my phone on the way there, but I did, and I just saw something that has me in my head. But the food was wonderful. The steak damn near melted in my mouth."

"That's good to know, and I thought I told you to stop stressing."

"That's easier said than done," she admitted.

"Would you care to keep me company tonight, or would you like for my driver to take you home?"

The idea of a distraction from her troubles sounded like heaven to Dillon. It was as if she was getting to know Heavy all over again, because he was a different person, but she knew that dick was the same, and it had always been heavy indeed. She couldn't believe how he'd managed to change her mind about dealing with him again.

"I would love to keep you company."

Heavy took some business calls, and Dillon stared out the window to see in which direction they were headed. Before long, they were pulling into a beautiful subdivision that, ironically, was only a few miles from the mansion where Dillon's girls used to live and work. Small world. She had seen plenty of gorgeous, fancy homes. She owned one, so she wasn't overly impressed when they arrived at Heavy's mini mansion. Still, it was a very nice house indeed. It was also a far cry from the home they had shared when they were a couple. They had both leveled up in more ways than one.

"This is a big house for one person," she pointed out as he led her into the grand foyer.

"It is, but condos and townhouses aren't my thing. I like big-boy shit. I thought we established that on day one." He winked at her, and Dillon smiled.

"You've come a long way from the old days."

His home was grand and spotless. The marble floors were so shiny that you could almost see your reflection in them. It was like they'd been waxed just before Dillon and Heavy entered the home. The décor was classy, expensive, and eccentric. The huge floor-to-ceiling windows in the living room gave the home a very modern vibe. There was a grand staircase, which led up to the second floor, and Dillon could only imagine what was up there. She saw an elevator in a corner, and she smiled.

"Some days you don't feel like taking the stairs, huh?"

"Hell nah. Especially when I have mad bags and shit. I have a room up there that's like a mini pantry, so I don't always have to come downstairs for snacks and drinks. There are times I can be in the crib for two days and never have to go downstairs, because I have everything I need upstairs. There's a microwave up there and all. Some call it lazy, but when I'm on the go, I'm on the go. I've seen times that I've gone more than fifteen days straight without seeing my home or sleeping in my bed, so when I'm home, all I do literally is chill."

"I get it. One doesn't become a billionaire by not being a hustler."

Dillon followed Heavy into the kitchen, where he removed a bottle of champagne from the fridge. He then grabbed two champagne flutes and led her to the elevator. She assumed they were going upstairs to his bedroom, and she didn't mind. Inside his bedroom, which was large enough to accommodate fifteen people, they sat on a chaise by the window, and he popped the cork on the champagne. He filled the flutes and gave her one.

Dillon's feet ended up in Heavy's lap and he rubbed them as they talked about any and everything. Heavy's company had managed to make her forget all about the newspaper article that she had read earlier. She could worry about that another day. For now, she just wanted to enjoy Heavy.

Which was why, almost an hour after they entered his bedroom, when his lips found hers, she didn't protest. Dillon took the lead by climbing into Heavy's lap as they continued to kiss. His hands roamed all over her ass, and he gave her cheeks a slight squeeze. The kiss they were sharing intensified, and Dillon moaned into Heavy's mouth as he pushed her dress up over her hips. Dillon began to grind on his lap, and she felt his manhood growing beneath his jeans. Dillon found herself yearning for him to be inside her.

Heavy scooted to the edge of the chaise and stood up while still holding on to Dillon. He carried her over to the bed and dropped her gently on his plush mattress. Dillon felt as if she'd landed on cotton. She eyed Heavy hungrily as he undressed. Heavy had always prided himself on his appearance. His body was a work of art, and even as busy as he was, she could tell that he still made sure to take care of himself. She missed his physique. She was jealous of how easy it was for Heavy to keep himself in shape, whereas she had to work out for hours at a time and watch what she ate.

Heavy rolled a condom onto his manhood, and he began to undress Dillon, admiring her body the same way that she had admired his. To Heavy, she looked just as beautiful as she had the first time they were together. His tongue circled around her belly button, and he placed a trail of kisses up her tummy. He stopped at her succulent breasts and pinched her nipples between his teeth.

Dillon enjoyed every moment, remembering how good Heavy had always made her feel, as she arched her back and moaned while Heavy rolled his teeth over her nipples. When he crushed his lips into hers, Dillon raked her nails down his toned back. Heavy pushed himself into her with a grunt, and Dillon's eyes closed, and her head rolled back. Heavy placed her feet on his shoulders, and he moved his hips in a circular motion. Dillon pulled at her own hair as Heavy brought her to the highest levels of ecstasy. He rubbed her clitoris with his thumb, and Dillon's breathing became labored.

"Heavy. Oh my goodness. You feel so damn good," she moaned, turning him on.

With a layer of sweat decorating his forehead, Heavy roughly turned Dillon over and slammed into her from behind. In the doggy-style position, Dillon made her ass cheeks clap for Heavy. He spread her cheeks wide and watched his dick glide in and out of her, the volcanic eruption rapidly approaching.

"This pussy good as fuck," he breathed as he fucked her hard and fast. "Damn, I missed you, baby!"

"Oh, fuck! Oh—" Dillon's cries were cut short by an orgasm that ripped through her like a tornado.

"Shit," Heavy grunted as he came right behind her.

They both collapsed on the bed.

He pulled her close and mumbled into her back, "Stay right here, because I'll be ready for round two in a minute."

Dave stared into space while clutching a glass of scotch in his hand. He had long lost count of how many drinks he'd consumed, and he was damn near seeing double. Alcohol was a friend in the Prescott household after all that he and Mallorie had been through. Dave just couldn't understand how he had got to where he was at the moment. In the back of his mind, he had always known that thinking with his dick would one day get him into trouble, but he hadn't foreseen it being this kind of trouble.

Everything he had worked so hard for was being flushed down the drain because Alleyne didn't know her place. Mallorie was a bitch, but she cared too much about her image to ever out him publicly. She might have made his life hell behind closed doors, but the world would have never known about Alleyne if Mallorie had to be the one to put it out there. Admit that her husband was sleeping with a gorgeous woman who was much younger than her? Never.

Arrogantly and foolishly, Dave had thought he had Alleyne under control, but he'd been sadly mistaken. Her ability to piss people off had Dave and his wife in hot water now. In a way, he wished he was a cold-blooded killer. If he could have gotten to Alleyne before her real killer did, he would have made sure that her body was never found. Dave lifted his glass and drank the remaining scotch in one swallow. It was hard to think when his head was spinning, but he had to find a way out of this mess.

As soon as he found out who the judge would be for Mallorie's trial, he could go ahead and attempt to grease palms. There were people who couldn't be bought, but they were the minority. Dave had to hope that he didn't get some morally upstanding person overseeing Mallorie's trial, or they just might be fucked.

"What the . . . ?" Dave squinted as he sat up in the desk chair and leaned forward.

In his study the floor-to-ceiling windows were behind his desk, but Dave wasn't working at his desk. He was facing the windows and admiring the view, and he had just glimpsed a figure off in the distance. Dave's estate was massive, and his vision was slightly blurred due to all the alcohol that he'd consumed, but he knew he wasn't tripping. He had seen something.

"Probably just the fucking paparazzi," he mumbled. The more he thought about it, the angrier he became.

Dave was tired of hiding out. He was tired of not saying anything and just letting people speculate. If one of the newspeople had gotten into his house, which was gated and supposedly secure, there was going to be a problem. Dave got pissed off at the thought of people going to such lengths to invade his privacy. He stood and swayed a bit. After he composed himself, he left the study and headed for the kitchen, so he could go out into the backyard.

If he caught anyone lurking around his home, he was going to beat their ass. He didn't care if the entire incident got recorded and leaked to the press. Enough was enough. Men cheated every day. That wasn't a reason for him and his family to be harassed and falsely accused of murder. The entire ordeal had gone too far, and he had reached his threshold for bullshit.

After crossing the kitchen, Dave walked out into the backyard and closed the door behind him. His eyes darted around as he looked for signs that he wasn't alone. He didn't hear anything, but the hairs on the back of his neck stood up, prompting him to want to turn around. Before he could do so, someone wrapped their arm around Dave's neck and cut off his air supply. Dave grabbed at the arm, but it was no use. The person wasn't letting up, and he was becoming lightheaded. Before he could lose consciousness from a lack of oxygen, the man behind him snapped Dave's neck, killing him instantly.

Chapter 14

Three days after her date with Heavy, Dillon walked into Meredith's grand estate house. Dillon and Heavy had had sex three times before they parted ways, and she still felt like she was walking funny. Dillon had been a little confused when Meredith summoned her. It was something that her friend never did, but she had done so much for Dillon that she had no choice but to go running when Meredith called. Meredith was sitting back on a plush couch, looking rich, as usual, as Dillon's Louboutin heels clicked on the hardwood floors and echoed throughout the sitting room.

"Hey. Is everything all right?" Dillon asked before she took a seat in one of the armchairs next to the sofa. It was a question that Dillon had been dying to ask ever since Meredith sent her private jet for Dillon.

"Dillon." Meredith's eyes sparkled. The life she lived could be a lonely one, and it was always good to see a friend. "You look amazing," she gushed over her friend.

"Thank you, and so do you, but that's to be expected. To what do I owe this pleasant surprise?"

Meredith picked a remote control up off the coffee table and used it to turn on her seventy-inch television. "I'm sure it's all over the news by now."

Dillon's heart pumped wildly as she waited to find out what Meredith was talking about. She had just begun to panic when Meredith found what she was looking for.

"It is a sad day in Charlotte, North Carolina," said the news announcer. "Senator Dave Prescott was found hanged from a tree in his backyard. While some are speculating that his death is a suicide, his wife, Mallorie Prescott, says that Senator Prescott would never harm himself. Drama has been swirling around this family lately, as Mrs. Prescott is on house arrest and is a suspect in the murder of Senator Prescott's mistress, an alleged sex worker."

Dillon gasped and looked at Meredith with a horror-stricken face. "How did you know this would happen?"

"Because it was my idea. I waited until you were safe on the jet, because I didn't need you being a suspect in this, but Dave had to go. Had he kept cooperating and talking in an effort to clear his wife's name, eventually, it would have put you in hot water. I had my men eliminate the problem. The same men that framed Mallorie by putting Alleyne in her condo."

"This was the last thing that I expected," Dillon admitted. "Do you really think it was for the best?"

Meredith was heavily connected and very rich. She had reach and power, and if she felt that Dillon was better off with Dave being dead, Dillon didn't see how she could fight it. Dillon also couldn't believe that she was getting sentimental. For a brief moment, she felt for Corey and Mallorie. They had already been through so much. But then she remembered the way that Mallorie had threatened her. In the world they lived in, one had to be cold and callous at times, but Dillon was still stunned at the person that Meredith could be.

"It was absolutely necessary," Meredith declared. "If Dave spoke about a brothel, the city wasn't going to stop until they found the person behind it. He would have kept the investigation going in order to protect his family. A high-profile madam case, he hoped, would distract the

world and divert attention away from his wife as a mur-
derer. And with her having an airtight alibi, the blame
would have shifted to him. And he would have used all
his connections and power to shift it to you. That's why
I made sure you were on the flight before the deed was
done, and I also wanted to make it look like a suicide."

"Wow." Dillon didn't know what to say. Meredith had
gone all out in trying to protect her. Dillon was flattered
and very appreciative. She could only hope that this
would be the end of the police effort to find her and bring
her brothel down.

But it also made her realize just how powerful Meredith
was. If Dillon wanted to step away and do her own thing,
would Meredith be okay with it? Dillon was the face of
the business because Meredith had to lay low. If Dillon
left Meredith to do her own thing, then what? Surely,
Meredith wasn't ready to retire and give up the money
that she earned from owning a brothel. It seemed as
if every time one problem was solved, Dillon found
something else to stress about, and it was all becoming
overwhelming. Maybe she should find something else to
do and leave the escort business alone for good.

Mallorie had been drinking for hours, and she was now
seeing double. Her life had gone from sugar to shit in a
matter of weeks. She couldn't stand Dave's cheating ass
before he died, but that didn't mean she wanted him to
die. Mallorie wanted to be adamant about the fact that
Dave wouldn't hurt himself. But if he had really taken
the coward's way out and offed himself, she would be
tempted to beat his ass dead and all. She looked over at a
defeated-looking Corey.

"Dave was too arrogant to kill himself. That's just not
something he would do," she announced. She knew in

her heart of hearts he wouldn't take his own life, but Mallorie didn't want to think that his death could be a murder either. That meant that someone had been in her backyard. They had hanged Dave from that tree right underneath her nose. What was so bad about it was that he wasn't in the house when she woke up that morning, and it took her nine hours to go out back and discover his swinging body. If someone had really framed her for murder and then killed her husband, that meant someone really hated them, and that made the hair on the back of Mallorie's neck stand up.

"Maybe he would if he felt your alibi would aid in your charges being dropped. What if *he* was the one who killed Alleyne, and he felt that death was better than prison?"

"That bastard is selfish even in death," Mallorie hissed. "Whether I'm found innocent or not, he left me here alone to pick up all the pieces by myself." Tears filled her eyes to the brim.

Corey felt lost. He was sleep deprived and had huge bags underneath his eyes. He had been shocked more over the past few weeks than he had in his entire life.

Mallorie sipped more wine and had an epiphany. "Where was that Dillon?" she spat. "No one can make me believe that whore isn't upset because her little business was outed. What if she had someone kill him?"

Corey shook his head. "I saw her post on her Instagram story. She's not even in the country."

Mallorie rolled her eyes and looked at Corey like he was the dumbest person that she knew. "I doubt that she could have gotten him up in that tree. Which means she had someone do it. Use your common sense."

"And with no proof, that would be like searching for a needle in a haystack. There are obviously plenty of things about my own father that I didn't know. We don't know a person's every thought. Maybe he had a moment of weakness, and he did do something stupid. I just say we focus on getting the charges against you dropped and leave everything else alone."

Corey had just lost his father, and there was no more fight left in him. Especially when he wasn't even sure what he was fighting for. It appeared to all that Dave had taken the coward's way out, thus continuing to shame the family. Their names were as good as tarnished, and he doubted he would win the mayoral election.

Mallorie finished her glass of wine. This way, maybe she was free. Free from the shame and the scandal of having a husband who slept with prostitutes. Once she was found innocent of murdering Alleyne, maybe her life would go back to the way it was. It might take a while, but she was certain she'd get there faster without Dave and his bullshit in her face. Mallorie refused to go down without a fight. She had more balls than Dave, and she planned to use all her resources. She wasn't going to reveal her plans to Corey, but calling her private investigator, Dan, was at the top of her to do list. For the moment, she'd play it cool.

"I guess we have a funeral to plan."

Chapter 15

Dillon swept her hand in a circular motion as she stood in the center of the living room. "Welcome to your new abode." She smiled widely at the girls. "It's not quite as extravagant as the last house, but it's still gorgeous, and it's what I could find on short notice. I still have to get my clientele back to where it was, but for now, we're back in business."

"About time," Tonia exclaimed. "Trying to get these men to pay top dollar on my own is too stressful. These cheap whores have messed the game up. I actually had a man that offered me three hundred dollars to spend the night with him, and he actually said he felt that was too much, but he wanted me really bad." There was a frown on her face, which told of just how offended she was by that offer.

Even Dillon had to scoff at that. "Yeah, these men are batshit crazy. You shouldn't even have been having a conversation with anyone who thinks three hundred dollars is even worth you speaking to him. He must be broke, on top of not knowing what grade A pussy is." She gazed around the room. "In any event, I met a man who is connected to the music industry as well as the sports industry. He knows a few moguls and quite a few rich men. Some of you have had dates already with someone that he referred to me. Business might be a little slow at first, but we will get back to where we were," Dillon told the women confidently.

Dillon's expression turned serious. "But there will definitely be some changes. That 'falling in love and getting too close to johns' shit is a no-no, and it will get you put up out of my shit with a quickness. Should a wife, girlfriend, or baby mama find out what her man is up to and confront you, under no circumstances are you to ever go back and forth with them. I damn near lost everything I had over an arrogant side chick and a pain-in-the-ass wife. The men we service have money, which means their significant others may have money, as well, and a little pull. I'm not losing what I've worked for behind a scorned woman."

Just thinking about it had Dillon pissed. Mallorie was rich even without Dave's money, and if he had refused to be faithful, all she had had to do was take him for half of everything he had and been even richer. The threatening to bring her down and being a headache had gotten them all more trouble than it was worth. All for a man who couldn't keep his dick inside his pants.

Dillon got them settled at the new house, and then she had plans to go meet Heavy at his office. He had just gotten back that morning from a business trip, and Dillon wanted to fuck him in his office. Heavy had grown on her quite a bit. As she was contemplating Heavy, Dillon's work phone rang, and she was shocked to see that Dria was calling. Dillon was suspicious, so she stared at the phone for a moment, trying to decide if she was going to answer. Finally, she decided to see what Dria wanted.

"Hello?" she answered cautiously.

"Dillon, I need to speak to you. It's very important. I just wan—"

"No, ma'am," Dillon said, cutting her off abruptly. She wasn't sure if she could trust Dria. There would be no talking over the phone. "When people just up and disappear, I don't want explanations over the phone. Where are you?"

"At the Ritz-Carlton."

"I'm on my way. Meet me downstairs at the bar."

Dillon knew that Dria wasn't broke, but if she was spending more than one night at an expensive hotel like the Ritz-Carlton, her money was going to dwindle fast, unless she had access to making money. Dillon couldn't wait to get answers.

Dillon wasn't far from the Ritz, and she got there in no time. When she walked into the bar of the luxurious hotel, she didn't see Dria. She had better not be on any funny shit.

"Let me get a lemon drop," she said after sliding onto a barstool and being greeted by the bartender. Lemon drops were cute little feminine drinks, but they got the job done. And Dillon needed about three of them.

Before the bartender could place her drink in front of her, Dria entered the bar area. She sat down beside Dillon and offered her a nervous smile.

"Hi, Dillon. I kn—"

"Let's skip the pleasantries and the bullshit, Dria," Dillon muttered, cutting her off. "Tell me what made you hightail it out of the house like your ass was on fire."

"I went to get coffee, and some guy called me by my name. As I was walking to my car, he approached me and said he knew all about me and my family in Albania. He threatened me and basically told me that if I got arrested, my family would know how I was really making my money in the States. The way he was coming at me, I felt like he was a police officer or something. I got spooked."

Dillon frowned. "No, he wasn't a police officer. Not just threatening you. If he was a police officer, and he knew everything about you, he would have been asking you to bring him to me. That was more than likely someone that Mallorie or Dave Prescott sent. They knew they could hurt me by sabotaging my girls. Huh," Dillon scoffed.

"I saw on the news that Dave killed himself."

Dillon sucked her teeth. "That's what they say. Whether he did or didn't, him and his wife are still a thorn in my side. Who knew Alleyne's pussy would cause all this drama."

The bartender set her drink in front of her at the perfect time. *Fuck sipping*, Dillon thought. She down the drink in four gulps and ordered another.

"Wow. So, it was either Dave or his wife that messed up my money?"

Dillon looked around the room. "Your living accommodations aren't too shabby. You don't look like a person that's pinching pennies."

Dria shook her head. "I've been dancing at a local club. I felt no one could fuck with me about that, because stripping isn't illegal, but it's for the birds. On a slow night I barely make enough to cover a room here for one night. I'm trying not to spend the money that I have saved, but I feel like I'm living like a pauper."

Dillon smiled as the effects of the lemon drop took over. "Today is your lucky day. I have some connections, and slowly but surely, the girls are getting back to work. We're under the radar and discreet, as always. Dave is dead, and Mallorie is trying to keep herself out of prison. I don't think anyone else will be bothering us."

"That's great to know." Dria smiled, feeling as if a heavy weight had been lifted off her shoulders.

After Dillon left the bar at the Ritz-Carlton, she couldn't stop smiling. She had Dria back on the team. Things finally seemed to be picking up for Dillon. As she made her way through the hotel lobby to the valet, she began getting those back-to-back annoying alerts and notifications, and she smacked her lips. Anytime that happened, it was always bad news. Dillon opened the attachments, and her heart sank when she saw an article with a picture of herself and Heavy leaving their dinner date a few nights ago. Then she read the caption beneath the picture.

Is heavy, of heavy paper entertainment, dating a rumored madam? Is she his girlfriend, or is he paying for her services?

Dillon was livid. She wished the people that wrote this tabloid stuff would get a damn life. And the fact that they even insinuated that she was an escort was enough to make her head spin. Dillon's fingers were itching to respond, but she decided not to. She powered her phone off and had the valet bring her car around. Instead of going to see Heavy, as she had planned, she took a detour to a nearby bar in downtown Charlotte. She needed a few drinks to take her out of the sudden foul place that she'd been taken to. Every time she thought she was past the bullshit, something else was tossed her way.

Dillon wanted to scream. She couldn't be on a high for ten minutes before she got knocked right back down. Every time she took one step forward, it felt as if she took ten more backward, and it was beginning to get very draining. She saw that Heavy had texted her a few times, and she replied with a simple I'm on my way.

After downing a few drinks, Dillon drove toward Heavy's office, wondering if he would feel some kind of way about the headline she'd just seen. He was a re-formed street nigga, and she knew niggas like him didn't want all the attention, but she could never be too sure. He had every right not to have certain things attached to his name. He was a young, rich black billionaire. There was no time for dumb shit in his world.

After she parked, Dillon went inside and told Heavy's receptionist that he was expecting her, and the receptionist told her to go on back. Dillon knocked on the door and waited for Heavy to tell her to come in.

As soon as she entered the large office, which smelled like the masculine candles that Bath and Body Works sold, he peeped her glassy eyes. "You got sidetracked, I see."

Dillon sat down and stared over at him. "I needed a few drinks after the headline that I saw, so go ahead and give it to me. Do you hate me?"

Heavy chuckled. "Hate you for what? I already knew how you made your money, and the fact that you didn't lie about it tells me that I can really fuck with you. You didn't come in the door, keeping major secrets, and let me be blindsided by some bullshit. You've always kept it real with me. I'm grown as hell, and I didn't get as far as I did by caring what people think. Get your paper, Ma. I don't care what those people think, and neither should you. And even if you were an escort, it's not like I've never paid for pussy before." He shrugged casually. "Buying females bags, shoes, clothes, cars, jewelry, it's all the same thing."

"I love the way you think," Dillon noted and smiled. "But, damn, you bought a woman a car before? Let me step my pussy game up," she joked, causing Heavy to chuckle.

"Baby, that Bentley you drive is shitting on that li'l Benz I bought her. But stick with me, kid," he said and winked. "A car isn't shit to me. Go ahead and be thinking about the model and color you want."

His words turned Dillon on so much that she stood up and sauntered over to him. She ran her hand over his crotch, and though his manhood was still soft, it was thick. His dick was definitely heavy, and he couldn't have had a more fitting name. Deciding to give him a little treat, she dropped down to her knees and unzipped his jeans. Heavy looked down at Dillon and licked his lips. He was a boss. He'd received head just about everywhere. The club, the movie theater, his office, his car, on a private jet, a yacht. There was never a shortage of women that were willing to please him in any and every way. He was also not a stranger to women of Dillon's caliber. But she was something serious, and the fact that she was down on her knees, servicing him with a devilish grin on her face, stroked his ego just a bit.

Heavy tossed his head back just as Dillon took him into her mouth and went to work on him. Her mouth was warm and inviting, and he had to let out a grunt as she deep throated him. Heavy wanted to see her pretty lips at work, so he looked down and watched her as she pleasured him with her mouth. The shit was getting sloppy just like he liked, and he was pleased to see that Dillon wasn't afraid to be a freak when it came to pleasing a man. All that bougie and classy shit had disappeared, and she had turned into his personal porn star.

If the head was top-notch, Heavy could cum from it, but he preferred to cum from pussy. He opened his desk drawer and pulled a condom out before standing Dillon up and bending her over his desk. She didn't even blink at the fact that he had condoms in his desk at work. They were probably in his car too. She didn't give a damn. If there weren't women willing to give Heavy pussy at any given time and anywhere, then he had the wrong women around him.

Heavy rammed his dick into Dillon from behind, and she grabbed the edge of the desk and gasped. "Heavy," she moaned in a throaty tone as he pounded into her.

Heavy grunted as he assaulted her vagina. Having sex in an office with a view of the city was amazing for both of them. Heavy felt like he was that nigga every day of his life, and being with him in that way had Dillon feeling giddy as well. She also appreciated the fact that so far, he hadn't asked for a percentage of any of the money that she made off the clients he'd referred to her. So, it wasn't business. He was doing it simply because he liked seeing her get her own money.

Heavy deposited his load into the condom, and he pulled his dick out of Dillon's gushy, wet pussy. She walked into his adjoining bathroom to clean herself up. When she walked out of the office, Heavy was staring at her with a smile on his face.

"What?" she asked bashfully.

"Come to Aruba with me next week. I'll be gone for four days."

That was short notice, but Dillon was getting used to it. Heavy was a man who was always on the move, and she was either with it or she wasn't. She knew that a lot of men in Heavy's position switched women the way they switched their boxers, so she wasn't going to get her hopes up about anything long term. Instead, she would take what she could get for however long it lasted and would pray that she'd stick around long enough to get that car.

Chapter 16

Dillon was nervous, more than she cared to admit, as she wasn't sure why Meredith had summoned her yet again. Since she'd been lying low, Dillon had barely seen her, yet, here she was visiting Meredith yet again. She was sure that Meredith had the resources to keep herself occupied, but Dillon couldn't imagine having to hide out and not being able to move around the States freely. Foreign countries were nice to visit, but Dillon wasn't sure she'd like being confined to one and not being able to visit family or show up in the city in which she was born and raised. Meredith didn't seem to have too much of a problem with it, and if she did, she never voiced it to Dillon.

"If you miss me, you can just say that." Dillon was smiling on the outside while praying on the inside that Meredith didn't have news of another dead body to report.

In the heat of the moment, and in self-defense, Dillon had killed Alleyne, but that didn't mean she wanted to have bodies racking up left and right. At the end of the day, she was a madam, not a mobster. Dillon wanted to make money and sit pretty. Killing people and potentially going to prison for life didn't sit well with her.

Meredith smiled. "You know there are certain things that just can't be discussed over the phone. Not even a burner phone. I won't take much of your time. Please sit."

Dillon took a seat on Meredith's plush couch.

"I'm ready to throw in the towel. P H I has been very lucrative, and even before that, I had money, since I come
from old money. I'm wealthy, and to continue in the
business might be more trouble for me than it's worth. I
have enough money to be set for the rest of my life. If you
choose to walk away from the brothel business once all
this nonsense blows over, I understand. However, if you
want to continue to use the girls and make money off my
connections, you can. I just ask for a small monthly fee,
but P H I would no longer be *my* brothel. You won't work
for me. You'll be the boss."

Dillon couldn't believe her ears. She didn't want to
appear too excited, because she'd never expressed to
Meredith that she wanted to do her own thing. "I'm
shocked."

Meredith shrugged one shoulder. "I've had a good run.
There's a difference between taking risks and just being
greedy. I want to leave the game on my own terms."

Dillon was elated. It was the last thing that she had
expected to hear, but it was wonderful news. If the whole
thing with Alleyne, Dave, and Mallorie would die down,
Dillon might be able to get back to business full throttle.
With her being able to keep a larger percentage of the
money, she, too, could choose a time frame in the near
future to leave the game, just as Meredith was doing.

"I would love to keep the business going for a short
time. I do agree with you on the being greedy part and
leaving the game on my own terms. Hearing my name
on the news had me shitting bricks. I am not trying to
see prison, but I'm just not ready to walk away from the
money this soon."

Meredith gave Dillon a warm smile. "I completely
understand. Not many can walk away from this kind of
money when we don't have to work hard for it. Being a
madam is the epitome of working smart, not hard."

The wheels in Dillon's head were turning. Meredith had a powerful family and a team behind her. If anything happened, all she had to do was call Meredith, and problems would be solved before she could blink. Heavy had connections, but there were certain things she didn't want to involve him in. He had street ties, but he made a lot of legit money. Money that she didn't want him to risk for her.

Meredith could see that Dillon was stressed out. "Relax, Dillon. You've been running things for a while now. I'm behind the scenes, but you're on the front line. You can do this."

"But you've always had my back. Look at how fast your people came when I needed help with the Alleyne situation. They showed up for me quick as hell. I don't have a team of mobsters ready to move dead bodies for me."

"Money talks, dear. It always has, and it always will. We deal with elite men. Wealthy men that have a lot to lose. There have never been any issues from them. All the drama that has occurred happened because of women. I'm sure you won't need any mobsters too often, but in the event that you do, you can always call me, and if I can help, I will."

"Thank you so much, Meredith. For everything."

Mallorie sat anxiously in front of Corey, waiting for him to get to the point of why he had come over. Since Dave was dead, Mallorie and Corey usually talked only about her case. Mallorie had no way of knowing why he had killed himself, but if it was going to work in her favor to suggest that he might have killed himself out of guilt, that was what she would go with. Her trial was in three weeks, and Mallorie hated that she'd have to sit in a packed courtroom and be put on the chopping block while he'd taken the cowardly way out.

Alcohol had become her best friend, and Mallorie sipped from a whiskey glass while she waited on Corey to fill her in.

"So, there are a few things that I found that just may work in your favor," Corey revealed.

"Oh really?" She raised her eyebrows. "Because it was my private investigator who found out about the hotel security guard who suddenly quit his job, and when his wife was questioned, she admitted that he had left town."

Corey sighed. Dealing with Mallorie hadn't been the easiest. He knew the pressure that she was under, and he was trying to be patient, but she was beginning to work his nerves.

"And we're checking on that, I promise you. But I also just found out that a very thorough investigation was done of the building. From the elevators and stairwells to the hallways. Alleyne's blood was found in a stairwell. It was just a miniscule drop, but that alone is evidence to prove that she didn't die in the condo. She died somewhere else, and the body was moved. That will help us argue the point that someone framed you. Or maybe they wanted to frame Dave."

For the first time since the entire ordeal had started, Mallorie felt hopeful. "Oh my God. Corey, this is great news. Please tell me you can use all this information to get me off. After all, you don't have to prove my innocence so much as having to make the jury have doubts that it was me that murdered Alleyne." Mallorie literally had her fingers crossed.

"I am hoping that all this evidence is enough to vindicate you."

Mallorie wanted him to do more than hope. He needed to guarantee her freedom.

Chapter 17

The smell of food woke Dillon up from a deep sleep. When she opened her eyes and saw Heavy walking into the room, carrying a tray with breakfast on it, she smiled at him and sat up. It was her birthday, and they were starting it in the right way. Heavy didn't have a lot of money. Well, he didn't when they first met. His empire was growing, and it was causing him to be away from home more. He felt that she shouldn't complain, because he was out making money, but breakfast in bed prepared by her man, that was one of the things that she loved. Who cared if he came home with a nice gift for her if she hadn't seen him in days and had no clue what he was doing in the streets in addition to making money? But Heavy couldn't seem to grasp that concept.

"This smells good! You mean Heavy actually cooked? I can't believe it."

"Anything for you. You know that. I was going to make reservations so we could go to brunch, but I felt like cooking for you would be more thoughtful. See, I do listen when you talk." He placed the tray in her lap and kissed her on the lips.

"I see you've been listening." Dillon couldn't stop smiling as she eyed the pancakes, bacon, eggs, and fruit.

"I got you a li'l mimosa action going on. We turning up all day."

Dillon said grace, picked the fork up, and dug into her food. "This is good, babe. You said we're turning up all day, so does that mean you're going to actually spend the day with me?"

"I do have a meeting in an hour, but that won't take long. While I'm gone, you can get dressed, and I'll come back and scoop you, so we can hit the mall. Gotta take the birthday girl on a shopping spree." Heavy's smile was contagious.

"Best birthday ever," Dillon laughed. "Go fix your plate, so we can eat together." She picked up a strip of bacon and munched on it while waiting on Heavy to come back with his plate of food.

They ate the delicious meal, and Dillon sipped her champagne and orange juice while Heavy washed the dishes and cleaned the kitchen. She could get used to that kind of treatment. She had gone shopping and purchased a few different outfits, so mentally, she went over which one she wanted to wear today. Once the kitchen was clean, Heavy came back in the room and gave her a kiss.

"I'll be back in an hour, tops." He passed her a fresh glass of mimosa.

"Okay. I'm about to take a shower."

Dillon drank her second mimosa, and by the time her feet touched the floor, she had a slight buzz going on. It was her birthday, and she was in a great mood. Dillon sang and danced around the room while she made the bed and got out her clothes for the day. It took her more than an hour to get ready. It was more like an hour and a half. She got lost in putting together the perfect look and doing her hair and makeup, but when she realized that Heavy had been gone for almost two hours, she got a sinking feeling in the pit of her stomach.

"I am not going to trip," Dillon said out loud. "Maybe he got caught up, and he's on his way home now."

The more she tried to tell herself that she wouldn't get worked up, the more her mood soured. Dillon was pissed, and there was no use in her trying to pretend that she wasn't. By the time Heavy had been gone for three hours, she picked up the phone to call him. She *didn't want him to be hurt or in trouble, but something very serious had better have occurred for him to do her like this on her day. As she picked her phone up, a text message from Heavy came through.*

Dillon's heart raced as she read a long text from Heavy apologizing and telling her that he had to run out of town unexpectedly, and he promised he would make it up to her. After the message, a Cash App notification came through for fifteen hundred dollars. Dillon's upper lip curled as she eyed the notification. She was mad enough to spit nails, but she refused to let Heavy ruin her day. She would cry over his no-good ass another day. Dillon grabbed her things and left the house to take herself shopping.

When Heavy wasn't home by the next morning, she packed her things and left. That was the beginning of the end.

Dillon suddenly woke up from this dream, and the first thing she saw was the beautiful view from their villa in Aruba. She had no clue why she had dreamed of the day that she left Heavy. Was that some kind of a bad omen?

Heavy emerged from the bathroom, wearing swim trunks, and there was a towel draped over his shoulder.

Dillon laughed. "You aren't playing any games, are you?"

"Hell no. I'm eating breakfast and then going straight in the water. I'm on vacation, baby." There was a broad grin on Heavy's face, and Dillon could only laugh at him.

"I'm starving myself, and I don't want to be the one to hold up the festivities, so let me get up and get ready."

She decided not to dwell on the dream that she had had. The past was just that. The past. They were starting over fresh, and Dillon doubted they'd have the same kinds of problems this time around. She wouldn't complain about him being gone a lot. Now, if he decided that he didn't want to keep his dick in his pants, that might be a problem. Just about every client she had from the brothel was a married man. It made Dillon shake her head to think about how many men out there cheated on their wives. But sadly, a lot of the wives knew about their husband's cheating ways, but for various reasons they, like Mallorie, chose to stay.

Dillon got dressed and joined Heavy out on the balcony for breakfast.

"I know this is vacation, and we aren't supposed to be talking business, but I know someone throwing his man a bachelor party in two weeks," Heavy told her. "After the party, he wants to get one of your girls for the groom-to-be."

Dillon frowned. "I'm not turning down a bag, but the groom to be wants to have sex with an escort? Better yet, his friend is going to pay for it? That's some sick shit. And you wonder why I don't trust men."

Heavy held his hands up. "How did I get in it?" he laughed. "Don't shoot the messenger, babe. Listen, we all know there are some men out here that aren't shit. Some get it together, and some never do. Maybe this will be his one last little hurrah before he says, 'I do.' Who knows? Just get the money and keep it moving. I've learned my lesson. I'm older and wiser now, and I'm not with all that cheating shit."

"Uh-huh," Dillon replied before putting a scoop of breakfast potatoes in her mouth.

She was going to do what he said and get that money. It wasn't her place to care or worry about who the client was and what he did in his personal life. Dillon was going to enjoy her Aruba trip without a care in the world. She felt she deserved that much.

Once Dillon was back in the States, it was back to business as usual. Dillon had been able to contact her old clients, and more than a few of them were more than ready to utilize her services again. There were two or

three who were so spooked by what had happened with
Dave that they wanted no parts of it. Dillon assumed that
they had been scared straight and were no longer cheating.
Or were no longer cheating on their wives with escorts.

Dillon took a break to grab some lunch and then some
coffee before getting back to work. She had taken time
off during the scandal, and she'd just come back from a
beautiful vacation. Dillon was working her ass off now,
and she didn't have one complaint about it. There was a
certain tax bracket that she was trying to reach, so every
time money was deposited into her account, it made
Dillon's pussy wet.

"Dillon? Hey!" exclaimed a young woman standing on
the sidewalk outside of Starbucks.

Dillon gasped softly when she recognized Jada. She
hadn't seen her in what felt like ages, and the sight of
her hurt Dillon's heart. She thought of Jada and her kids
often. Neither Jada nor her mother had reached out to
her, so Dillon had hoped that meant Jada had herself
together. She could see clearly that wasn't the case. Jada
was rail thin and had to have lost at least twenty pounds.
Her braids were piled on top of her head in a messy bun,
and the new growth told Dillon that the braids should
have been taken out at least a month ago.

The white shirt that she wore was dingy, and her face
was riddled with acne. Dillon would have given Jada as
much money as she needed to go somewhere and buy
some clothes, take a good shower, get her hair done, and
eat a good, hot meal, but she knew that if she put any
money in Jada's hands, it would go to drugs.

"Hi, Jada." It was hard for Dillon to mask her heart-
break. Jada looked terrible.

"Girl, this has to be fate. I lost my phone a minute ago,
and I wanted to call you so bad. I know I need my hair
done, and I came out of the house looking raggedy today,

but you know I clean up nice. Please let me work. I really need the money."

Dillon couldn't hide her shock if she tried. She had heard of people being delusional before, but Jada had to be more than delusional. She had to be high to think that a man would pay thousands of dollars an hour to sleep with her when she was standing there looking like charging forty dollars for a night with her would be too much. Dillon didn't want to hurt Jada's feelings, but maybe tough love was what she needed.

"Jada, you look more than raggedy, baby. You look like you need some real serious help. Why don't you let me send you to rehab?"

Jada threw her hands up in exasperation. "I get tired of being judged because I'm not walking around in thousand-dollar shoes and carrying five-thousand-dollar purses. I don't need all that shit. I don't want all that shit. That doesn't mean I'm not worthy of making money."

"Jada, let's cut the shit. I love you. I do. Rehab is far from cheap, and I'll pay that shit right now in full if you agreed to go. I want the best for you, and we both know this isn't about the price of your clothes. You don't look clean, and if that hurts your feelings, I'm sorry. You look malnourished. None of my clients would pay to sleep with you."

"Fuck you, Dillon." Jada's voice cracked. She knew she was down bad, but her clouded judgment made her think sometimes that if she acted normal, other people would assume that her issue wasn't as bad as it was. She had let herself go terribly, and she knew it. The day Jada lost her kids was the day she hit rock bottom, but she still wasn't ready to get help.

She knew she was breaking her mother's heart. She knew she was hurting her children. But Jada was addicted to drugs. The monkey that was on her back weighed a ton.

"You can turn your back on me, and you can count me out," Jada muttered. "But I promise, I'm going to come out on top one day."

"Jada, please be for real. If I didn't want to see you on top, I wouldn't be standing here offering to help you. You're just upset because I'm not helping you in the way that you want me to. If you're willing to, take my number. When you're ready to get that help, you can call me, and I'll answer."

"Nah, I'm good." Jada walked away, and all Dillon could do was stare after her and shake her head.

For Jada's sake and the sake of her kids, Dillon hoped that she got it together soon.

Chapter 18

The next day, when Heavy was back in town from a business meeting, he popped up on Dillon at work and brought her flowers. She had to admit that not having to keep her profession top secret when it came to the man she was dealing with felt nice. There were times when she was dating Corey that she had actually got tired of being secretive and evasive. This time around, being with Heavy was definitely a breath of fresh air.

"Thak you so much! These are beautiful," Dillon gushed before she kissed him and pulled back.

"You're welcome." He placed his lips back on hers and parted her lips with his tongue. The sensual kiss that he was sharing with Dillon turned Heavy on, and his dick stiffened.

He immediately concluded that he wasn't the only one who was turned on when he felt her nipples harden through the thin fabric of her shirt. Heavy wanted her, and he didn't want to wait until later, when she got off work. The great thing about being her own boss was that she could do whatever, whenever. He picked her up and placed her on the huge desk in her office after closing the door behind him. Heavy removed the flowers from her hand and placed them beside her on the desk. With a sneaky grin, he placed his face in the crook of her neck and began to kiss on her.

Dillon moaned, and she bit her bottom lip between her teeth while Heavy devoured the flesh on her neck. He was hitting her spot, and she became insanely wet and turned on as her chest heaved up and down. The way her clit began to throb for him, she knew it was about to get real nasty in that office. Both of them knew there was a great chance that someone could knock on the office door, but they didn't care. Heavy removed his mouth from her neck and pulled her to the end of the desk, where he then hiked her skirt up and eased her panties off. Heavy licked his lips before he dipped his head low, spread her pretty pussy open, and admired it before he began to probe her slit with his tongue.

Dillon's body jerked at the sensation of his tongue going up, then down, then circling her clit. He sucked on her clit so gently and tenderly that a low whimper fell from her throat. Dillon lifted her hips a bit to give more of herself to him and looked up at the ceiling as Heavy performed tricks with his tongue that had her letting out all kinds of low moans, hisses, and whimpers. She didn't want anyone to hear her, but controlling her cries of ecstasy was becoming very hard. When Heavy went back to sucking on her clit and her vagina began pulsating, Dillon grabbed the back of his head with one hand and locked her thighs around his head as she bucked against his face.

That only inspired Heavy to go harder, and he locked his hands around her thighs as he feasted on her pussy and slurped at her like she was ice cream melting off a cone on a hot sunny day. Heavy devoured her with the skills of a professional pussy eater. Dillon almost drew blood from biting her lip so hard in an effort to contain her cries. She came, and their low, deep moans filled the office. They couldn't help it. The feel of his mouth on her body was nothing short of amazing. Dillon was ready to swear on a stack of Bibles that she had never felt anything so good. Meanwhile, Heavy would declare that he had never tasted pussy that was so fresh and sweet. Her body jerked a few times as Dillon rode the waves of her orgasmic high. Heavy came up for air and multitasked with a lust-filled grin by both unbuttoning his jeans and gently stroking her pearl. When Heavy's dick was free, they engaged in a deep and passionate tongue kiss that had her tasting her juices off his tongue.

Dillon cupped the sides of his face as their tongues swirled, and he pushed his thick dick inside her. "Fuck. You feel so fucking good," Heavy groaned in her ear.

He had never been big on lovemaking, not even when they'd been together the first time. But Heavy was older, more mature, and much more sexually experienced now. He had abandoned the mindset that sex was for his pleasure only. And in that moment with Dillon, he realized that he could show her with his body the things that he might not be able to convey with words.

Heavy's strokes were slow and deep. The way he was staring into her eyes while they made love had Dillon's pussy contracting on his dick. She became lost in his eyes, and she wasn't able to look away until he hit a spot that made her eyes roll back in her head and her back arched so much she swore she heard her spine crack. Heavy moaned as he went back to gently biting and licking on her neck. Heavy pushed her shirt up and ran his tongue over her nipples. She wasn't wearing a bra. It wasn't needed, because her breasts were perky and perfect.

He pulled his dick out of her and sensually kissed her from the bottom of her breasts down to her stomach. Heavy's kisses were wet and juicy, passionate and deliberate. He wanted to bring her to the ultimate heights of pleasure. When he dipped his head back between her thighs and his mouth locked around her clit, Dillon thought she was going to lose her mind. The things he was doing to her body were going to have her hopping out of bushes and acting like a certified ghetto ass if he moved wrong. Heavy plunged back into making her have an orgasm almost immediately. Dillon's body was as limp as a rag doll. Her energy was depleted, and she wanted to go to sleep right there on the desk. Not long after he entered her again, he released his seed inside her.

"That was good as fuck," he exclaimed and chuckled. "Your pussy ages like fine fucking wine."

Dillon finally found her voice. "Sir, I don't know what it is that you're trying to do to me, but when you have a stalker on your hands, it will be your fault."

Heavy laughed and pulled her up off the desk. "I will never be mad at being stalked by a pretty lady."

Dillon gave him a knowing look. "Um, if that lady isn't me, you better have a problem with it."

Heavy laughed again and pulled her into his arms. "I just wanted to come brighten your day. I hope I did that."

"You did more than that." Dillon smiled. "Thank you."

Dillon went into the bathroom that was connected to her office and cleaned up before putting her panties back on, fixing her shirt and skirt, and walking Heavy to the door. She was in love, and she couldn't believe it!

The next day, Dillon paced back and forth, nervously wringing her hands. She was in the master bathroom of her home, and she was shitting bricks. Her stomach was in knots. *How could I have been so stupid?* Dillon had been chastising herself for half the morning. When she woke up at five in the morning to pee, she'd been hit with a wave of nausea that felt like a punch to the gut. Dillon rarely threw up. Even when she drank too much, it was rare that she vomited. That morning, however, she'd been on her knees twice, emptying her stomach into the toilet. With all the nasty sex that she'd been having with

Heavy, it hadn't taken Dillon long at all to put two and two together.

After brushing her teeth, she had found some crackers in the pantry and had managed to calm her stomach down long enough to get dressed and run to the store to get a pregnancy test. Heavy had already called her once, but she hadn't answered. Her nerves were shot. Financially, Heavy and Dillon combined could afford all the kids that they wanted. Money wasn't an issue.

And since they'd been back dating, he had shown her that he was more reliable and more responsible. But they were still enjoying life. They were jet-setters. If Heavy decided at the drop of a dime that he wanted to leave the country or fly to LA to shop, they did just that. Having a child would change a lot in their lives, and she wasn't sure how she felt about that.

Dillon made it to the store and back in record time, and as soon as she walked back in the door, she took the pregnancy test. Her phone rang as she walked over to the sink to peer at the test results. She once again ignored Heavy's call while she contemplated the two pink lines on the test. Dillon stared at the test for almost two minutes, as if her staring at it would make one of the lines disappear. With a sigh, she finally sent Heavy a text message and asked him to come over right away. This wasn't news that she wanted to give him over the phone.

While she waited on Heavy to arrive, Dillon went over many different scenarios in her mind. Maybe she shouldn't tell him about the baby. Maybe she could just sneak behind his back and get an abortion. No, she couldn't do that. That would be wrong. If she wanted them to be on the same page, she had to be honest with him. What would he say? Would he be happy? How would she feel if he was the one that suggested an abortion?

Though Dillon was stumped, she continued to ponder how Heavy would reaction as she got dressed and made herself look decent. She had just slicked her hair back into a low bun when her doorbell rang. Dillon's stomach was doing backflips as she walked to the door to let Heavy in.

"Hey. Is everything okay?" He was concerned.

"Yes. I just have to show you something."

Dillon turned her back, and Heavy followed her to the bathroom. She picked up the test and passed it to him, and he stared at it for a few seconds. Then a broad grin broke out on his face.

"Are you serious?" He didn't even let her answer before he pecked her lips over and over again.

All her nervousness went out the window, and she giggled at his reaction. "You aren't scared? Nervous?"

"Hell nah. Scared of what?"

His passion and conviction melted Dillon's heart.

"I've had enough pussy to last a lifetime. I've fucked women in damn near every state and several other countries. I've gone weeks and had a different woman every single night. That shit doesn't faze me anymore. Since we broke up, I never thought I'd see a time when I wanted more than sex from a woman, but I do. The way we ended traumatized me a li'l bit, and I swore it would always be money over women, but you're a boss, and I fuck with you the long way. We have history, but we've both changed so much since we were a couple. We've been having fun for the past six months, with no real issues. It just reminds me of how we've always been. So why don't we get that old thing back? Only a better version of our old selves?"

Dillon couldn't believe her ears. She'd never been pressed to be in a relationship, but there was no way she was passing up the chance to be with a billionaire. And now it wasn't even just about his money. Heavy was a boss-ass nigga who had an amazing dick, and he treated her like a princess. She had always loved him. It didn't get any better than that, and Dillon knew she'd be stupid as hell to pass him up. When she was with him, everything was on him, so she rarely had to spend her money for anything. Her man was rich, and so was she. But above all else, he made her feel things that no other man had. They could make one hell of a team, and she was with it.

"I'm down for that," she said cautiously. "But are you really ready for a relationship again? I don't want to be out in the streets, getting embarrassed. We've been down this road before, and it's not one I want to go back down. So, I need to know if you're serious."

"If I say it, I mean it. You being embarrassed is the last thing you have to worry about. You're about to be envied by damn near every woman in the world, baby. You got a one-of-a-kind catch." Heavy winked his eye at her, and all she could do was laugh at his antics.

"It kills me to stroke your ego, because you already have an enormous head, but you just might be right. Our breakup hurt me, too, and I swore I'd never put myself in a position to be hurt that way again. But looking back, we both needed that time away from each other to become the best versions of ourselves. I'd be honored to be your girl. Again."

Heavy grabbed her hand and peered into her eyes. "And this time, we do it right. Not to mention that since we already know one another, it might not be long before I'm ring shopping."

"What do you mean?" Dillon asked.

Her heart galloped in her chest. *Ring shopping?* She didn't picture Heavy as the "walking down the aisle" type. But then again, he liked to do everything big, so if he did get married, she knew a courthouse wedding wouldn't do.

"I, um, I don't know what to say," she added. It was rare that Dillon found herself speechless.

"Just say you'll rock with me. I'm not letting you go this time." Heavy kissed her hand, and it felt as if Dillon's heart skipped a few beats.

She almost felt silly for being so smitten with Heavy, because it could very well blow up in her face. However, Dillon was done worrying about the what-ifs. She was going to enjoy the moment for what it was.

"I'm definitely rocking with you, Heavy."

Heavy chuckled and kissed her on the lips.

Dillon prayed this was her happily ever after, and if it couldn't be that, she hoped it was her happy for a little while.

Epilogue

Six months later . . .

Dillon's phone screen lit up, and she saw the notification that forty-two hundred dollars had just been deposited into her bank account, and that was just from *one* transaction. Her girls were booked and busy for the rest of the day. Dillon was officially back in business, and London and the rest of the staff were back at the house, handling things, because she was in Greece with Heavy. They had been there for two days and had another four days to go. The view from their hotel balcony was absolutely beautiful.

Dillon was eating breakfast, enjoying mimosas and life. Well, he was enjoying mimosas. Dillon just had orange juice. She had carried small for the first five months, but out of nowhere, it seemed as if her belly had doubled in size overnight. Dillon couldn't believe that she liked being pregnant. Aside from morning sickness the first month, pregnancy had been a breeze, and she was glowing.

She and Heavy were still in a great place. Dillon trusted him wholeheartedly, because if he was cheating, she wasn't sure when the other women got any of his time, as he invited her everywhere he went, and she always tagged along.

In the past six months, he'd gifted her a Birkin bag, a beautiful diamond-encrusted Patek, and a charm bracelet, and he'd taken her on a shopping spree in Milan. Whenever they traveled, they had plenty of nasty sex, ate like royalty, and hit all the finest stores. Dillon was having the time of her life with Heavy. A baby hadn't been in her immediate plans at all, but she was elated. Dillon had been keeping her pregnancy on the low and enjoying life. They had had an intimate gender reveal with her and Heavy's families, and they had found out they were having a boy. The nursery was already halfway done, and the baby's closet was filled to the brim with clothes, diapers, and wipes. Heavy and Dillon had moved into together when she was four months pregnant.

Heavy came out on the balcony to join Dillon and said, "You're almost as bad as me with that phone."

Dillon smiled at him. "When money is calling, I have to answer. I'm all yours now, though. I know when we get back to Charlotte, you'll be in business meetings and in your bag."

"And I'll still be in the house every night at a decent time," he promised.

"I love you."

"I love you too."

Dillon almost passed out when Heavy got down on one knee. Her hands flew up to her mouth and her eyes doubled in size as she watched him pull a ring box from his pocket.

He gazed into her eyes. "What's understood doesn't have to be explained. I'm rocking with you, and I know you're rocking with me. We have history together, and we're about to be someone's parents. I'd love nothing more than for you to have my last name. Will you marry me?"

"Yes," Dillon squealed as tears filled her eyes.

She had known a proposal might come in the near future, but she was still shocked. Heavy opened the lid on the ring box and revealed a beautiful rock that almost blinded Dillon.

"Damn! I'm going to need security wearing this bad boy," she quipped.

"And we can definitely get you that," Heavy asserted.

Dillon was in awe. She couldn't stop staring at the ring. She felt like she was in a Disney movie. The hood version, of course. "I love it." She tore her eyes away from the ring long enough to kiss Heavy; then she went right back to admiring it.

"Did I do good?"

"Babe, you did great. I can't get over it."

"And you're still going to get a push gift." He winked at her. "We're in the big leagues now, baby."

"If I wasn't the size of a whale, I'd jump into your arms and kiss you all over your face," Dillon laughed. "I can't be breaking your back, though."

Heavy licked his lips. "You're not the size of a whale. You're thick in all the right places. That ass is damn near bigger than your stomach. If pregnancy will have your ass and thighs looking like this, I'm going to keep you pregnant."

"Let's not get too ahead of ourselves. I can see myself doing this one more time in three or four years, but that might be it."

Dillon's phone rang before Heavy could respond, and she saw that Nilda was calling. Dillon was going to keep her engagement to herself for the time being. She would announce it next month at her baby shower.

"Hey, Nilda," Dillon said cheerfully when she took the call. She was in a great mood.

"Dillon, have you seen the news?"

Dillon's eyes fluttered closed. She didn't miss the somber tone in Nilda's voice. "I just want to go a week without hearing bad news," she sighed. "What's on the news?" It never failed. She'd be floating on a cloud for all of an hour or two before trouble came along and knocked her down.

Dillon knew by Nilda's silence that nothing good was coming. "A body was found two days ago in an alley. The victim apparently died from a drug overdose. The body has been identified, and once the family was notified, they released the name to the public. It was Jada."

Dillon wasn't surprised, but it wasn't the news that she wanted to hear. In the past few months, Dillon had been through a hell of a lot. And none of it made her cry the way hearing about Jada's death did. Since seeing her former friend, Dillon had hoped at least once a week that Jada would call her and tell her that she wanted Dillon to take her to a rehab facility. Her death wasn't the news that anyone wanted to hear, but Jada was finally free.

Mallorie's knees buckled when the juror read the not guilty verdict. Corey made a move to hug her, but Mallorie felt as if she was frozen. While waiting to hear her fate, she had almost urinated on herself. She had never been more afraid in her life. Mallorie wasn't meant for prison, and she knew it. She didn't have a lot of faith in Corey, but he had managed to get her off, and she would forever be grateful to him. Mallorie had never been a weak woman, but taking the easy way out had crossed her mind a few times. She would rather hang herself the way Dave did than rot in a prison cell for the rest of her days for a crime that she didn't commit. If she had been convicted, Alleyne would still be taunting her even in death. Mallorie didn't deserve that.

For the first time since the whole ordeal had begun, Mallorie smiled as the lights from cameras flashed in her face. The moment another scandal rocked the city, all would be forgotten, and people would no longer be gossiping about her, Dave, and the dead body that had ended up inside their condo. People had the attention spans of fleas.

Mallorie rushed out of the courtroom and made a beeline to the bathroom. She had a fifteen-minute ride home, and she wasn't sure she could continue to hold her water. Despite how badly she had to use the bathroom, Mallorie stopped short when she saw Dillon standing at the sink, washing her hands. Her blood began to boil as she eyeballed the well-dressed woman with a noticeable baby bump. The bitch was pregnant. Mallorie's eyes went to Dillon's hands as she dried them, and she spotted the massive rock on Dillon's finger. That little bitch had been having a grand ole time living life while Mallorie had literally been fighting for hers.

"You came hoping to see me nailed to the cross for a crime I didn't commit, huh? Seems fitting for a person like you," Mallorie snarled as she looked Dillon up and down with disgust all over her face.

Dillon smirked at the woman. "I didn't come expecting anything. I never accused you of killing Alleyne, but you and Dave sure accused me plenty of having something to do with it. This was a very high-profile case. I was interested just like everyone else in the city. Congratulations on your win. How does it feel to be vindicated?"

Mallorie smirked at Dillon. "Cute. Real fucking cute. I can't wait until the day karma serves your ass up a nice dish of humble pie."

Dillon laughed. "Like the humble pie you had to eat? *You* were the one harassing me and promising to bring me down because *your* husband was a lying, cheating sack of shit. God rest his soul. Your anger was misplaced. You even had your flunky of a private investigator stalking me and my girls. So humble pie? Oh, you were the one that needed that, and you damn sure got it."

"We may never know who killed Alleyne, but it wasn't me, and all that I care about is whoever killed her and got away with it didn't ruin my life in the process. I hate that my husband felt the need to step out on me, and I argued with Alleyne due to her being disrespectful. I'd never kill a woman because my husband couldn't keep his dick in his pants, and I'm glad the jury ruled in my favor."

Dillon shrugged her shoulders. "You were found not guilty, Mrs. Prescott. You don't have to try to convince me. Once again, congratulations on your victory."

Dillon sauntered past Mallorie, and Mallorie wanted to grab her by the hair. Dillon was a smug little bitch, and Mallorie didn't like her. What Mallorie had said was true. Someone else had killed Alleyne, and she was glad that she didn't go down for it. If Dave took the life of his mistress, then he was already suffering. And if it was Dillon or anyone else, Mallorie had to believe that he or she would receive their karma. As for Alleyne, play stupid games, win stupid prizes. Mallorie didn't care that she was dead. *May she and Dave both rot in hell.*

The next day Dillon looked down at the iced-out watch on her wrist. She had arrived at the restaurant a few minutes early and ordered a glass of sparkling water. Dillon planned to breastfeed, but she missed mimosas so bad. As soon as she got home from the hospital, she planned to pump enough milk to last a few days and then have a few glasses. Her mouth was practically watering for a mimosa already. Dillon wasn't sure if it was her hormones or all the extra water that she'd been drinking, but her baby had her glowing. Dillon was the happiest that she'd ever been.

Corey was supposed to arrive in less than five minutes, and she hoped he wouldn't be late. Dillon had no clue why he wanted to meet with her, but she assumed it was for closure. Mallorie's trial was over, and she'd been found innocent. As much as Corey had been afraid that the scandal would damage his chances of being elected the city's new mayor, it had actually seemed to work in his favor.

A lot of people empathized with the fact that he had lost his father so soon after finding him. They also admired how he'd been able to clear Mallorie's name. Anytime he was interviewed, Corey made it a point to explain that he didn't approve of his father's affair, and he wouldn't have approved of an affair with any woman, but damn sure not a sex worker.

He had assured the public that he had no knowledge of any kind of brothel when he was dating Dillon, and the fact that he hadn't been spotted with her, and she was now linked to Heavy, made him believable. People, women especially, felt sorry for Corey. He seemed like a good guy who had been surrounded with lies, deceit, and betrayal. When he showed up at interviews with weary smiles and bags under his eyes, it made people aware that all the drama in his life was causing him to stress and lose sleep.

Dillon had just finished her water when the hostess led Corey to the back of the restaurant, to the table where she was seated. Corey looked better. He had a fresh haircut, and there were no longer bags underneath his eyes.

"Hi, Dillon," he said as he sat down, and his tone seemed pleasant enough, but Dillon wasn't sure she should let her guard down just yet.

"Hi. You look well."

"Thank you. So do you. I'm sure you're wondering why I asked you to meet me here, so I'll make it quick."

"That would be very much appreciated."

Corey licked his lips, sat back in his seat, and studied Dillon. She was so poised and beautiful. So classy. But she could also be sneaky and conniving. "In an effort to clear her name, Mallorie had a private investigator do some digging. I mean, I'm sure you know that, because you were at the trial. The security guard who just up and disappeared? Well, he showed his face back at home once the trial was over. He finally confessed to me that two Irishmen approached him and threatened him that if he didn't turn over the hotel security footage, he would be sorry. He gave them the footage because he feared for his life, but as an incentive for him to leave town and not talk, he was also paid sixty thousand dollars."

It took every ounce of restraint that Dillon had to remain calm on the outside. On the inside, she was panicking. "Okay. What does that have to do with me?"

Corey was silent for a moment, as if he enjoyed toying with her. "I'd be willing to bet my last dollar that neither Mallorie nor Dave killed Alleyne. Her body was placed in that condo. Who would have wanted to set either one of them up more than the person that they were threatening to expose?"

Dillon felt an immense sense of relief. He didn't know anything for real. He was still grasping at straws. She sucked her teeth and placed her purse strap on her shoulder. "I thought that maybe you invited me here for closure. Maybe to see if I ever really liked you or had any intentions of being with you, but you're still stuck on the bullshit with Alleyne. I wasn't arrested, I wasn't the one on trial, and Stepmommy dearest has been vindicated. I refuse to keep doing this shit with you. Have a nice life and please lose my number," Dillon scoffed as she stood up.

He eyed the ring on her finger and her huge belly. "Wow." He chuckled. "Did you ever really like me?" Corey asked, trying his luck. "I mean, you can be honest about it now. What do we have to gain from lies?"

"Fuck off." Dillon sauntered away from the table with a frown on her face. She was irritated. She didn't owe him an explanation. Not after the way he'd come at her. He might have been hurt, but Dillon was truly over it all. The situation with Alleyne had taught her a lot, and she was ready to move on from it. Maybe she shouldn't have killed the woman, and maybe she shouldn't have tried to pin it on Mallorie. But it was all in the past, and it couldn't be undone.

At the moment, she was happy with Heavy, and if anything ever happened with them, she'd be happy with someone else. Dillon refused to keep reliving the past with Corey or anyone else.

When she got in her car, Dillon saw that she had a client who wanted to be serviced by Dria for four hours. A smile spread across her face. Money was the motive for Dillon. Anything else was irrelevant.

The End

Also Available

My Woman His Wife:

20 Year Anniversary Edition

Anna J.

In the Beginning . . .

Chapter One

Jasmine

Imagine that, imagine that, imagine that, imagine . . .
At five foot two, 136 pounds, dark chocolate skin, and almond eyes, sexy Monica was standing over me topless in a red thong, giving me one hell of a show. My girl was popping it like she was trying to get rent money and she only had two days left to scrape it up. You would think there was a pole in the center of the bed the way she was rotating and grinding her body to the beat of the music. Heavy on the guitar, the sound making her body contort in ways that shouldn't be possible. She was a professional and knew how to reel me in. It was more than her body though, but we'll get into that later.

My eyes were fixed on hers as she did a sensual butterfly all the way down until the lips of her vagina kissed my stomach, leaving a wet spot where they landed. She bent over and a tattoo spelling her name in neat cursive peeked out over the band of her thong. She took her right nipple into her mouth and caressed the other as she continued to move to the beat of the music. Her body seemed to shimmer as light from outside landed on her skin, making her almost glow. She worked up a light sweat, making her glisten a little in the sparsely lit room.

Stepping off the bed, she bent over to remove her thong, afterward hooking it onto my foot. A double-headed dildo magically appeared as she crawled toward me. My legs spread invitingly when her lips made contact with the space behind my right knee. I heard R. Kelly hyping it up with the guitar, making the love of my life sweat just a little more, and my body was shaking in anticipation for what was to come. She had yet to disappoint me, and I'd bet my last dollar that today would be no different.

Well, the second love of my life. While I was lying here, legs spread-eagle, playing with my clit, I couldn't even fully get into it because I should have been at home with my husband and two kids. Yeah, you heard that right. A bitch was married, but I was out in these streets acting single. I could have just gotten up and gone, but I didn't feel like the drama and tears I had to see every time I was ready to leave. Monica was so damn dramatic sometimes, and today I just didn't have the energy to do it with her. I knew in my heart that I had no damn business being here in the first place, but I was thinking with my pussy in anticipation of all the wonderful orgasms I would have. Shit at home died down a long time ago, but it wasn't until I found myself lying here looking up at another woman's breasts did the guilt set in. I'd been here many times, but today it just hit different and I felt like crap about it.

It wasn't supposed to be like this. I knew I should be at home making love to my husband, but he wasn't producing multiple orgasms like Monica. She did things with her tongue no one has written about yet. She had ways of making me have blinding explosions that left my brain scattered. My husband had no idea on how to even find the spot, and I could forget about him lasting all night. The five minutes he gave me I could do myself with just a flick of my middle finger in the right spot. I needed satisfaction that my own hands didn't produce, and Monica gave me what I needed without any questions. Well, maybe some questions, but that's beside the point. Stay focused.

I didn't want to have to tell my partner what I wanted. After all these years, he should already know what made me cum. *If you're going to hit it from the back, put a fin-*

ger in my asshole or leave a handprint on my ass cheek. Take it with one of my legs on your shoulder while you use your thumb to play with my clit. While I'm riding, take both of my nipples into your mouth at the same time. Hell, I like it a little rough sometimes. Toss me around a little bit. Choke me out. Do something besides pound me all hard for five minutes then roll over and fall asleep.

Then if that weren't enough, this fool wanted to invite company into our bedroom! The blackassity of a minute man killed me every time. He could barely handle me alone and he wanted company? He was very bold for that move, but I agreed to those shenanigans and that was why I was in this mess now. If nothing else, know for sure that once a person shenans once, they will shenan-again!

It all started about two months before the twins' fourth birthday. It had already been eight months since my husband and I had so much as fondled each other, let alone had any actual sexual contact. We were literally passing each other like ships in the night, merely escaping colliding into an iceberg. I tried to pretend like I was unfazed by it. Moving along with raising our children like our lack of bedroom action didn't matter, but the truth is I wanted to get fucked. Good at that. Not this mediocre shit I was getting from James's tired ass. He had been on my last nerve about having a threesome with some chick he'd met from God knows where, and I was about tired of hearing it. All I got was five minutes. What was he gonna do? Break it down to two and a half minutes between the both of us? He must have been suffering from hallucinations from sitting up in that news station all day or something. And what the hell was this girl and I supposed to do? She could eat all the cat she wanted to, but I didn't get down like that! Never did. Never would. Wasn't about to start.

Back in the day, my husband and I made love constantly. It was nothing to be bent over the kitchen counter getting served from behind. He would be stroking me from the back with one finger playing with my clit, and the other

in my asshole while kissing me on my neck and talking
dirty to me all at the same time. I loved a man who talked
dirty, and he had the gift for real. Talking me through an
orgasm was probably the best thing you could do for me
in life. I would ride him in the dining room chair until my
legs hurt, and he would then pick me up and lay me on the
table, devouring me from feet to head, and not necessarily
in that order. He liked for me to hold my lips open so that
my clit stood right out as he simultaneously sucked on
it and fingered me with three fingers the way I liked it. I
would lean up, and watch his tongue go to work, sopping
me up sloppily until I squirted in his face. He didn't mind
it at all and would just lick the mess up while still teasing
my overly sensitive clit. My body would feel like it was on
fire, and I loved every minute of it.

All of that stopped for one reason or another, and I
didn't feel like him or this girl he was trying to sell me on.
It got to the point where this fool started leaving notes
around the house, practically begging me to jump on
board. One night he tried to show me a picture of the girl,
and I just snapped the hell out. What part of no didn't he
understand, the "n" or the "o"?

"Babe, just hear me out," he said, pleading on his knees
at my side of the bed. "You won't even listen to what I
have to say."

I remembered the days when he would be on his knees
on my side of the bed, only my legs would be thrown
over his shoulders as his lips and tongue would have me
squirming and begging for mercy. Right then, the sight of
him was contributing to my already-pounding headache.

"James, I done told you fifty thousand damn times that
I'm not doing it, so why do you keep asking me?" I almost
reached up and throat punched his ass. He was working
the little bit of nerve I had left, and I just wasn't in the
mood for this. He didn't even realize that I was ready to
bust him in the head with the alarm clock. Why wouldn't
he just go to sleep?

"Because you're not keeping an open mind."

"Would you want me to bring another dick into the bedroom? A little friendly competition?" I asked and waited for a reply. It was always some double standard with men. They wanted what they wanted, but when you flipped the script, all of a sudden they were mute. He looked at me like I was crazy and got up to go on his side of the bed.

That shut his ass right up, if only for a second. I was so damn tired of hearing about this Monica chick, I was ready to just go ahead and get it over with so he would just shut the fuck up about it. This entire scenario was making me sick to my stomach. What his dumb ass didn't realize was I might have gone along with it just to please him, but I'd be damned if I would be pressured into doing anything I wasn't down for. *We aren't teenagers. We are grown, and I will not be bullied by my spouse to have sex with strangers because essentially that's what this is.*

"So, is doing it in the bedroom the problem?" he asked in a desperate voice.

"What? Didn't I just tell you I didn't want to talk about it?"

"I'm just saying that if your concern is bringing her into our home, I could easily get us a room over at the Hyatt or the Marriott."

"James, how do you even know this girl? What kind of shit are y'all into over at TUNN?"

I was guessing this fool couldn't see the big-ass pile of salt on my shoulders. *If this were a cartoon, steam would be coming out of my ears right about now.*

"My buddy Damon hooked it up for me. It's his wife's sister or something like that. They do it all the time."

"He fucking on his sister-in-law, too? What kind of shit they into over there?" I asked, my face showing the disgust of what I just heard.

That only made me wonder what kind of freaky shit her family was into. I didn't know too many people just putting their own flesh and blood out there like that. Was

Damon doing both the wife and the sister and just passing her off to us? Or as a collective, this was just some shit they were all into. My head was swimming just thinking about the many scenarios, and none of it made me feel better about it. It all sounded absolutely ridiculous to me, but James's slow ass was game for anything apparently.

"No," he said, just as irritated, putting his head in his hands. "Not with his sister, with other women."

"What do you know about her, James? This chick could be HIV positive for all we know. There is no cure for that!"

"We would all be using protection," he said as if he was offended. *Shit, I'm offended he won't let it go.*

"Will she be putting a condom around her mouth?" I asked. "Semen and saliva can carry the same shit."

"Here you go taking the conversation to another level. Why can't you just relax and enjoy life for once? It's only this one time."

"What I'm about to do is enjoy this six hours of sleep. Good night!" And with that said, I turned my behind over and went to sleep. Enjoy life? Was this man serious? I was five seconds from enjoying bashing his damn skull in, but I digress. The headache I was trying to avoid was slowly creeping in, and I did my best to fight it off so that I could get some sleep.

Of course it wasn't over. When I woke up, James was in the shower. As much as I hated to go in the bathroom while he was in there, I figured if I could at least brush my teeth, I could shower real quick and be out of the house before he had a chance to come at me with some bullshit. I was hoping he wouldn't bring this Monica shit up at 6:37 in the morning because I would hurt him.

By the time I was done brushing my teeth and cleansing my face, James was stepping out of the shower. Through the mirror I peeked at his toned body and semi-erect penis. At the age of 32, standing at least six feet three inches, he still had the body of a college football player. He's definitely well endowed, but what difference did it make if he was only good for five minutes? He caught my eye as he was drying off, and a sly smile spread across his face as he covered his midsection with the towel and went into the bedroom. I hopped in the shower and lingered a little longer because it was his morning to get the kids ready.

We used to fuck in the shower all the time. Many mornings I woke up early just to ensure we had time to get it in. I closed my eyes as my soapy hands started to roam my body as memories of James banging me against the wall infiltrated my brain. I'd be hanging on to the showerhead for dear life as our bodies would collide under the spray of the water. Many mornings I ended up with my hair brushed into a bun because the water ruined it. When he told me to grab my ankles, I obliged, enjoying the water running over my shoulders and head. The grip he had on my hips was the only thing keeping me standing as he brought me one climax after the next. Those were the good old days, and I briefly wondered what happened to them. I couldn't keep my fingers off my clit as I rubbed one out while I leaned against the back of the shower wall. These days I had to take what I could get, even if that meant me doing it myself.

When I stepped out of the steamy water and into our room, I could still smell his One Million by Paco Rabanne cologne. That made me wet instantly, but he'd never know. I'd just as soon please myself than waste my shower on a few minutes with him. After putting my outfit together and plugging in the flat iron, I was finally able to sit on the bed and moisturize my skin. Out of the corner of my eye I noticed a single yellow rose on my pillow and a piece of heart-shaped chocolate with "I Love You" printed on the foil resting next to it. I smiled but continued to rub my Coach Floral body lotion into my skin.

I loved my husband, and maybe we could talk about this entire Monica thing later. I mean, I wanted spontaneity, right? I couldn't keep complaining about what I wasn't getting if I wasn't at least trying to get something. Right? All of this shit was exhausting, and I just wanted to be left alone for the moment.

Surprisingly he had nothing to say at breakfast. He smiled a lot, and that just pissed me off. Not that I had any conversation for him, but his being quiet made me nervous. At least if he were talking, I'd know how to vibe off him. He just sat there smiling the entire time, and that just made me suspicious.

When I started gathering my stuff up to leave for work, he already had my briefcase and files along with my lunch stacked all nice and neat in the passenger seat of my 2003 Blazer. I got a kiss on the cheek, and he even offered to take the kids to childcare for me. Something was definitely up, and I wasn't at work for five minutes before I figured it out. I was looking through the files that I was supposed to be working on over the weekend when a hot pink folder that I didn't remember having before caught my eye. When I opened it, a five-by-seven photo of Monica was pasted to the left, and a three-page print-out about her was on the opposite side. I was too shocked to be offended.

The pages included her date of birth, zodiac sign, likes and dislikes, a copy of her dental records, last HIV test results, and the results of her gynecologist exam, which I was glad to see were all negative. Her being a Virgo might have piqued my curiosity because I heard they were some undercover freaks and all that shy shit was just a game. Her address and phone number were also included, along with directions on how to get to her house from my job off Google Maps. I had to laugh to keep from being pissed because I was sure my husband was going crazy.

As if that weren't enough, further inspection produced a key card from the Hyatt and an invite to meet him and Monica at the hotel restaurant for dinner. A note, hand-written by James, said the kids would be at his mother's house and I should be at the hotel by 7:00 p.m. I put everything back in the folder and went to my first meeting of the day. I didn't even want to think about that right now, and I had a few choice words for James later on.

When I returned to my office for lunch, I opened my door to ten bouquets of yellow tulips crowding my space. On my desk sat a bouquet of tulips and white roses mixed in a beautiful Waterford crystal vase. My secretary informed me that they were delivered only ten minutes before I got there, and the card could be found next to the vase on my desk. I was too overwhelmed to think clearly and mechanically walked over to my desk to retrieve the card. It was in a cute yellow and white striped envelope to match the flowers and was written with a gold pen. It read:

> *Jasmine,*
> *You must know that you're the love of my life, and there is nothing in this world I wouldn't do to make you happy. This one time I want us to be happy together. Please reconsider . . .*
> *Love Forever,*
> *James*

In that instant, I knew I would be at the hotel later. If I'm being totally honest, I'd been considering it all day. When I saw her picture and put a face to the name it stayed on my mind during my entire meeting. I figured this one time wouldn't kill me, and it might spice up our love life so that it would be like it used to be. I hoped I wasn't making the biggest mistake of my life by doing this. After gathering my thoughts, I went on with the rest of my day trying not to think about what I would be getting into later. I had a trial at two o'clock that I had to go to, and on my way there I mentally checked my schedule to make sure I would be out of the office by five and chillin' in the suite by five thirty. That way I could freshen up and put on something sexy for dinner.

I got out of court at four thirty, having had my client's charges dismissed. That made me feel great, and I planned to take the next two days off to celebrate. When I got back to the office, my secretary was smiling at me and holding a vase with what looked like two dozen powder pink roses accompanied with another card. She gave them to me and offered to open my office door because my arms were full. When I walked in I almost dropped the bouquet I was holding because I was totally surprised. As if all the yellow tulips weren't enough, my office was now crowded with just as many powder pink and white roses and seemed to triple as I got farther inside.

"Someone is either madly in love with you or is apologizing. Whatever it is, let me know your secret," my secretary replied as if she really wanted an answer. I just turned to her with a smile on my face, stepped to the side, and closed my door. We were not cool like that, and now wasn't the time to start.

I sat the bouquet on my desk next to the one I received earlier. There was nowhere for me to sit, so I walked over to the picture window so that I could gather my thoughts while I looked down on the city from the twenty-third floor. The envelope holding the card smelled like Pleasures by Estee Lauder. I loved that scent and was pleased to find out someone else did as well. When I opened the envelope and pulled the card out, little gold hearts and stars fell from it. The card was from Monica requesting my presence at the hotel later. I was flattered and speechless. Maybe she wasn't that bad after all.

"Sheila, have the ladies on this floor come take a bouquet. If there are any left over once they are done, extend the invitation to the other floors. I want everything out before I'm back in the office. You can just leave these two to decorate my office," I instructed as I prepared to leave for the day.

"Absolutely. I'll get on it right now," Sheila replied, getting up to gather the ladies on our floor. A line quickly formed with smiling faces as each lady took a bouquet out. I left before they were done, knowing Sheila would lock my door once the flower parade was over.

I counted fifty flower arrangements. I didn't need that many. No one wanted to come back to a bunch of dead flowers. All of these flowers were taking up way too much space, and I really didn't have anywhere to put them all. On my way to my Jeep I called to check up on the kids before stopping at Victoria's Secret for something sexy. I wanted this to be a night to remember since it was a one-time thing. I wanted it to be perfect and was prepared to pull out all the tricks.

I decided on a cranberry spaghetti-strapped one piece with matching thong. The gown was ankle length with thigh-high splits on both sides, and the front dipped down all the way to my navel. The back opened to the middle of my back, showing off my curvaceous size ten, even after a set of twins. I purchased a bottle of Breathless perfume and a pair of sandals to match, then made my way to the hotel.

When I got to the suite a little flustered from sitting in traffic longer than I expected, I was taken aback by the decor. I didn't think that I would make it in time and started getting a little antsy. As I rushed up to the room, I was making a plan to get ready quicker than I originally anticipated, and it added to the already-nervous energy that I had about the evening ahead. Pink and white rose petals decorated every inch of every room and floated in the Jacuzzi on top of rose-colored water. Yellow tulips sat in crystal vases around the living room and bedrooms, and Maxwell's *Urban Hang Suite* played softly in the background from invisible surround-sound speakers. A mixture of pink and white rose petals and yellow tulip petals covered the California king–sized bed. A bottle of Passion Alize sat in a crystal ice bucket accompanied by three long-stem wineglasses on the end table closest to the bathroom door. On the other a glass bowl was filled with condoms of different textures and colors.

A note was tucked into the mirror in the bathroom with instructions to meet my dinner guests in the dining room at seven o'clock sharp. It was already six thirty, judging by the clock on the bedroom wall, so I stepped up the game as I showered, dressed, and did my hair in record time all while not disturbing the romantic setup. I was walking into the dining room at five of seven. The waiter sat me in a cozy booth away from the other guests with a glass of Moet and a yellow tulip and a powder pink rose courtesy of my husband and Monica. At seven sharp my dinner guests walked in. I briefly wondered where they were all this time since I had the suite all to myself to get ready. Did Monica have a room here too? Were they engaged in anything sexual before getting here? It was taking everything I had to stay seated, and before I could bail out, I just took a sip of my drink and held my breath, releasing it calmly. Tonight was going to be a good night. It had to be.

James was sharp, dressed in cream linen slacks with dark chocolate gator shoes that matched perfectly with the button-down shirt with different shades of browns and tans swirled through it, compliments of Sean John fashions. His wedding band glistened and shined from the door, and the light bounced off it all the way across the room. I could smell his cologne way before he reached the table.

Monica was equally impressive in a short, champagne-colored one piece that showed off perky breasts and fell just above her knee. The bottom of her dress had that tattered look that people are wearing nowadays, and it accented her long chocolate legs. Her toes peeked out of champagne stiletto sandals, and her soft jet-black curls framed her face. Her makeup was flawless, and she smelled sweet.

I stood up as they made their way to the booth, and I couldn't stop staring at them. When my husband and Monica reached the table, he gave me a soft, lingering kiss on my lips that made me wet instantly. He hadn't kissed me like that in months. Monica gave me a soft kiss on my cheek, and James made sure we were both seated before he took his.

Before we could start conversing, the waiter was at our table with appetizers. We were served seafood-stuffed mushrooms and Caesar salad with glasses of Moet to wash it down. I glanced over at my husband periodically and couldn't believe the thoughts I was having. For the first time in months, I wanted my husband the way a woman wants her man, and I couldn't wait to get upstairs.

"Did you get the roses I sent you?" Monica asked between small bites of the crab-stuffed mushroom she was eating. She had the cutest heart-shaped mouth that made you want to kiss her. Her tongue darted out every so often to the corners of her mouth to remove whatever food or drink was there. That turned me on and made me wonder how her tongue would feel on my skin.

"Yes, thank you. They were nice."

"Did you enjoy the tulips?" my husband asked, his eyes never leaving me. "I know yellow is your favorite color."

Tonight, he looked different. Kind of like he was in love with me all over again. His eyes twinkled with mischief, and his lips begged for me to kiss him. I wanted to so badly.

"Yes, baby, I did. Thank you."

"You're welcome, baby. How'd your day go?"

Me, Monica, and James made conversation over the smoked salmon, wild rice, and mixed vegetables we were served for dinner. Before dessert was served, James and I slow danced to "Reunion" by Maxwell as I watched Monica from the dance floor. She swayed from side to side in her seat, never taking her eyes off me. I didn't know what she did when I wasn't facing her, but when I did, she looked me right in the eye, her facial expressions telling me what I had to look forward to.

As we danced, my husband held me close, his mouth on my ear, singing the words to the song. His warm hands felt good on my bare back as he made small circles, massaging me. I truly felt like this was indeed our reunion because it had been a long time since we'd been like this. I closed my eyes, and I tightened my arms around his neck, enjoying the feel of him in my arms, and me in his.

Slices of double chocolate cake waited for us when we got back to the table. I couldn't touch mine because I was ready to go upstairs. James fed me and Monica his cake off the same fork, and that only made me more excited. I wanted to get this party started, but I went with the flow because I didn't know what they had planned.

"Are you ready for ecstasy, baby?" my husband asked me after we finished dessert. Instead of answering, I grabbed both of them by the hand and led them upstairs.

Chapter 2

Jasmine

Once we got into the elevator, James pulled us into a group hug with my and Monica's heads resting on his shoulders. We looked at each other curiously, probably thinking about how far the other would go. Before I could react, Monica leaned over and kissed me, and it wasn't a peck on the lips, either. She slid her tongue into my mouth, allowing my taste buds to sample the chocolate cake left on it from dessert. Her lips felt soft as she sucked on my bottom lip, then my top, causing a tingling sensation to shoot down my back straight to my toes, and finally resting warmly on my clitoris. My body was buzzing with nervous energy, and I willed the elevator to move a little faster. I wasn't ready just yet, but from the way Monica was moving, I didn't have a choice but to get ready.

I could taste a hint of her cherry lip gloss when my tongue touched the corner of her mouth. A moan escaped my lips when her hand made contact with the left side of my neck, pulling my face closer to hers. I opened my eyes to look at her facial expressions while she kissed me, and to my surprise, she was already watching me. I blushed, a little embarrassed at being caught, but she let me know it was cool by kissing my eyelids. She kissed the tip of my nose and went back to my lips while my husband made small circles on my back with his fingertips. Her kiss was slow and sensual and thankfully not wet and sloppy like most men do. She allowed me to lead, and then I allowed her to teach me what she knew.

My right hand found my husband's erect penis just as we were approaching the fourteenth floor. When I stepped back to adjust my hand around his shaft, the elevator suddenly stopped and the lights went out. We were all stuck on stupid for about thirty seconds before either of us moved. We were on our way to erotica beyond our wildest dreams and the damn elevator stopped! You talking about pissed? I finally got up the nerve to go through with this wild night and here I was stuck in a hot-ass elevator. Oh, how I was *so* not in the mood for this.

"James, do something," I said while slightly hyperventilating. We were stuck between the thirteenth and fourteenth floors, and I wanted out.

"Baby, just calm down. I'll call the service desk to see what they can do," he replied as he stepped from between us to get help.

While James was on the phone, I sat down in the corner to slow my heart rate and collect my thoughts. I didn't know how long we were going to be stuck, and this was not the place to pass out from lack of oxygen. I was hoping to still be in the mood when we got out because at this moment, I wanted to be off this elevator and in my bed.

Just as I leaned my head back against the wall, I felt a pair of warm hands parting my legs. I still heard James on the phone, and my body tensed up because I couldn't believe Monica was trying to sex me at a time like this. Having an orgasm was the last thing on my mind at the moment, and I was almost certain everyone felt the same way. Before I could protest, Monica had my thong pulled to the side and her tongue stroking my clit. Her tongue felt hot on my panic button, and the way she used her fingers made my knees touch the elevator walls instantly. She sucked my clit up into her mouth softly, sliding her tongue back and forth across it, making my breath come in shallow pants. My hips involuntarily ground into her mouth, and she pushed back, snaking her tongue from my opening up to my clit and back down again.

She took her time moving two fingers in and out of me in a "come here" motion that was playing havoc on my G-spot while she sucked, licked, kissed, and played mercilessly with my clit trapped between her lips. My body shook involuntarily because I was trying not to explode. I didn't want to moan aloud while James was on the phone, but it was killing me trying to hold it in. She held the lips of my cave open and her tongue twisted around inside me, my walls depositing my sweet honey on her tongue. For a second, it felt like we were the only two people trapped in that hot box.

"Okay, ladies, the attendant said we'd only be in here for a . . . damn."

When James hung up the phone and looked over at our silhouettes in the dark, he was speechless. I guess the sight of his wife being pleased by another woman shocked him. It wasn't completely dark. The little track lights they had around the edges gave very little light to the room. We couldn't see clearly, but we could see enough to know what was going on.

His back was to us the entire time, so it had to have been a pleasant surprise to see Monica and me the way we were. James never could do more than one thing at a time, so it didn't surprise me that he didn't pay us any mind until he was done with his call.

He stood back and watched for a while, taking in the sights and sounds of what was happening. With the little bit of light coming from the call box, I could see James massaging his strength through his pants. He squatted down behind Monica, lifting her dress up over her hips, exposing her plump ass. My eyes were now adjusted to the dark, and even though I couldn't clearly see what was happening, his outline said it all. I could make out in the mirror on the ceiling of the elevator what was happening right in front of me. Monica was in the doggie-style position with her head buried between my legs. James had inserted his fingers into her walls just as Monica did to me only moments earlier. I could see James maneuvering his body so that he could taste her. In the meantime, Monica was pulling another orgasm out of me.

She moaned against my clit from my husband pleasing her. The more James pushed and pulled on her, the more intense her pleasing me became. I scooted forward so that I could lie flat on the floor. Monica stood up and positioned herself over me. She pulled her French-cut panties to the side and placed her lips on mine. I just imitated what she did to me, switching from kissing and sucking her clit and sticking my tongue inside her. James was inside of me, stretching my walls to fit him.

He stroked me slowly, teasing me with just the head before sliding it all in. His thumb created friction on my clit and before we could stop it, I exploded on his length and Monica exploded in my mouth. We were about to switch positions when the lights came on and the elevator started moving. James pulled out of me still rock hard, making it a little difficult to pull up the zipper on his pants.

When the elevator door opened, the attendant and the security guard were waiting on the other side. They tried to apologize but we just rushed past them and scrambled down the hall to our suite so that we could finish what we started. We didn't think about the fact that they could probably smell sex in the air, and I don't think we really cared.

Upon entry to the room, Monica went to run hot water into the Jacuzzi because the water that was in there got cold. I sat on the side of the bed, anxiety covering me like a blanket. I couldn't believe what I'd just done and what I was about to do. I was excited and scared at the same time. Excited because I was finally letting go of my inhibitions and stepping outside the box. Scared because I didn't want to disappoint my husband.

I'll never do this again, I thought, but I did want him to enjoy this night of pleasure.

Monica came out of the bathroom in her bra and pant-ies. I was hesitant about looking her in the eye because I knew my cheeks were red from blushing. We were all silent, not wanting to be the one to say something first. James changed the CD in the stereo to a slow-jams mix he put together. When R. Kelly started crooning, "Come to Daddy," Monica started doing an erotic dance in front of the full-length mirror. James leaned back on the dresser to watch the show, and I just sat there with a shocked expression on my face. She danced like she had ballet lessons but with just enough eroticism to make you think she might have been wrapped around a pole in a strip club once or twice.

As she got closer to me, I scooted back on the bed to keep her at arm's length. What we did in the dark eleva-tor was cool because I couldn't see it, but now we were in a well-lit room with my husband able to see everything. I wasn't sure if I wanted to go through with it, but when I looked over at James stroking his length and gazing at us I couldn't stop. Just the fact that he had been hard for more than five minutes was amazing.

The look on my face screamed, "Help," as I looked from James to Monica. Monica advanced toward me slowly, and James smiled as he watched us work. I was now up against the headboard with my legs up to my chest. When Monica reached me, she took my feet into her hands and started to massage them one at a time. I was as stiff as a virgin on her first night, and Monica did her thing to help me relax.

She took my toes into her mouth one at a time. My moans escaped involuntarily. Her soft lips traveled up my thighs until they rested against my pelvis. Her tongue dipped in and out of my honey pot. She held my lips open with both hands, exposing my now-wet pearl to my husband.

"James, can I taste it?" Monica asked my husband in a husky voice. I looked over at him to read his face. It showed nothing but excitement.

"Go ahead and make her cum," he responded in a deep, passion-filled voice. His hand moved at a slow, lazy pace, up and down his erect shaft. A hint of pre-cum rested on the tip of his penis, and I motioned him over to the bed so that I could taste it.

He disrobed on his way over, his body looking like he should be on the cover of *GQ* magazine. Monica had her full lips pressed against my clit, causing me to squirm and breathe heavily. James stood beside the bed with his chocolate penis standing straight out. I didn't hesitate to wrap my lips around him, taking as much in as I could without choking.

James fondled our breasts simultaneously while trying to maintain his balance as I gave him head. Monica held my legs up, and kept her face buried in my treasure chest. Our moans were bouncing off the walls, tuning out the music that was playing. If there were people in the suite next to us, I was sure they heard everything. Monica moved back off the bed and pulled me with her. James lay down in the middle of the bed on his back, his erection pointing at the ceiling. I straddled his thickness like a pro, dipping all the way down until my clit touched his pelvis, then coming back up until just the head was in. James leaned up on his elbows and took my nipples into his mouth one at a time. Monica had my ass cheeks spread so that her tongue could make acquaintance with my asshole. I was having orgasms back-to-back like I used to when me and James first met. I was damn near about to pass out from exploding so much.

We switched positions in order to relax a little more. Monica put on a strap-on vibrator with clitoral stimulators around the base. I looked at her like, *who does she think she is using that on?* She took James's place in the center of the bed and motioned for me to get on top of her. I looked at her and my husband like they were crazy.

"James, I am not getting on her like that. She done . . ." The mood was changing quickly, and Monica was looking frustrated. Ask me did I give a damn. Some shit just ain't meant to be tried, and she was one of them.

"Baby, it's okay. It'll feel just like the real thing. Trust me on this one," James said to me in a calm, soothing voice. I wasn't buying it.

"And what are you going to do with that?" I asked, referring to his erect penis.

"You'll see, and you'll enjoy it. Just trust me."

He gave me a reassuring look as he led me to the bed. I closed my eyes and got on top of Monica, doing to her what I did to my husband. It was feeling good, and I really got into it. When I bent over to kiss Monica, I felt a warm liquid oozing down the crack of my ass. My husband held my back so that I couldn't move, and I could feel him inserting a finger into my forbidden place. I tensed up automatically, and he whispered to me to try to relax.

I didn't do back shots often, and my husband knew that. Literally I'd never taken anything more than a finger from him, so anything bigger than that had me nervous. I wanted to get an attitude, but what they were doing felt so damn good. I reminded myself that it was only one night, and I tried to relax myself so that my husband could join in the fun. I wondered how he was going to fit it in because my husband was definitely blessed in the dick department. He's long and thick, with a big mushroom-shaped head that I knew was way bigger than the hole he would try to get it into. It would be like trying to put a block into a round hole. A finger in the ass was one thing. He could do that all day, but ten inches in the ass was something to scream about.

"James, I don't think I'll be able to take it back there, baby," I whispered. "You're too big."

I was hoping he would have second thoughts when he heard how scared I was, but that wasn't the case.

"Jasmine, I won't hurt you, baby. I'll take my time, and I'm using this so you'll be okay." He held out a bottle of KY Warming Liquid for me to view.

"Won't it get too hot back there?"

"You'll be fine, just relax," Monica responded before taking my nipples into her mouth. A moan escaped from my lips, totally catching me off guard.

I tried to relax as James eased himself into my back door. Lord knows it was killing me, but I stuck in there. He slowly pushed the head in, which was the most painful part. It felt like he was ripping me a new asshole, and tears gathered at the corners of my eyes threatening to fall and land on Monica's forehead. Once he got in as much as he could comfortably, he began pleasing me with long, slow strokes. In combination with Monica pushing and pulling on the bottom, I was going crazy from the new feelings I was having. When James pulled out, Monica pushed in, causing me to lose my breath on more than one occasion. James reached around my waist and teased my clit while Monica held my lips open for him. His other hand fondled my right nipple while Monica's mouth warmed the other one.

I didn't know whether I was coming or going. Sometime during the mix, the pace quickened and we were going at it like animals. Monica sat on the lounge chair with the vibrator in hand, watching me and James become one. He held me by my ankles, pushing my legs all the way back, my knees touching my ears easily. He was driving his dick deep in me with slow strokes, and I never wanted him to stop.

"I'm cumming, baby," I said to my husband between inhaling and exhaling. "Cum with me."

James slowed it down, and we looked at each other as our orgasms played out. My legs wrapped around him tightly until our rapture subsided. Monica looked spent as she, too, was exploding along with us. James pulled out of me, and rested with his head between my breasts while we caught our breaths. The session we just had was the best thing since sliced bread.

"I'll meet y'all in the Jacuzzi," Monica replied as we reluctantly untangled ourselves from each other. At that moment, I wanted Monica to leave so that James and I could enjoy our weekend alone, but I didn't want to be rude. I later found out that was mistake number one. The red light was practically blinking right in front of my face, but for reasons beyond even me, I went with the flow instead of stating my wishes. She served her purpose, and now it was time for her ass to go.

We joined Monica in the Jacuzzi a little while later. James popped open one of the Alize bottles, and we sat back and chilled. *Friday After Next* was playing in the DVD player, but I paid it no mind. I wanted some more of my husband, but with Monica there I knew it would be a group thing. We relaxed a little longer, and before the movie was over, we scrubbed each other clean and dried ourselves off.

James had another movie playing in the room while we fell back on the huge bed. He told us of our plans for the next day. Monica would only be with us for tonight. After breakfast, she would be heading home, leaving me and James to enjoy the rest of our mini vacation, which was cool with me because I was ready for her to leave anyway. I didn't see why she had to stay the entire night. I mean, he could have easily put her in a cab and sent her on her merry way. I started to suggest that to James, but I didn't want to spoil the mood. He also made mention of a shopping spree and a couple's spa treatment we would be attending here at the hotel.

I half watched the movie and half played back what went down earlier. Out of the corner of my eye, I took in Monica. She was definitely gorgeous, and I could see why James thought her to be the perfect candidate for our evening of adventure. She had skills and knew what she was doing, but I couldn't help but wonder how much it took for her to be here. Had she and James hooked up before? I tried not to entertain the thought, but it was bugging me. Then on top of all that, I was wondering if I could maybe hook up with her on the low at a later date. She was phenomenal, and I wanted to see exactly what she could do. Maybe it was just the liquor talking, but I was definitely thinking about meeting up with her soon.

We gave each other full body massages and orally pleased each other until we drifted off to sleep. The next morning, we showered together and had breakfast over conversation of our activities the previous evening. When James got up to use the restroom, Monica just kind of stared at me. I wanted to ask her if I had a boogey in my nose or something. For some reason I felt a little uncomfortable.

"So, Jasmine, did you really enjoy yourself last night?" she asked as if she really wanted to know. I answered after watching her tie the stem of a cherry into a knot with her tongue.

"Yeah, it was different. I had fun," I said nonchalantly. I did not want to have this conversation with her. I was still thinking about having her one on one, but I wouldn't dare approach the subject. I was a heterosexual woman. Surely this one event did not change that aspect, or did it? Monica got dirty in the bedroom, and although my mind was telling me to leave it alone, my body was buzzing just being in her presence.

"Well, if you want us to hook up under more private circumstances, you know how to contact me."

"I'll do that," I said coyly, not wanting to show my hand just yet. Just that quickly I had made up my mind that Monica would get to have me again. I just had to figure out how to go about it without damaging my marriage. Keeping us together was the most important thing to me, and I couldn't let Monica fuck this up for us. We were barely hanging on by a thread as it was.

Just then James joined us at the table. He thanked Monica for a wonderful evening and put her in a cab to go home. I saw the envelope he slipped her, but I decided not to comment on it. I might need that bit of information later on. We went back to our suite to change, and then we went on the shopping spree. We only had three hours to shop because James scheduled our spa time for early afternoon.

We made it back to the hotel with ten minutes to spare before we had to go and get pampered. Instead of shopping, we ended up going to a miniature golf course. We had a ball as we missed hole after hole because neither of us could hit the ball straight. After that we had lunch at the Hibachi, a five-star Asian cuisine bar located on Delaware Avenue. It felt like we were dating again, and I didn't want the day to end. I did pick up a pair of sexy stiletto sandals from Charles David before we went back. I had a thong to match them perfectly, and that's all I planned to wear with them later that night.

Thoughts of Monica kept trying to infiltrate my thoughts, but I was determined to concentrate on the moment I was having with my husband. That entire threesome thing was cute, but that was supposed to be the gateway to bringing us back together. With that being said, she definitely came in and rocked the damn butt, and now my silly ass was feeling confused. I didn't like girls like that, but I really liked Monica, at least on a sexual level. Maybe if I had her just one more time, I'd be good. You know, just to flush her all the way out of my system. That way I could give James my full attention, and we could start to build again.

All too soon our weekend was over and it was time to go back to work. We had a good time just hanging out and being stress free, and we got into some hellified sex sessions that left me speechless and smiling every time. No more of the five-minute poundings were going on. We made love for hours. Sometimes it was slow, sometimes it was heart-pounding fast, but it was more than five minutes and that's what mattered. We took pictures on the strip and some nude ones in the room. We also climbed into the big champagne glass–shaped Jacuzzi and had our picture taken, and once the picture guy was gone, we got it on something fierce, splashing bubbles all over the place.

Before we left, I made sure everything was packed and we weren't forgetting anything. I sat on the lounge chair to catch my breath and enjoy the room for a second longer. James was in the restroom making sure he packed all of our toiletries. When he came back in the room, he kneeled in front of me and put his head in my lap.

"Jasmine, I am so happy you are my wife. This weekend was wonderful, and I appreciate you going through with our plans. You have made me very happy," James said while rubbing the backs of my legs.

"I'm glad you enjoyed yourself. We needed to get away for a second," I responded while fondling the wavy texture of his hair.

Instead of responding, he reached under my skirt and pulled my panties to the side. I couldn't protest because he was already tasting me. We went at it for another hour and were late checking out. We had to pay a fee, but it was well worth it. Hopefully this was the start to how our lives would be moving forward. This, minus Monica's contribution, was all I ever wanted from James. For us to connect again on a level beyond just surface. To be in love like we used to be. To turn the heat up so high we would both feel the burn and wouldn't care. This was the man I married. This was who we were. Unfortunately, there was a nagging feeling in the back of my mind telling me I played myself, and I couldn't let the feeling go.